A
Beckoning
Silence

By
Jim Brewster

PublishAmerica
Baltimore

ISBN: 1-4241-8122-4
PUBLISHED BY PUBLISHAMERICA, LLLP
www.publishamerica.com
Baltimore

Printed in the United States of America

Also by Jim Brewster

The Silver Star
Midnight of the Phoenix
The Vicar of Afton

Dedicated to Sophia Diptee Wilson,
my Nepalese Grand-Niece

St. James Church in Afton

The church lay on a long-sloping rise overlooking the north shore of the Susquehanna River as it flowed into the Chesapeake Bay. From the vantage point of a fishing boat on the Bay, it arrested the eye. Closer, the beauty of a flowering dogwood nestled to the west wall denied the finality of the graveyard beyond. Familiarity had mellowed the simple lines of the church, especially when the western sun tinted the light yellow walls to gold.

It had stood the test of changing times—first as a private chapel, then as a mission. The needs of the Second World War had established a Naval Training Station at near-by Bainbridge and thus began St. James gradual transformation from a rural country church to a congregation that each week counted new members.

The priest at St. James, modest, literate, alert to the use of humor where appropriate, intensely aware of human frailties, and a man in his own right, had become known in the area as Father Sam. Those who knew him well shared his enjoyment of a perfect martini. Life and death passed quietly each year under his gentle care.

In the normal cycle of time, little upset the daily comings and goings of Aftonians until one day *The Baltimore Sun* emblazoned the headline of a gruesome murder in a town north of Afton. As the investigation proceeded, it became evident that a man from Afton was implicated. This had no sooner been headlined in the local paper than the suspect had been found dead of a narcotics overdose. The man, the paper reported, had some relationship with the female curate at St. James. Time took the headlines away, but gossip enjoyed a much longer life.

BOOK ONE

CHAPTER ONE
The Doorbell?

She inched herself across the rumpled bedclothes and squinted at the clock. It seemed to read ten-thirty. Was that night or day, she wasn't sure? She lowered her head to the pillow, very slowly; it felt as though the pain might explode in her skull.

There it was again—someone at the front door. Need she answer it? Would they go away? Reluctantly, she dragged herself out of bed and, groping for a robe, shuffled to the door.

"Dr.Crawford, hello. Won't you come in?" She pushed tangled hair away from her face.

Jim Crawford saw that he had wakened her from rest he knew she needed.

"I'm terribly sorry to get you up, Rachel." He stepped in and closed the door. "I won't stay, but I wanted to give you this. Ben left it for you. I assure you, I have not read it. I didn't see any reason for the police to find it—there is no question that it was a suicide."

The ugly word once again sent a shock through her body leaving her trembling.

Crawford handed her a crumpled piece of paper

She held out her hand automatically, but instinct warned her not to accept it. She drew her arm back.

Crawford reached forward and gently placed the paper in her hand.

"I am terribly sorry, Rachel, I really am. He almost made it." Then, looking at her as a doctor might, he asked, "Are you all right? I could give you a sedative?"

"I'm—fine, Dr. Crawford, thank you," her voice barely a whisper.

"Call me, please, if I may help." Excusing himself, he left Rachel staring down at the crumpled paper. Involuntarily her fingers opened and she let it fall and went unseeing to her bedroom. Shrugging on clothes, any clothes, she began an aimless wandering from room to room. Passing a mirror, she found herself staring at an image with no recognition. She busied herself doing unnecessary cleaning and straightening, anything to resist the urgent cry of her bed. The phone rang once, a call from Father Sam, but she begged off at his invitation to dinner.

Toward evening, falling exhausted on the sofa, she saw the threatening piece of paper. She hated it, refusing to touch it, yet it was all that was left of Ben. With a feeling of nausea, she picked it up.

"Dear Rachel,"

How could she read beyond those words?

*"I'm sorry to do this—I tried, but things just don't seem to work out. You—*his writing was getting hard to read—*you did everything and more for me. The night we spent together is the dearest memory of my life. I know you can't love me—maybe it's the man who went to India? It is important to me now to tell you one more time how much I love you, Rachel—another time perhaps? I need to go where it's quiet—away from the bad noise of my life—I feel it beckoning me. Please don't hate me—Elkton was a mistake—I did nothing wrong, believe me. I am not a coward, but I have to find a silence, it may give me peace.*

Goodbye, my dearest Rachel.
Ben

Rachel stared unseeing at the paper. No longer able to cry, her trembling fingers gripped the letter and pressed to her breast.

"May God give you the silence you are seeking, my dear, dear Ben."

No sooner had she whispered the prayer than the doorbell shrilled, shocking her to consciousness. Against her will, she opened the door. A man in a policeman's uniform stood there, a large female officer behind him. Her skin crawled with apprehension.

"Reverend Mason, I'm Steve Mooney, Chief of Police in Havre de Grace. This is Sergeant Cloris Beechamp. She assists me on occasion. May we come in, there are a few questions I would like to ask you in regard to Mr. Stoddard's death?"

Rachel could no longer be shocked by what was happening. She numbly replied,

"Please come in. Call me Miss Mason, please."

"Miss Mason, we are wrapping up the Stoddard case. I'm sorry to have to bother you, but there is a detail that we need to clarify. The Mexican boy told us that Mr. Stoddard had written…."

"Chief Mooney, may I interrupt you?"

"Yes, of course, Miss Mason."

"Ben did write me a note that Dr. Crawford gave me and that I still have, if that answers your question?" Her voice was soft, but her eyes were challenging.

"Well, yes, it does. However, it is the contents of the note that would be of interest to us. I mean by that, could it provide information that might affect our investigation? As you know, Mr. Stoddard was considered a suspect in the Elkton murder. I wonder if you would let me have the note, Miss Mason?"

Rachel paused only a moment, "Chief Mooney, the note is personal. It was written to me and intended for me alone to read. It was a very personal goodbye. I'm sorry, but I feel very strongly about this! What's more, I consider it an invasion of my privacy to show it to anyone." Her face flushed with anger.

Taken aback, Steve Mooney hesitated before answering; before he could, Miss Beecham spoke.

"Miss Mason!" Her tone was a monotone, as though reading from a script. "You realize you can be charged with obstruction of justice?"

Mooney interrupted, "I don't know that that will be necessary, Officer Beecham. I'm sure we can rely on Miss Mason's integrity. I do, however, need to remind you that we are still conducting an investigation into Mr Tribuzzio's murder. Mr. Stoddard, who was at the scene the night of the murder, has to be considered a prime suspect in the case. I say this only because withholding evidence is considered a crime, Miss Mason."

Officer Beecham, not mollified, cast a baleful look at Rachel.

"I'm sorry Mr. Mooney, but I feel strongly about this. Ben was a close friend of mine and that is all that the note is about."

Seeing that she would not voluntarily surrender the note, Mooney stood and extended his hand, "Thank you, Miss Mason. We've taken too much of your time." He and Miss Beecham left without further words.

Rachel was left with an angry, helpless taste in her mouth. Show them the note and be done with it! No, it was too personal and did not add anything to their investigation, or did it? She knew Ben was capable of irrational rages, could he possibly have murdered the man in Elkton? *"Elkton was a mistake,"* what did that mean? In her heart, she wanted to believe he had not done it, but until the police found the person who did, Ben would be the silent victim—guilty until proven innocent, she thought.

* * * *

The shock of Ben's suicide reverberated in Afton, especially among those who knew of his relationship with Rachel. Tongues quickly created a tragic love story with Rachel as the cruel-hearted lover. Already crippled by remorse, Rachel knew she would have to leave St. James; not because of peoples' tongues, but because her faith in herself had been shaken. She did not know where, or really why, but she knew in her heart that if she were to become whole again it would have to be a place far from Afton— perhaps Nepal, Scott had loved it?

* * * *

The day after Mooney's visit, Rachel stopped at Father Sam's office. She managed to maintain a superficial objectivity while she told him her reasons for needing to leave St. James—and possibly going to Nepal.

Sam did not attempt to dissuade her, but he emphasized the many good things she had accomplished both in the parish and in helping Ben regain his self-respect—that he had finally committed suicide was *not* her fault—it was vital that she understand that Ben had simply been too burdened with society's cruelties to fight back any longer.

"Rachel, I wish you wouldn't leave, I will miss you sorely, but I will try to understand why you feel you must go. Wherever you do go, as you attempt to listen in the stillness of your search, don't make a friend of loneliness—there is too much that God needs you to do."

Rachel had been able to control her emotions until these last few words, then, unashamed, she wept, gripping Sam's hands as if she were drowning.

* * * *

That afternoon, Sam called Bishop Phillips' office.

"Karen, Sam Adams, how are you? I wonder if the Bishop is available?"

"You sound so serious, Father Adams?" Karen was used to a light, humorous greeting from the rector of St. James.

"Sorry, Karen, must have been bad eggs this morning." Sam's attempt to lighten the mood was an effort.

"Let me see where he is." Karen quickly sensed it as not a time for levity.

There was a short pause before Chauncey's modulated tones came on the line.

"Samuel Adams, of the Afton Adams, I believe, how are you? Turning the corner, I hope, after the nasty business with that fellow—Ben?"

"Yes and no, Bishop."

"Hmm. What may I do for you, Sam?"

"Bishop, this would be better done face-to-face, but I thought you should be aware of it as soon as possible. Rachel has asked to leave St. James. I wish she would stay, but she feels very strongly that she needs to stand back and reassess her life."

"I'm really sorry to hear that, Sam. This is, of course, because of her involvement with Ben, I assume? From my brief acquaintance, she seemed a very fine person—one who would strengthen the Church. Should I talk to her?"

"I'm sure she would like that, Bishop, but I suspect her mind is made up. She thinks of going to go to Nepal. Nepal, of course, is where Scott Barton, her friend, disappeared several months ago."

"Oh, I had momentarily forgotten that tragedy. Does she harbor the hope that he's still alive, Sam?"

"No, I don't believe she does, but where his life ended, she is hoping to find a new beginning in her own life"

"Dear me, that is upsetting. Of course I will give her my blessing if *you* support her reasons. When will she leave, Sam?"

"She is very anxious to go, but she will be guided by our advice."

"Well, that part is good—gives us time to hunt up another assistant for you, Sam. Hopefully we can get this done expeditiously.

Say, it just occurs to me that I met a man, the Anglican Archbishop of Singapore, at the last General Convention. We talked a bit about a health clinic for Tibetans he has just organized somewhere in central Nepal. I wonder whether Rachel might be interested in such a thing?"

"I don't really know what she plans to do in Nepal."

"I'll just drop him a line and see if he could use someone like Rachel. I'd not mention it to Rachel just yet."

"I shan't, Bishop. Oh, by the way, Caroline has consented to be my wife; in fact, she seems to think that February 8th would be a suitable day. If it is at all possible, we would hope you and Nancy might attend the wedding."

"You rascal,'oh, by the way', indeed! Nancy and I have been hoping this would happen. I know she will be as delighted as I am. February 8th? Karen! See that I am free on the 8th of February! Sam would you do me the honor of allowing me to marry you?"

Caught off guard, but pleased, Sam stammered, "Bishop, Caroline and I would be honored if you would. Yes, of course, how gracious of you!"

"Done! I will be there with ecclesiastical bells on, Sam!"

"I can't think of a more harmonious sound, Bishop. Thank you so much!"

* * * *

That evening when Sam told Caroline that the Bishop wanted to perform the ceremony, she fell strangely quiet, disconcerted. She had been thinking of their wedding as a quiet ceremony with her son and possibly her brother and a few guests attending and then a quick get-away on their wedding trip. Sheepishly she realized that of course it would need to be a parish celebration with an all-inclusive reception, especially now that the Bishop would attend. Eager as she was to marry Sam, she blanched at all the necessary folderol that would be necessary. Neither of them wanted a really formal ceremony, those designed for expectant young couples.

"Oh, Sam, I guess I didn't think this through. My romantic mind saw us being married in a simple chapel, perhaps on the Eastern Shore, with only a few of our friends and family."

"I don't relish a large church wedding either, Caroline, but how can I not be married here in this parish and especially now that the Bishop wants to participate?"

"At our age, it seems so silly to stage a major wedding. There should be a law that over the age of fifty-five only small, intimate ceremonies be allowed. Oh, woe is me! Well, this is what I get for snagging the "Archbishop" of Afton. Why couldn't you have been someone so-so, Sam?"

"Just call me So-So-Sam, the Archbishop of Afton. That sounds great! Bow down, woman, and make way for the aged patriarch!"

Finally able to laugh at the corner they had painted themselves into, they realized there was no alternative; they'd just have to enjoy it.

"I'll make the announcement in church on Sunday, publish the banns, as it were—assuming you get an OK that your son, Russell, is clear to come—better try to reach him tomorrow, if you can. Your brother may be more of a problem."

"My brother has always been—if not a problem, let's just say a *challenge*," she responded wryly.

* * * *

The Reverend Samuel Adams was not, by nature, a methodical man. On the contrary, he knew some critics might have called him disorganized. The threat of that opprobrium did not concern Sam; he had his own methods that had served him well for years.

Every January since his ordination forty-four years ago, he would sit down and mark his own year-end "report card." Though he never showed it to anyone, even dear Beth, he was scrupulous in asking himself the tough questions and answering them honestly.

On a bright Saturday morning, before the Annual Meeting, he sat down to assess the past year at St. James. The year had ended tragically with Ben's death. Sam had struggled hard over his role in this heart-breaking event. He sincerely believed that both he and Rachel had tried as hard as they could to help Ben restore his shattered confidence, but they had both failed. Why? He could not find the answer. Ben, like an exhausted swimmer, had run out of energy fighting the opposing surf and had quietly slipped under the waves in surrender. Why they both had failed, he left to God to understand. He gave himself a very dubious C minus.

He ticked off the other plusses and minuses of the year.

He, of course, did not like the idea of Rachel leaving, but he had become resigned to her decision. Should he be able to alter her decision—on what grounds? He gave himself a dissatisfied B-.

On the plus side, he felt that the pulse of the parish had been quickened by all the new communicants and that this year, finally, might prove to be the year for making the long-delayed improvements to the church buildings. The Annual Meeting would be the kick-off for that adventure. That should be a hopeful A.

The Bishop continued to be very supportive of his efforts at St. James. A modest B seemed fair.

Although well aware of his advancing years, he felt he was still able to respond to the needs of the parish both spiritually and physically. He gave himself a cautious C.

Having said that, he felt some inability to communicate with a few members of the church, his talent for so many years. He was beginning to sense a restlessness with the old forms of the Service among the young people, but, always willing to listen, he believed he was as permissive as he could be in responding to their needs. He gave himself a C, with a question mark.

He had always made sure that the Vestry was representative of the congregation but, somewhat skeptically, he recognized Lance Bosley as the spokesman for any changes that were certain to come. He allowed himself a cautious C+.

He felt thankful that his parish was peopled by young spirits although he would admit, privately, that he sometimes yearned for the older, more familiar patterns that he had grown up with and loved. This was worth a sentimental C.

He assigned 90's for A's, 80's for B's and 70's for C's; adding up his score for last year he came out with a 77, or C+.

"Amazing!" He scowled. "I thought I deserved at least a B+ or a low A. Oh, well, it seems always to be the same every year—maybe, as I get older, I need to lighten up on the grading a bit?"

Looking up from his scores, disappointed that he had shown no gain, he spotted Xavier entering the Parish House. Now there was a success! Sam vividly recalled how grudgingly the boy, who had insisted on calling himself Mike to hide his Mexican heritage, had started his work at St. James six months ago, substituting for the ailing Toby. It had been a hazardous gamble on Sam's part because of the boy's drug history, but looking at him now, he could not feel anything but pride in how he had matured and become a confident, contributing member of society. Sure, Sam had "bribed" him with the goal of working a year and then buying Sam's car for $2000, but he preferred to think of it as an "incentive." Anyway, Xavier had become a man in the short span of six months and Sam was very proud of him. Sadly, he could not take credit for it; it had been Xavier who had grown through his own efforts, not Sam's manipulation. He gave himself a psychological A, but did not put it in his record.

He carefully put the score sheet into the file labeled C.P, for Clerical Performance.

Looming on the scoring horizon next year, he was certain, would be the politically generated angst on same sex marriage, and abortion. That he had not been conscious of any violent reaction to the election of a homosexual Episcopal Bishop surprised him. He knew his beliefs in these areas would complicate his marks, and severely test his scoring honesty.

In summary, he felt it had been a good year and he looked forward to an even better one this year, beginning auspiciously, with his marriage to Caroline.

* * * *

Sam was now having dinner most evenings at Caroline's, and because he could not check the answering machine at the Rectory as a normal routine, he had reluctantly acquired a cell phone. After several lengthy discourses to Caroline as to why the cell phone was an abomination, she politely but firmly asked him to either accept the concept or cancel his contract. Suitably chastened he tried manfully to adjust to the phone's imperious demands. Such a time occurred as they were sitting down to dinner one night.

"Hello, this is Sam Adams speaking. May I help you?"

"Reverend Adams, this is Steve Mooney. Hope this is not a bad time to call you?"

"No, not at all, Chief. What may I do for you?" Sam raised his eyebrows in Caroline's direction, as if to say, you see what happens with cell phones?

"Shouldn't take long. I just talked with Miss Mason, but thought you should know, too. We've had some news on the Tribuzzio case. Mrs. Tribuzzio has testified to us, under oath, that there were two men who came into the house the night her husband was murdered and that he was dead when Stoddard arrived. I believe we can rule out Stoddard as a suspect in the case with Mrs. Tribuzzio's testimony. We have admitted her to the Witness Protection Program because she is terrified that she will be killed. So, for whatever it's worth, I think we can absolve Stoddard although it doesn't help him any, I guess."

"Oh, that is good news, Chief! I do thank you very much for telling me. I know Rachel has to be vastly relieved!"

"Reverend Adams, that is one tough cookie!"

Mooney did not expand on his comment nor did Sam choose to follow it up.

"Thanks, again, Chief! Good evening." He hung up and felt as though a ponderous weight had been lifted from him. He related the conversation to Caroline as she brought back their dinner plates.

No sooner had they said Grace than the phone rang again.

"This is Sam Adams. May I help you?"

"Father Adams, I am terribly sorry to bother you at dinner time, but you asked me to call you if Toby took a turn for the worse. I'm sorry."

"Lacey, thank you for calling me. May I come over in a few minutes and visit?"

"Yes, Father, if you would be willing to? Toby is not good. The doctor is with him now, but he says he may not go the night." Lacey's voice was weary and resigned. She had suffered with Toby's illness for several years, but in the last six months she had been virtually chained to him as he became weaker and weaker.

"Lacey, I will be there in a few minutes."

"If you can come, Father, I think he would want to see you."

"I'll be right there. Your faith has gotten you this far, Lacey, hang on a little longer."

Caroline had come up behind him as he finished the call. Putting her arms around him, she rested her head on his shoulders. "I'm sorry, Sam, but it is all for the best, isn't it? He can't be happy the way he is."

"He is a skeleton, Caroline. I wish God would take him home. Let me eat a piece of this beautiful roast and then run—I'm terribly sorry, Caroline. I should get over there as soon as possible."

"Of course. I want you to go, Sam."

Sam wolfed down the outside piece of roast beef that he loved, drank most of his milk, and then drove off for the Tobias'.

Jim Crawford was just leaving as Sam drove up.

"Hi, Sam. How you be?"

"I'm fine, Jim, you?"

"Not always chipper when I leave Toby, I'm afraid. He can go anytime, Sam. I'd be surprised if he sees tomorrow. I have to run to the hospital, but I'll be back in an hour or so. I have given him a shot of morphine so he may or may not be awake."

"You're the best, Jim! Thank you so much for all you have done for Lacey and Toby!" He took Jim's hand and gripped it firmly.

"Not enough, I'm afraid. Those damn weeds!"

Sam nodded and turned to go into the house, knowing this night's vigil might be long, he also knew that he would not want to be any other place than with this quiet, hardworking man who had suffered for so long and so patiently.

He had told Caroline that he would not return to her house unless it was before eleven, so turning the ignition key and heading out of the drive at five in the morning, he headed back to the Rectory. He was not tired. Rather he felt an indefinable warmth that was seldom possible with another human being until all pretense falls away and two souls are able to speak the simple language of love.

Toby had passed beyond the reach of Jim Thompson and Sam, yet each felt that Toby's body had now been restored to full health.

* * * *

After Sam had left for the Tobias', Caroline cleared the table and loaded the dishwasher. Her mind was a long way from what she was doing; it had drifted to memories of her marriage to Don. She knew her life with Sam would be far different than with Don. In the early years of their marriage, he had been a salesman for Bethlehem Steel and his territories usually did not require him to be away over night so that their home life was very normal. Later, when he was promoted into management, he did travel some, but again it was infrequent—sudden phone calls never required him to leave home.

Hanging up the damp dishtowel, she turned out the kitchen lights and wandered out into the living room as she recalled the "old days." She kept a picture of Don on the living room table. It had been taken when he was made Vice President of Sales at fifty-eight. Picking it up, she was reminded again of how handsome he had been, with silver gray borders to his hair, a "strong face" with penetrating blue eyes and just the suggestion of a smile, curling up the corners of his mouth. He had been fun, but single-minded in whatever he attempted, whether it was his sales goals or getting his golf score down, and he had been a wonderful father to Russell. It had been a very happy marriage, cruelly ended by the plane crash. She put the picture down, not with a sense of sorrow, but with the feeling that she had been so lucky to have met and known him for forty years.

And now she was embarking on her second voyage, with an entirely different kind of man. There wouldn't be the excitement of promotions, sudden transfers to strange cities, company rumors and personnel changes, instead, now she would live in Afton with the same people, in the same beautiful setting. It was this very sameness in her life that she found she was more than ready to enjoy, with a husband who was a shepherd. She smiled as an image of Don's *Bethlehem* Steel and Sam as *shepherd* of St. James, popped into her mind; it was her own intimate Christmas fantasy.

Picking up Don's picture again, she murmured, "Don, I know you understand what I am doing. My marriage to Sam in no way diminishes what we had. I shall always love you in the many ways that I did. I feel I have your blessing." Then feeling that she was getting too introspective, she kissed the picture and put it back in its place.

"You better get used to losing Sam to other people's needs at inconvenient hours. That's life; not in the fast lane, but life in the fasting lane," she laughed to herself. Is that sacrilegious, she wondered, but only briefly.

Chapter Two

Sam gently, but insistently, urged Rachel to stay involved with parish work, at the very least, to keep her mind occupied until she had more concrete plans for where she would go. On her part, Rachel was in a lonely quandary as to how to plan her life after she left St. James. Nepal had stayed a fixed goal in her mind, but how realistic was it? She knew no one in Nepal. She was aware that the Chinese occupation of Tibet had forced Tibetans to migrate to Nepal and she vaguely remembered hearing that refugee camps had been set-up to care for them. If she could somehow make contact with someone, it might be work she could do. On the off chance that Scott's father, who had gone to Nepal at the time Scott disappeared, might know someone she might contact she had asked Sam if she might take a few days off to visit the Bartons. Sam, already uneasy with some of the comments that he had heard from a few parishioners after Ben's death, urged her to go at the time of the Annual Meeting to avoid any unpleasantness.

Sam's lament to Caroline had been, "Oh, my dear, how my heart aches for this girl. I am at a loss as to how to advise her. What can I do?"

"I don't know, Sam. I love Rachel very much, but I feel, intuitively, that she needs this time of searching to find herself. You mustn't try to do her thinking for her."

* * * *

Russell hung up from his mother's call, telling him her plans to marry the Episcopal priest, with some surprise. He did not know the Reverend Sam Adams, but he knew that his parents and the Adams had been good friends some years before his father's death. He decided then and there that he would go to Afton a little early to spend some time with his mother and get to know the gentleman. He had been very close to his father, but enough time had passed since his death that he could be cautiously pleased that his mother had found a companion.

It had taken some time for Russell to accept his father's sudden death. He had, in fact, pressed the National Aviation Safety Board for a thorough investigation of the circumstances of the crash. Knowing the many flight hours his father's friend, Jack Downey, had, who was piloting the plane, he could not accept the official statement that a freak weather system had hit the airport as they were landing; that a downdraft was the cause of the crash. What Russell questioned was the lack of warning about the storm. Official recordings, however, seemed to verify that Downey had over-ruled the air traffic controller's advice to divert the landing.

Russell had followed his father's path to Johns Hopkins and then taken an MBA at Harvard. He was, in turn, both a brilliant and a sporadic student depending on the specific course. His engaging personality, however, placed him high on the lists of those recruiters who had come to Harvard in his final year. Several of the largest US companies made him generous offers, but, given his freedom from the demands of graduate school, he decided to turn them all down in order to spend the summer in Europe. His father, proud of what his son had achieved, encouraged him to relax for a while.

Russell had been an aggressive lacrosse player and mountain biker at Hopkins where his father had been a four-year starting catcher on the baseball team. Both men liked sports that challenged them with a taste of "living on the edge." Russell was at his best when the possibility of a violent collision or fall might be seconds away. That he avoided serious injury was a tribute to an innate sense of seeing how close to the "edge" he could go, yet not overstepping it.

It seemed perfectly natural to him, in planning his trip to Europe, to set standards more rigorous than some might. He got himself hired as a deck hand on a freighter destined for France, with intermediate ports of call at Buenos Aires, Lisbon, and, finally, Le Havre.

Buying a bike in France, he began a thousand mile tour of virtually every country in Europe, Scandinavia, and some of western Russia.

Finding himself only as far as Odessa in mid-September, he decided that the three-month time schedule was too restrictive, so he added nine months more by working, as his financial needs demanded, at a number of seaside resorts along the Mediterranean coast.

After a year of sporadic correspondence, his father made it abundantly clear that "enough travel was enough"—it was time to come home and find a job. Russell, ruefully, had to acknowledge his father's logic, realizing he had probably over-stayed his "European summer." Making the decision to come home, however, was more complicated than his father knew. Early in his tour, he had established a very comfortable relationship with Denise, a blonde cyclist from Finland. She became something more than a companion and one who matched his ability to survive on whatever food they were able to afford. She was as able as he to find employment when they would decide to stay in a particularly attractive location.

As they toured a coastal town, they would compare its beauty to the last place they had stayed. If the waters were a particularly languorous shade of blue-green and the fishing boats outnumbered the multi-million dollar yachts, they would stay. Or, if at another town the narrow winding streets worked uphill in a gentle curve, exposing second-story flower boxes filled with yellows, reds and blues, they would stay. The cardinal no-no was any sign of self-conscious wealth. It was a time of raw sensation with no thought given to anything but pleasure.

Confronted with the realization that he should get back to business-America, they decided there was no alternative but to get married. It was a logical, not an emotional decision. Knowing his mother would be hurt if they were married quietly in Monte Carlo, they agreed to wait until they had returned to Maryland.

Russell's father paid for Denise's family to come to the United States for the wedding. Her father was a hardy farmer from Kuusamo, Finland, about as far north in the country as humans can go. The family spoke little English so communication during their visit was limited, if not almost impossible. The wedding, charming and austerely simple, in deference to Denise parents, was perhaps not what Caroline had romantically envisioned; it, nonetheless, appeared to achieve the stability she wanted her son to have.

Russell had no difficulty finding lucrative employment with a software manufacturer in Seattle. The location seemed ideal because at every opportunity they would head north along the Canadian coast camping, cycling or kayaking.

Although children had not been a major consideration in their decision to marry, Denise gradually began to make it the centerpiece. After three years and no pregnancies, she seemed to lose interest in their relationship. At the same time, Russell found he was getting bored with the rigorous, almost primitive, recreation they imposed on their spare time.

The nature of Russell's job allowed him to live wherever he chose, so, with discontent obvious to both of them, he suggested a radical relocation to Florida, to which she half-heartedly agreed. Florida's exotic but alien climate did nothing to fulfill Denise's maternal needs, and as a result, during Russell's frequent business trips, she drifted into a variety of relationships at their country club. Her relationships were not motivated by any desire to find another husband, but rather they were caused by the emptiness and the seeming pointlessness of her life without children. She finally unburdened herself to Russell, telling him of her unhappiness at their barren marriage, and asked him for a divorce. It was accomplished amicably—she refused support and, in not too long a time, he learned she had returned to Finland. He heard nothing more of her. The whole experience faded into a dream-like unreality when he allowed himself to reflect on it, but it convinced him that marriage was an extremely hazardous adventure, overstepping that *edge* he had been so careful to respect.

And so Russell looked down at the phone, perhaps skeptically, hoping his mother was making the right decision, but she did sound happy.

* * * *

Dwight Brown, Sam's Senior Warden, had asked the Vestry to come to his home for a private meeting to discuss what the parish might do for a wedding gift for Sam and Caroline.

Dwight's maid saw that everyone was offered coffee or soft drinks while he handled bar requests. After the men had settled down, Dwight opened the meeting by asking for individual ideas as to what would be appropriate as a wedding gift. Hesitant at first, the men slowly began to offer ideas: a silver tea service appealed to a couple of the men, a weekend in Manhattan was another idea, someone suggested a check for a thousand dollars, Ed Swan, the Treasurer, uneasy with too lavish an expenditure, suggested a weekend in Ocean City in the coming summer. They soon ran out of other ideas.

"Friends, this is a gift from the parish—it needn't be blatantly lavish, but it should demonstrate the feeling of affection of the parish. Could we think in terms of something in the neighborhood of ten thousand dollars, of which I would contribute half," Dwight suggested.

There was an undertone of approval to this idea.

Lance Bosley cleared his throat, "Gentlemen, I've given this gift idea a lot of thought. I agree it should be a very generous outpouring of our affection for the couple, especially our Rector. Along that line, try this idea on for size: our Rector is nearing retirement, he has had heart problems; though they have not reoccurred lately, they have to weigh heavily on him. He is soon to marry a very charming lady. These circumstances suggest an imminent retirement, quite possibly this year. Why not anticipate this; send them on their way, by giving them a two-month vacation in Europe this summer? It would be a fond farewell—well deserved. I would combine Dwight's generous contribution of five thousand dollars with my own of ten thousand. Fifteen thousand would allow them to enjoy themselves comfortably."

There was a stunned silence and then a sudden babble of excited comment. "Wonderful!" "How generous, Lance!" "Boy, what a gift!" "We think that is just so generous, Lance!"

Dwight had not commented.

"Dwight, what do you say? Pretty wonderful, isn't it?"

"It most assuredly would be a wonderful gift, Lance. A couple of considerations, however: to my knowledge, Sam has not even hinted to me that he is planning to retire any time soon. The mandatory retirement age for a priest is seventy-two, which leaves him almost four more years. Under those circumstances, I am quite sure he would be loathe to leave the parish for two months this summer."

"Dwight, you are quite possibly right, however, let me tease this idea a bit more. Our Rector is, first and foremost, a loyal, hard-working man. He would be reluctant to leave his parish if he were forty. Might it not seem logical, however, that with his new marriage and his questionable health something like this might prompt him to say, 'Now's the time!'" Lance was obviously enjoying his role as prosecuting attorney.

"Lance, you seem to emphasize Sam's health as an imminent issue. I grant you he had a pretty good scare last year, but he has been reassured by his Hopkins' cardiologist that he is in good shape." Dwight, having witnessed the frightening episode when Sam had fallen from the pulpit during his heart attack, was well aware that there could be a reoccurrence, but he also knew that Sam was feeling better than ever lately.

"Of course I'm not privy to the kind of information you have, Dwight. I do know the statistics, however and sixty-eight year old men who have suffered a heart attack are cautioned not to over-do. This parish is growing so fast it would be a challenge for a much younger man. Must we watch this noble man die in the traces, so to speak?"

The extreme civility of the exchanges did not disguise the tension between these two men.

"Without straining the point, I would argue that it is the heart-felt meaning behind the gift that gives its value. We really can't know what is in our Rector's heart, can we? I wonder if we could hear from some of the other men?" Lance turned to the group, ending the private conversation with Dwight.

Ed Swan spoke up, "What's the harm, Dwight? Let him *carpe diem* the day."

"I agree with Ed, Dwight, I don't see the harm in it."

"Dwight, I'd be tickled pink if my company would send me to Europe for two months!"

Lance interrupted, "Let's take a vote—what do you say, Dwight, shall we?"

Dwight had counted heads as he listened to the comments and knew Lance would win.

"Well, I am impressed that you, as a very new member of St. James, feel you need to do this. Everyone, naturally, is going to want to know how the Vestry came up with this amount of money."

"I think how we did it is our business, not theirs, as long as we didn't jeopardize our finances," Lance replied.

"We do *represent* them Lance, we are their representatives, so to speak. They have a right to know how we do their business."

"Again, Dwight, it seems like nit-picking, but you raise an interesting internal point: each of us was *elected* to the vestry except yourself who was *appointed* by the Rector. Presumably, we represent the attitude of the congregation more than an appointed official, and this is said with the greatest respect for the role you *do* play."

The men listening to this debate began to realize they were also watching a power struggle not the simple discussion of an appropriate wedding gift.

"That is perfectly true, Lance, and all I am doing is trying to interpret how I think Sam and Caroline might see this gift. I do not want this discussion to turn personal, Lance. If the consensus of the group favors your idea, I will simply want my vote recorded as opposed, but I will, of course, make the contribution I offered."

The decision was then made to give the Rector and Mrs. Pickering a two-month, all expense trip, to Europe next summer.

Lance was thanked for his extreme generosity and rewarding solution to the problem.

Dwight watched with long experienced eyes, and no little amusement, as Lance was being lionized as the new power on the Vestry.

* * * *

The next evening, when Caroline was waiting for Sam to arrive, the phone rang.

"Hi, Mom. How are you?"

"Hello, Russ. I'm fine. What exciting event stirs you to call at this hour, my son? You are not going to tell me you have a conflict on the 8th, are you?"

"No, no, nothing like that. I wouldn't do that to you. No, I just wanted to call and ask you a question."

"Make it simple, you know my age."

"Mom, how would it be if I came up a bit early, say on the 4th of February—it would give us a chance to get reacquainted and me get to know Reverend Adams?"

"Why that would be just wonderful! I'd love that! Please do come."

"Great. Oh, and what if I were to bring along a friend of mine? She'd only be able to stay a few days, but I'd like to have you meet her, you'd like her."

Already feeling the pressure of planning a larger than hoped for wedding, Caroline's reaction was guarded.

"Well, how nice. This is someone who is special to you, Russ? You know, I mean, someone you are serious about?"

"Oh, yes, I'm always serious about my girl friends, Mom. She's a lot of fun. I've dated her off and on for a couple of years."

"That doesn't sound too serious—not someone you are thinking of marrying?" Caroline had hoped her son might have found one girl he could settle down with, married or not, but, once divorced, he had shown little interest in monogamous relationships.

"Oh, probably not, Mom, but she's fun to be with, you'll like her."

"Oh, I'm sure I will. Sure, bring your friend along. What is the young lady's name?"

"Allison Thomason. Her father's some kind of hell-fire and brimstone evangelical preacher—runs one of the big charismatic churches here in Naples."

"Oh?" If there were such a thing, Caroline's brow would have broken out in psychological sweat. She knew only too well, the Pat Robertson type of politico-religionist called for all of the Christian restraint Sam was able to muster. "Well, Russell, you realize that the man I am going to marry is an Episcopal priest. He has his own peculiarities as far as some of the Southern evangelical ministries are concerned. I just don't want this time before our wedding to be, in any way, turbulent."

"Oh, she's light as a breeze, Mom, nothing heavy about Al. She won't upset the good Reverend."

"I hope so, Russ. Well, we'll look for you on the fourth of February. Do you need to be picked up in Baltimore?"

"Oh no, I'll rent a car. I'll get your directions later. Bye, Mom, I'm looking forward to seeing you."

"So am I, darling. Bye."

Caroline's conventional mind fretted over this untimely intrusion. Why must he bring along a girl at this time? She would definitely insist on their staying in separate bedrooms, but, of course, she knew her son well enough to know he would think that ridiculously archaic and unnatural. Why was he bringing her now if it was just another "lots of fun" girl? Oh well, another complication she would deal with later.

* * * *

The Annual Meeting had gone smoothly, as Sam expected it would. The one discordant note occurred after Ed Swan had given his annual financial report. One of the younger men, whom Sam did not know very well, stood and asked why the parish should be liable for Miss Mason's salary for this indefinite period in view of the fact that she had asked to be released in late December.

Dwight, sensing a rather strong reaction from Sam, immediately responded.

"That is a reasonable question, sir. However, the rector has asked her to stay to complete several of the projects she had under way. Were there to be an overlap between her leaving and the arrival of a new curate, I will underwrite Miss Mason's salary. The rector does need an assistant, sir."

Lance Bosley asked for recognition. "That is extremely generous of

Mr. Brown, but, as a Vestryman, I would think that such monetary decision would be made by the Vestry?"

Dwight, well aware of the challenge, did not choose to reply, simply nodding his head in response.

Sam closed the meeting with a prayer, then he and Dwight left. He had wanted to remove himself and the Senior Warden as quickly as possible so that the group would feel free to discuss anything without their inhibiting presence. He knew that Marcy, his prickly, built-in vigilante, would hear and report on every detail if he needed to hear it.

Walking back toward the rectory, Sam could sense that Dwight was fuming.

"Sam, I have often had young Turks in my business, but, mark my words, the honorable Lance Bosley will be a handful in a year or two—if it takes that long. He made it pretty clear he is challenging me as Senior Warden."

Sam, ever the optimist, said, "I choose my Senior Wardens and my clergy, otherwise decisions should be made democratically. Lance is a little pushy, but he's a source of energy, Dwight. We need to harness that energy and let it help us all."

"I hear you, my friend, but a young Turk, like an unbroken stallion, fights a harness."

* * * *

Sam's first inkling of Lance's activity came, as expected, from Marcy the day after the Annual Meeting. She had overheard talk of an "unofficial" meeting he had held.

"Sam!" Marcy continued before he could even say hello, "There's something going on with that idiot Bosley!"

"Marcy, easy does it. What are you talking about?"

"He had a meeting the other day at his house to discuss where the parish is going. Did you know that?"

"No, but that is not a criminal act—I'd like to know where it's going myself."

"The way I hear it, there isn't a question of *where*—he seems to think he *knows*."

"Oh, good. He's a member of the Vestry, maybe he'll share that important knowledge with them?"

"Sam, listen to me! Something is fishy here. The way I get it is that he is actually organizing people to *force* changes *he* thinks are necessary!"

"Marcy, you make it sound like a conspiracy to overthrow the Episcopate. Is it really that dangerous?"

"Samuel Adams, I think it is serious and I don't like it! He's a new boy in the parish—shouldn't be on the Vestry in the first place! How does he have any idea what should be changed? If he has ideas, let him start with the Vestry! Anyway, I'm going to keep my ear to the ground and I will keep you informed whether you want me to or not!"

"OK, agent M, thank you. Agent S signing off."

Although Sam had treated Marcy's story flippantly, he was vaguely uneasy with what she had told him. He had been uncertain about Lance ever since an October Vestry meeting when he had implied, quite suggestively, that there was misconduct between Rachel and Ben. Sam wouldn't let himself dislike Lance, but their relationship had not been as warm as Sam would have liked it to be. He ended up, however, dismissing Marcy's alarm as a tempest in a teapot.

CHAPTER THREE

Caroline had tried in vain to reach her brother. His agency told her he was at the Hotel Davenport in Spokane, but the hotel denied he was registered. The evening after the Annual Meeting, he finally called.

"Leigh, I have been trying to reach you to tell you I am going to be married the eighth of February. I know it is short notice, but I've had a terrible time trying to get a hold of you. Is there any chance that you could come to the wedding, I'd love to have you."

"Oh, marvy, Sis, that's really great news! Another steel man, like old Don?"

"No, Leigh, Sam is a priest."

"Sis, no! Don't do that to me! A priest? Ye gods, I thought they had to be celibate?"

"An Episcopal priest, you idiot!"

"Oh, a watered-down priest—well, that's a little better, I guess? By the way, did you get my letter on Patrice?"

"Patrice, I assume, is the child you just married?"

"Oh, now, Sis, don't be old fashioned. Patrice and I are soul mates; our ages are immaterial. Don't be stuffy."

"Whatever, Leigh, whatever. Would it be possible for you to come to our wedding on the eighth?"

"I haven't the foggiest, Sis. Let me call you when I find out where we are going after this iceberg. I'd like to bring Patrice, you should get to know her, but, on second thought, I doubt they'll let her go, she's just been cast."

"Oh, I'm sorry, Leigh, I could have found some children for her to play with."

"Caroline! Oh, Caroline, you were meant for a nunnery."

After she had hung up, she raised her eyes to heaven and thanked the Lord that Leigh's "child bride" had "just been cast."

* * * *

Xavier had been sweeping off the pathways to the church when a car drove up and stopped near him. When he turned, he did not see just a car, he saw the ultimate car in his opinion. It was a Jaguar XKR, convertible with a newly waxed Jaguar Racing Metallic finish. He knew a lot about this car, having studied its specifications carefully in several car magazines. He stopped making any attempt to sweep the snow and stood drinking in the beauty of the vision in front of him. Here was a bomb that Blue Booked at ninety thousand big ones, that developed 390 horsepower from a 4.2-liter V8 engine and weighed a hefty 2 tons. Checking the 18-inch alloy wheels and whistling softly, he stepped back in order to better see the shark's mouth grill and the sinister, slanted headlight treatment.

"Excuse me!" a voice called. "Hello!"

Xavier really did not hear anything, absorbed as he was. "Awesome!"

"Sir! Could you help me?"

Surprised as though the car had spoken to him, he peered through the side window. Inside was a girl somewhere about his age and she, like the car, was not just a girl, she was a really cool blonde.

"Sorry, I didn't hear you."

The girl lowered the window.

"That's OK. I was looking for Rev Adams. Would he be in the church, do you think?"

"Father Adams is in his study in the Parish House—there, back there, that building." He pointed behind her so she could not really see it. "Can I help you, I work for Father Adams?"

Xavier felt very bold offering to help the girl. She appeared not to need his help, but he wanted to delay her leaving.

"That's nice. I guess I can do it. It's just a note from my grandfather, Mr. Brown. I'm Lisa Brown."

Xavier suddenly realized that this was the Lisa Brown whom one of Mr. Brown's caretakers had told his mother about. She was staying at the Browns.

"I can take it to him, Miss Brown, or, you could back up and park over there," pointing to an area by the Parish House.

"Why don't you hop in and show me where his office is?" She smiled at him in a way that would have made him swim the Gulf of Mexico.

"I shouldn't, I'm kinda dirty."

"Dirty? Shoveling snow? Come on, get in."

Poor Xavier, on the verge of sitting in the ultimate automobile and, on top of that, next to this cool girl, was paralyzed.

"C'mon, please."

No man, least of all Xavier, could have refused this girl's "please." Obediently, he opened the door and very gingerly slid onto the platinum colored leather seat.

"There! See how easy that was?"

"It was the hardest-easiest thing I've ever done. This is such a beautiful car, Miss Brown."

Lisa turned to him and gave him one of her practiced pouts, "Car!" She laughed, "OK, car, but please, no more Miss Browns, you make me sound like somebody on Dr. Phil." She reversed gears and spun the wheels, launching the car back so fast Xavier gasped.

Lisa laughed delightedly and skidded to a stop perfectly parked next to the door of the Parish House.

"Phew! Has this baby got it!"

"Are you talking about me, sir?" She looked over at Xavier, a mock scowl on her face.

Xavier blushed bright red, "The car—I meant the car—Miss Brown—Miss Lisa."

The most beautiful laugh Xavier had ever heard wafted from the girl's lips. The combination of this girl and the unreal car had left him limp and spellbound. To make his paralysis even more immobilizing, she leaned over and put her hand on his arm. He knew she must have felt the tremor that shot through him.

"I'm naughty, aren't I? I'm sorry. Please tell me you name—and I am not Miss Lisa!"

"Uh—Xavier." It was crazy, but he had a moment of terror when he couldn't remember his own name.

"Oh, how lovely—Xavier! I love it—Xavier. That's Spanish, isn't it?" Her hand was still on his arm.

"Mexican,…. Lisa."

"How fun! Xavier, you are my first Mexican boyfriend!"

A scene from the movie *Pretty Woman* flashed though Xavier's mind—Julia Roberts, totally overcome by the music of La Boheme, exclaims, "I nearly peed in my pants!" He knew the feeling at that moment.

"Come on, Xavier, show me where Rev Adams hides." She released his arm and stepped out of the car.

Xavier opened the door of the Parish House and pointed to Father Adams' office.

"Will you wait for me, Xavier?"

Her voice had the heartrending tone of one about to go before a firing squad.

"Sure, yes, yes, I'll stay right here!" Xavier knew an earthquake would not have moved him.

The girl was gone only minutes.

"He was on the phone so I put it on his desk. He's older than I thought. Come on!" She tugged his arm.

Back outside, Xavier had no idea what the girl intended.

"You like the *car*, obviously."

"Sure! It's the most beautiful car I've ever seen close to."

"Come on then, drive it."

"Oh, no, I couldn't. Thanks, but I can't. I—I have to finish with the walks. Thanks, though!"

"Oh, come on, of course you can! It drives just like your car—maybe a little more powerful, but that part is easy. Come on, Xavier!" She pulled him toward the driver's door.

"Honest, Lisa, I can't. I told Father Adams I'd finish the walks, really. I'd like to but....'

"When do you work here?"

"Oh, most days after school."

"What grade are you in?"

"I'm a senior."

"Then you are seventeen—eighteen."

"I'm going to be eighteen this month."

"Cool! I'm only seventeen. Tell you what, on your birthday, you'll drive the car, OK? What day is your birthday?"

"It's the eighth."

"Will you drive it then?"

"I guess I could."

"Don't you *want* to?"

"Yes."

"Then I'll pick you up here on Friday."

"Wait a minute, Lisa, I forgot, I've got to do some extra work before the wedding."

"OK, then Sunday?. My grandfather's in the wedding. The minister is getting married?"

"Yes, Father Adams is marrying Mrs. Pickering."

"Sounds like she's already married."

"No, no, her husband died a couple of years ago."

"Good. It wouldn't be too cool for a minister to marry an already married woman, would it?"

Uncertain whether she was teasing him, he tried a laugh.

"See ya!" Lisa laughed as she got back in the car. "Next Sunday at, let's see, three o'clock, OK?"

"I'll be here, Lisa."

"You better, muchacho!" And she laughed again, jamming the shifter into gear, she threw gravel from the wheels as she skidded out onto the roadway. Disappearing down the narrow church lane, she blasted the horn three times.

Xavier stood where she had left him, his world tumbling over and over like a ball in a giant lottery shaker.

* * * *

Caroline was restless the night before Russell was to arrive. She was sure she had forgotten something vital in her plans for the wedding and after he arrived, with the girl, she knew the remaining days until the wedding would be busy—too busy to calmly think of all the details. Leigh had still not phoned her with his travel plans, only that he would be there sometime the day before the wedding. Brother or not, she could not spend precious time worrying about Leigh, free spirit that he was.

She mentally reviewed her schedule for the umpteenth time: Bishop Phillips and Nancy would arrive about one-thirty on the seventh—they were reliable. She had bought a new coverlet for their bed and had had the curtains cleaned.

Russell and the girl—what was her name, she couldn't remember—would move to the Canvasback on the seventh, making room for Leigh and his child bride, if she were to come with him—aargh! She hated to move Russell, but she did *not* need to advertise their sleeping habits to the Phillips—it was safer this way.

She had asked a woman she knew in town to help her out in the kitchen and with the meals during her guests' stay. The only big affair at the house would be the Friday night dinner for which she counted eleven, assuming Leigh would be two rather then one.

She was very pleased with the dress she had ordered from Hutzler's in Baltimore. She had debated long and hard on the dress, not wanting it to be ostentatious in any way yet she wanted it to express a style, pride if you will, in her new life with the humble but remarkable man she had so long admired. The only adornment she would wear, aside from a white orchid, would be a single strand of black pearls that Don had given her on her 50th birthday. She had asked Sam if he would mind and, of course, he said it would be wonderful.

She had ordered the largest prime rib roast the butcher had. Very pleased, she had found what she thought was a good Cabernet Sauvignon in a wine shop in Baltimore—at least it should be good at $40.00 a bottle!

They would run through the ceremony at one on Friday. She didn't feel it was necessary, but Sam, strangely enough, said he would be more comfortable if they did. He said he had performed so many wedding services from the altar steps that he wasn't sure of how it all worked from the opposite position.

So, what else did she need to do? She rolled over and squinted at the time—two-thirty! It was going to be long day tomorrow—today!

* * * *

When they arrived at his mother's, Russell had to admit that Allison had probably stretched the Florida thing a bit. He had worn blue jeans and an open sport shirt; Allison had worn only an abbreviated blouse, scanty white shorts and flip-flops. He had thought she had looked really sharp leaving Florida, but as soon as he saw his mother's look of horror, he knew he should have forewarned her.

"Hi, Mom!" He kissed her and gave her a big hug, genuinely happy to see her, but also to divert her eyes from Allison.

Caroline's first impression of Russell's friend was not favorable. The weather had moderated some, but it was still freezing.

She hissed in his ear, "My lord, Russ, where are the girl's clothes?"

He turned and held out his hand to Allison, "Come and say 'hi' to my Mom—Caroline. She wonders whether you are warm enough?"

"Brr, not really. Hi, Mrs. Pickering, good to meet you."

Russell put his arm around Allison and urged her into the house. Caroline had gone ahead to pull a coat from the hall closet.

Slipping into the coat, Allison actually purred, "Ohhh! How luscious this feels. Is this an animal, Mrs. Pickering?"

"Well, yes, I suppose it was at one time."

"Russy, look. Don't I look sexy in this, really?"

"You look like a frozen Fiji Islander in a dead animal's coat. Is that sexy, I'm not sure."

"You must be tired from the trip, Russy," she teased.

* * * *

Caroline had invited Rachel to join them for dinner, but she had said she'd be a little late. Sam arrived about five-thirty; it seemed like midnight to Caroline. She had exhausted her small talk with Allison while Russell made a number of calls on his cell phone as he wandered around the house reacquainting himself with the once familiar antiques and photographs. The girl, still snuggled in the fur coat her legs curled under her on the sofa, had shown no signs of changing her clothes for dinner.

When Sam came in, Allison got up so that he, too, had a momentary shock when he saw her long, bare legs.

Caroline introduced them.

"Allison, very nice to meet you and to have you with us. Sam Adams." He extended his hand to her.

Her hand was ice-cold. "Hi, Mr, oops, sorry, Reverend Adams, really great to meet you. My Dad sends his regards."

Caught off guard, not knowing her father, Sam stammered something like, "How very thoughtful."

"He's a preacher, Reverend Adams," Russell said, as he came into the room. "How are you, sir? May I offer you my congratulations!"

"Why thank you, Russell. I have looked forward to meeting you for some time. Thank you for coming, it means so much to your mother having you here." They shook hands. "May I interject a comment here? It is always awkward to address a priest—is it *Father* So-and-so, or *Reverend*, or *Pastor*, or plain old *Mister*, or worse? My preference is to be called *Sam*, as long as you all keep it a secret." He turned to Allison, "Your father is a minister, too? What denomination, may I ask?"

Thinking of conventional churches, he was further confused when she replied, "Oh, he has his own church."

Intercepting an undecipherable frown from Caroline, Sam decided to let the subject go at that.

"Wonderful! How nice. Please return my greetings." He walked over to Caroline, crossing his eyes as he approached her, kissing her on the nose.

Not having relaxed since Russell and the girl arrived, Caroline felt a convulsive need to laugh. Coughing uncontrollably, she gripped Sam in an iron embrace.

"Gosh, Mom, are you allergic to your new husband already?" Russell was relieved to take the spotlight off Allison.

"You've noticed that, too? But she takes medication for it, in fact, I should excuse myself and concoct some medication right now."

"I'm sorry," Caroline apologized, non-apologetically. "I will go with Sam and put some refreshments together."

"What might I serve you, Allison?"

"I'd like a coke, please."

"Her dad's church forbids alcohol, ahh—Sam," Russell explained. "I'd have a Scotch or Bourbon, doesn't matter which."

"Good, Russell. Will you make allowances for us, Allison?"

"Oh, I have no problem with drinking. I think it's a silly rule of my Dad's, but I grew up that way—his rules are law."

"I see. Well I respect your respecting his rules, Allison." He nodded and joined Caroline in the kitchen

"Sam, what if she doesn't have any clothes or shoes to wear?" She was now so relaxed that she could not stop laughing.

"There's always the Salvation Army," he replied, enjoying her amusement

* * * *

Rachel did not arrive until quarter after six. Caroline had given her son some background on Rachel, including the suicide of a person she had been close to and the loss of another friend to an accident and her consequent decision to leave St. James in the spring. She had told him just enough to pique his interest in this woman. Without having met her, he was intrigued by the morbid complications of her life. He couldn't help comparing it to the apparently cloudless existence of his friend, Allison.

Caroline delayed dinner to allow a second round of drinks for Russell and Sam, and to allow Rachel time to get acquainted with Allison and Russell. Rachel, never an aggressive conversationalist, deferred to the more spontaneous repartee of the group; several times Russell attempted to draw Rachel into the conversation.

At one point he said to her, "Rachel, my mother tells me you are planning to go to India soon. That is an exciting prospect. May I ask, why India?"

Embarrassed to have to answer a question that hit so close to home, she hesitated and then stammered, "Actually I may go to Nepal—north of India. There probably is no logical reason for Nepal—perhaps *that's* the reason I'm going there."

That kind of answer, of course, could not have intrigued Russell more.

"I applaud that type of thinking!" He clapped his hands in approval.

Realizing her answer had sounded completely inane, she attempted to re-phrase it. "I guess I made the trip sound ridiculous. What I meant was, that many times a purely logical decision takes second place to a more— what should I say?—emotional one." As the words stumbled out, they were not at all what she wanted to say. She blushed and finished, weakly, "I don't know the reason, I guess?"

Caroline and Sam, empathizing with Rachel's embarrassment started on another conversational tack. Russell, too, saw Rachel's confusion and sensed the question must be emotionally charged and decided to laugh at himself.

"I'd love to go to India—Nepal, but the powers that be, namely my mother, long ago demanded that I come home to stoke the fires of industrial America. It *may* be possible, when I retire in thirty-odd years, that I will get to go there."

Sam, sensing it was time to eat, gave Caroline a wag of his head toward the dining room which was sufficient to prompt her invitation to sit down to dinner.

The dinner conversation went smoothly—Russell, aware there was a need to be cautious about kidding the young cleric and Sam moving conversational subjects along at a brisk pace, combined to keep things light—neither Rachel nor Allison contributed a great deal. Rachel, mentally kicking herself for unwittingly letting her guard down and then stammering out her adolescent attempt at an explanation, tried somewhat unsuccessfully, to appear interested and involved. Allison, at a more primitive level, concentrated on consuming several helpings of prime rib and mashed potatoes and did not let the conversation interfere with her gustatory pleasure.

* * * *

After dinner, they sat around the fire. Sam and Caroline had become more accustomed to Allison, helped considerably by Russell's perfectly normal acceptance of the girl's idiosyncrasies. It was apparent that she adored him. Nestling against him, warmed by the heat of the fire, she drowsed, blissfully unaware of the conversation around her.

Sam could not help studying the girl and, unconsciously comparing her to Rachel, and trying to define what the Allisons of the world meant. Aware that Caroline would accuse him of being too "heavy", he, nonetheless, could not resist running through his mental drill: what was this segment of the younger generation trying to say to life and, specifically, what was it they were trying to say to those, like himself who would very soon pass into history. He felt it immensely important to try to weed through all the overt differences—whether they be language, dress, puncture or garnishment, or P&G, as he called metal adornment and tattooing, so that he might be able to find a level of communication with them. He thought he had accomplished at least a superficial level of communication with Xavier, but even there he was not sure how deeply their understanding of each other went.

This girl was making a statement with her clothes; granted she was a product of Florida where sand and sun were king, but yet, wearing these briefest of shorts and flip-flops to Russell's mother's home in Maryland in the middle of the winter had to say something—defiance? He did not feel that was justified. Certainly it conveyed self-confidence, a strong ego, a take-it-or-leave-it philosophy. What, he wondered, had been the increments in building this philosophy—what made a difference to her? She had expressed her acquiesance to her father's strict rules, yet, at the same time, had verbally dismissed them as silly. Unable to pigeonhole Allison in a meaningful way, he, nonetheless, realized she was distinctly part of a force for change. This might especially be true because she was a product of the powerful evangelical movement in the South. Fascinating thought.

"Sam? Sam!" A voice seemed to be calling to him. His mind crept slowly back to the group around the fire.

"Sam? Where are you, my dear? I think it's time for you and me to say goodnight to these young people. You have a busy schedule tomorrow and I'm going to run to Baltimore to do some shopping. Incidentally, Allison, you are more than welcome to join me, you might see something you like?"

There was only a faint mumbling response that Caroline could not interpret.

"I doubt you'll make a sale, Mom. She's brought the clothes she likes. She can be a very stylish dresser; she may surprise you."

Caroline exchanged glances with Sam.

"Well, fine, just thought I'd ask. Rachel, thanks for coming, nice to have you here. Sam, goodnight—back to your monastic cell, my dear. Call me tomorrow after five sometime." She kissed him and opened the door for Rachel and Sam to leave.

CHAPTER FOUR

The following morning, Russell and Allison came down to breakfast at eight, each still waking up—hair tousled and pajamas askew. To call what Allison was wearing pajamas, Caroline decided, was as generous as she could be—it consisted, more precisely, of a wisp here and a wisp there.

During breakfast the girl slowly woke up. She asked Caroline about her wedding, what she would be wearing, what flowers would be appropriate in February, how many guests she expected, who was Sam's best man, where were they going on their honeymoon if it was not a secret, how long had she known Sam, etc, etc.

Caroline was both flattered and surprised by the girl's curiosity. It slowly dawned on her that weddings might be much on her mind. Knowing Russell's dismissal of Allison as a marriage candidate, she could not help feeling sorry for the girl's eager, but futile curiosity.

"Mrs. Pickering?"

"Why not Caroline, Allison?"

"Caroline, would you object to my changing my mind about riding to Baltimore with you today?"

"Of course not, my dear, I'd love to have your company. I'm hoping to leave as close to ten as possible, however." Looking over at Allison's somewhat less than Baltimore clothes.

Allison jumped up and ran to the stairs.

Russell laughed, "I wondered last night why she didn't want to go with you—she lives to buy clothes."

At five minutes to ten, Allison came downstairs. If Caroline had not known it was she who had gone upstairs, she would never have known the person who came down. This person was dressed in a silver-blue satin pants suit, her long blonde hair meticulously coiled, mascara making her large blue eyes luminus, silver drop earrings adding the final touch to her exotic image. Caroline noticed that she even had on silver slippers.

Caroline was speechless—it could not possibly be the same adolescent hoyden who had arrived yesterday afternoon!

"Allison, you absolutely take my breath away!" She was not exaggerating. "You are very beautiful, my dear!"

"Thank you." Even her voice seemed to have taken on a sophisticated air.

Caroline, who had dressed "down" expecting Allison to appear in her role as a teenager in Tahiti, excused herself and dashed upstairs. Ten minutes later she came down dressed in a tailored Harris Tweed suit with a turquoise necklace and earrings complementing the soft brown of her blouse.

"There! I can't compete—this is the best I can do on short notice!"

Russell, who had come into the hallway when he heard all the commotion, started to laugh, then Allison and Caroline joined in. He ushered them out of the house, delighted that his mother had seen the glamorous side of Allison.

Left to his own devices for the day, Russell found himself thinking of the young woman, Rachel. He had the feeling that she would be interesting to talk to if he could break through the barriers she seemed to have erected. He was fascinated that she was planning to go halfway around the world to the isolated mountain kingdom of Nepal. He was envious, in fact, that she could break away and explore such a unique place. It vividly brought back the exciting days he had spent during his "European year."

What the heck, he decided, call her up and see if they might have lunch and talk.

The phone rang several times, enough that Russell assumed she was not home. On the fourth ring, however, she answered.

"Rachel Mason speaking."

"Rachel Mason, this is Russell Wood Pickering speaking. Good morning!" He made no attempt to disguise mimicking her formal greeting.

"Good morning," was her flat response.

"Rachel, I have been left high and dry by everyone here—they've all gone shopping. I wondered if I might take you to lunch? I'd enjoy talking to you?"

"Sort of as a last resort type of thing?" It was an attempt at humor, but it did not work, it sounded plaintive.

"Oh, oh! Not well said, I gather. Let me try again. Rachel, I have been an irrational, inveterate, etcetera, explorer of strange places. I would love to talk to you about Nepal or any other country. Could we do lunch and talk?"

"I assume that both of us being irrational would be our common denominator?"

Russell felt he was losing points in this verbal sparring. "Rachel, may I make it less suspect if I simply say I'd like to talk to you—about anything?"

He suspected from her long hesitation that she was going to refuse.

Finally, short of enthusiastically, she replied, "That would be fine, I guess. Where have you in mind?"

"The only place I know about is the Canvasback, is that an OK place?"

"It is very nice."

Still her perfunctory tone told him there was little enthusiasm for the venture.

"Great! Would noon be convenient?"

"That's fine. I'll see you there." She hung up.

Russell felt like he did when he made a major software sale, but he also knew he had been through a rough negotiating trial. This should be fun, he thought.

* * * *

He was minutes late getting to the Canvasback and found Rachel seated at a table in the center of the room. Passing a waitress, he asked if they might have the booth in the corner.

"Good morning, again, Rachel. Nice to see you. Would you mind if we sat in that booth? I'm always nervous about leaving my back unprotected?"

"Yes, of course, if you prefer," she replied, picking up her purse as she got up.

Russell was still pursuing fragments that might add up to "what makes Rachel tick." He registered the fact that she had chosen the most central, most crowded area of the restaurant—certainly not one for quiet, reflective conversation. He had also noticed, however, that she was not wearing her clerical collar as she had last night. She was really very pretty, he thought. Though she still seemed reserved, guarded in her responses to his opening gambits, she, at least, did not seem as combative as she had on the phone.

After their salad and ice cream lunch, during which Russell had picked his way through innocent subjects like a soldier picking his way through a minefield, he suggested coffee.

He told her of some of his adventures in Europe, omitting any mention of his companion. Referring to Nepal, he told her as Far East as he had ever gotten was St. Petersburg, but he had always yearned to see Everest and the Himalayas.

She seemed interested in his bicycle adventures, but he had not elicited any response with his mention of Nepal. She asked a few questions about his experiences in Europe, what the accommodations were like, how the food was and then, companionship—how did he fare traveling alone for a year?

Given the option of lying to her or admitting he had not been alone, he did not hesitate to tell her that he had met his ex-wife in Finland and that they had traveled together.

"Oh, I'm sorry, I didn't mean to intrude into your personal life. I guess I hadn't known you were married."

"Divorced three years ago—no problem." He felt pleased she knew.

"That's too bad! Allison is certainly a very beautiful young lady. You are very fortunate."

"Rachel, let me cut through some of this: Allison is a *very* beautiful young lady, one I like very much, but one who will not be my second wife, if I ever have one. She's fun to be with, but that's about it." He was glad that Allison had come into the conversation, it cleared the air on that subject.

"Oh, again, I'm sorry, I really wasn't trying to...."

"Rachel, may I say something to you that could offend you if you want it to, or not. You are not wearing your clerical collar, but I get the feeling something other than that collar is constricting you. Where are *you*? You have let me babble on and on, but I don't hear *you*. Are you only a professional listener? You are an extremely pretty, *young* woman—I'd like to get to know you, but you're hiding from me, why?"

Russell knew he was throwing the dice; either he would break through or she would get up and leave.

She sat staring at him—did he see her eyes mist briefly as though she might cry?

"You are nothing if not direct, Russell Pickering. I could be offended, but I'll choose not to be. In my own defense, if I need one, we *have* just met, you know. Am I obliged to let my hair down to every person who invites me to lunch—'professional listener' that I am?" Starting defiantly, her tone softened. "I'm sorry to be deadwood, Russell, I've never been known as the life of the party, plus I admit to being poor company right now. I'd get up and leave right now, if I were you." Her expression seemed to say, "please don't." "Tell you what, just to show you I'm able to talk: you come over to my apartment and we'll talk all afternoon."

Russell heard challenge and defiance, but he also heard a plea to be understood, to be liked, and also a tone that seemed to accept him, trusted him enough to admit him to her secret hiding place.

He got up and took her by the hand, pulling her up out of the booth, "Boy, do I have a way with clerical broads! Let's go Sphinxy; drown me with words!"

She got up laughing happily for the first time in a long, long time.

* * * *

Rachel unlocked her apartment door and walked in ahead of him. "I wasn't expecting guests, Russell, so you will have to make allowances for my casual lifestyle."

"I'll just sit here by myself while you tidy up the place; I hate untidiness." He pulled off his jacket and threw it on the floor.

Rachel was functioning on a very thin veneer of bravado by inviting this man to her apartment; in fact, by the time they had gotten there, she was already regretting it. Why she felt the need to prove to him that she was capable of "talking" was ridiculous! She really didn't want to have to fend off his probing, challenging questions. As she busied herself straightening the sofa cushions and collecting the sections of the morning paper, she felt her resentment of him and her annoyance with herself build.

"Could I make you some coffee or would you prefer a soft drink?" She asked, struggling to sound solicitous.

"Just a couple of jiggers of single malt scotch will do, thanks."

"I repeat, may I make…." She could not disguise a note of impatience.

"Rachel?"

She turned toward him.

"Is this a bad idea, charging in on you like this? What do you think?"

There was her out, just admit that it would be better at another time maybe, but she found she was unable to say it.

He got up as though to leave, sensing her discomfort.

"Russell,…. please don't leave. I'm sorry. Chalk it up to the February blahs or something. Please, sit down, I'm sorry."

He sat down again. "I'm a coffee drinker, Rachel, if you please."

Going into the kitchen gave her time to lecture herself. *For goodness sake, snap out of it! Can you make yourself any less attractive? The hurt, emotionally bruised little innocent from the Kansas farm—grow up, Rachel!* These and other taunting words tumbled out of her mind. When she returned with the coffee, she hoped she had regained something resembling graciousness.

Their talk was a rambling, cursory feeling-out of each other. Russell was consciously less aggressive than at lunch and brought up subjects he thought she might be interested in. At one point, he asked her about her seminary life in Massachusetts. When she mentioned her love for hiking in the Berkshires, he discovered they had hiked the same trails when he was at Harvard.

"I really loved those hills," she told him. "I was something of a loner at seminary, not because I felt I was any different than the other students, but because I guess I needed to let nature overwhelm me; to give me a quiet time to think." She stopped, aware that she was exposing personal feelings.

"I can understand that. The wilderness has the same effect on me. It allows a certain kind of freedom, yet one that demands a sense of awe at the sheer power of it. Tell me how you decided to go to seminary."

It was an innocent question and logically followed her mention of the seminary.

Rachel looked at him trying to guess whether he may have been told anything about Ben's part in her life. She chose to guess that he did not know anything about him other than his suicide.

She started to tell fragments of her background, her life in Kansas, college at Kansas State, even, briefly about Scott's death in Nepal. Then, she suddenly found herself telling him about the episode at the restaurant with Ben; how he had escaped from the Colorado police and hidden in the restaurant where she worked; how they had talked and she had felt so sorry for this boy; then when the police arrived and the awful shooting; his capture; how she had testified for him at his trial and his imprisonment for seven years; then his unbelievable appearance in Afton.

Gradually she told him everything. It was as though, once started, she couldn't stop.

He listened intently, quietly, nodding, or occasionally asking a question. He saw her relive the experience, her facial expressions unable to disguise her emotions.

She struggled through Ben's suicide and then stopped, exhausted. She felt strangely relieved to have been able to tell a virtual stranger her innermost thoughts.

Apologetically, she said, "I'm sorry. Who wants to hear all that travail? Serves you right! See, I can talk my head off."

He came over and sat next to her. She did not know what to expect and was immediately uncomfortable with him so close to her.

He reached for one of her hands. "Rachel, thank you very much. That is as warm a compliment as you could give me to tell me that story. I know how difficult it was for you and I appreciate it even more because of that."

She didn't know whether to withdraw her hand, but somehow it felt natural.

"Oh, well, thanks for listening. As you said, you must have a way with clerical broads."

"Speaking of which, it's not that I have anything against women clergy, but I do feel easier without your clerical collar. I suppose that's because I'm such an inveterate sinner?"

Rachel's mind, her clerical mind, could not restrain the image of Russell and Allison living what amounted to a married life.

"It's not too late to change your evil ways and repent!" She laughed, but she was uncomfortable with the subject. He still held her hand and it felt good.

"I want to know more about the fellow who went to Nepal, but I've been here too long already so, if you invite me, I'd like to come back." He had seen her clock showing it to be five o'clock; he had been there three hours.

"Scott? Well, maybe. That's a different story. How about you and Denise? Would you tell me more about her?"

"Not yet, you are still proving to me that you can talk, remember? I'm still the listener."

"She laughed, "Well, we'll see."

He got up, letting go of her hand, and recovered his jacket from the floor.

"I really liked this, Rachel. Thank you. I hope you'll ask me back?"

"I enjoyed it too, and I thought I wouldn't. Thank *you*."

After he had left, she looked at the hand he had held. "You feel different, are you?" She laughed again.

* * * *

Caroline's shopping trip to Baltimore with Allison turned out to be very pleasant, so much so that Caroline wondered at how wrong she had been in judging the girl. Their conversation ranged over a wide variety of topics: politics, literature, entertainment and, fleetingly, religion. She learned that Allison had graduated summa cum laude from Stetson University in Florida and had been a member of the college tennis team.

When they began looking for clothes, Caroline was willing to let Allison guide her to areas where more youthful styles were featured. Although uneasy with several of Allison's recommendations, she ended up with three more colorful outfits that she never would have considered if left to her conservative habits.

The entire day was a smashing victory for a girl who wanted to impress her potential mother-in-law. Caroline couldn't wait to tell Sam how much she admired Allison and how wrong she had been with her first impressions.

They arrived back in Afton just as Russell was turning into the driveway.

"How did it go, ladies? I see bags so someone bought something."

"Your Allison was a dear, Russ. She convinced me I wasn't sixty-five, that I should pretend to be forty! That's a great gift, twenty-five years!"

"Great! How about you, Al, did you find anything?"

"I saw a number of nice things, but I guess I'm all set for the time being. And you, how did you spend your lonely hours without me?" She came over and nestled against him.

"Oh, this and that. Just sort of enjoyed the quiet, I guess." He was reluctant to mention his day with Rachel with her arms around his neck.

"You have one smart cookie here, Russ. I couldn't have enjoyed it more!"

* * * *

That evening after Sam had arrived, she continued to express her new appreciation of Allison. Most of what Caroline said reflected her true feelings, impressed as she had been by Allison's breadth of knowledge and obvious intelligence, but no small part of her motivation was the feeling that here was a wonderful mate for her footloose son.

Russell, pleased that his mother had had such a pleasant day with Allison, was convinced that part of her enthusiasm was, subtly, a sales campaign. He thought back on his afternoon with Rachel and, though knowing her only very briefly, compared her to Allison. He decided it was a premature judgment, but Rachel was an attractive girl, no, really quite pretty, complicated, confused, and intriguing.

* * * *

On the third day of Allison's visit, it became apparent that she had decided to stay through the wedding. It was not a problem for Caroline because she had become fond of the unorthodox girl, but it did seem to disturb her son. He had made several comments that sounded as though he would have preferred it if she had left.

The day before everyone was to arrive, he called Rachel on his cell phone to avoid using the house phone. When he suggested that they meet again before everything began to happen she hesitated. She told him of the various things she had to do, most of them to relieve Sam at this time, but he sensed she was only using these things as an excuse to avoid seeing him. As a last resort, he used his leaving on Sunday as a final plea.

"I really shouldn't, Russell—maybe for a short visit? When do you have in mind?"

"It's nine-thirty, how about ten-thirty?"

"Well, I guess. Sure, see you then. Bye."

Telling his mother that he wanted to do some personal shopping (he was perversely amused at that definition of seeing Rachel), he left Allison content with her several copies of People magazine.

When Rachel opened her door, he greeted her, "The Reverend Miss Mason, I believe?"

"I could be a little sensitive about your using the miss-ing part of Reverend, but come in anyway, Russell." She smiled. She realized how pleased she was to see him again.

"If you pick up on that, Rachel, you don't *miss* much."

"Enough already with the misses. Come in and sit down. Coffee, I assume?"

"That'd be great."

He couldn't help but notice that she seemed more relaxed with him and although he couldn't remember what she had worn on their last "date", she was wearing a bright blue blouse, printed with exotic flowers of some sort; her eyes seemed to pick up a luster from the blue of her blouse. Her hair seemed different though, again, he couldn't seem to remember how it had been. She looked fresh and pretty.

Rachel had anticipated that he would like coffee so had prepared a pot. He followed her into the kitchen. The kitchen being apartment-small, she was very conscious of him being so close.

"You cook, I assume?" She used the question as a sort of shield.

"I really don't. I can if I need to, but I'm not interested, I guess."

"Denise, being a Scandinavian, probably was a good cook?"

Russell didn't want to spend much time on Denise's qualities as a chef. She had, in fact, been a raw vegetable advocate.

"Not really, raw foods mainly."

Back in the living room, she sat in one of the armchairs as protection from him sitting with her if she sat on the sofa. Russell guessed why she did what she did.

"So, tomorrow is the big gathering, then the wedding the next day. Do I understand you will be assisting the Bishop in the ceremony?"

"Yes, a little nervous about that, as a matter of fact."

"I'm looking forward to seeing you in your vestments."

"If the Bishop is robed as I expect him to be, you won't even see me."

"Oh, I expect I will."

Uncomfortable with the implication that he would be focusing on her, she tried another tack.

"I'm terribly fond of your mother, Russell. She has been so kind to me."

"You probably know her better than I do, Rachel, but we have always been close. How about Mr. Adams, has he been easy to work with?"

"I couldn't have found a more perfect man to teach me how to take my first steps. I love the Reverend Samuel Adams as a priest and as a man."

"That gives other men a problem, Rachel, you know that?"

The conversation kept veering toward areas she was uncomfortable with.

"I don't have a problem. . . .." She couldn't finish, "with men", because that wouldn't be true. Certainly she had had such a problem with Ben. She finished lamely, "I guess I won't finish that."

"Rachel, honestly, I'm not trying to make you uncomfortable. You have to remember that I, like most men, don't know half of what I should know about women. Let's agree that neither of us really knows anything profound about the other sex. What I do know is that I like you and I'd like us to get to know a little more about each other on something more than a superficial level. How's that for being ultra suave?"

She couldn't control the skip-in-her-heart-beat feeling that she had not known since Scott—this was emotional territory she didn't know how to explore. Her reaction to her heartbeat, however, made her blush.

"You are almost too much for me, Russell. I don't like devious people, but flat out openness has its own problems."

"Gosh, what does that mean? The fact that I say I like you gives you problems?"

"Yes, I suppose it does in a way."

"You're not likable, is what you are saying, right?"

"Russell, I will hit you with this magazine if you don't stop!" Confused as he made her feel, she could only laugh at his bating.

"Tell you what. You are dealing with your tired old persona of Rachel Mason as I am doing with an even tired-er persona of Russell Pickering. To make things easier for both of us, let's take new names, known only to us, and write a new story on a fresh page. Want to try it?"

Rachel was instantly charmed by this fantasy; it would allow her to shed the burdens of the last few months, her guilt about Ben, Scott's tragedy and her unknown future.

"Oh, yes, let's do that!" She clapped her hands like a three-year-old at a birthday party.

"What shall I call you—no longer Rachel?"

"You choose my name and I'll choose yours."

"All my life I have been partial to Penelope and I've never met one. How's that?"

"Oh, yes, I love it! Let me see, no, that won't do. How about, no. I think you are a perfect Algernon."

Russell turned up his nose, but laughing said, "Thanks for the compliment. OK, we're all set; new names, new lives. Let's start by you telling me how old Penelope is?"

"She, I am twenty-five, soon to be twenty-six—and you?"

"Use my name, please."

"Algy, how old are you?"

"I'm thirty-two soon to be thirty-three. When's your birthday?"

"March fifth, yours?"

"Amazing! March sixth. The other person who was just in the room, why do you think she sat in that chair you're in rather than the sofa?"

There was a pause while Penelope tried to decide whether this violated the rules. She decided, what the heck.

"I would guess, not knowing her very well, that she might have been afraid the other person might have sat on the sofa, too."

"I know it is very difficult to figure out another person's motives, but why do you think she was afraid?"

"I would make a wild guess that she probably didn't know how to handle something that might have turned—emotional?"

"OK, if it were you, Penelope, would that bother you?"

"I'm not sure, Russell, that I can play this game."

"Oh, sure you can, answer me." He made his voice sound commanding.

Rachel stared at him for an intense minute then, in a small voice, she replied, "I don't think it would."

"Are you sure?"

"Yes, I think so."

"Good! Now, why don't we both go back in the kitchen and get a second cup of coffee. The other person seemed a bit nervous when she was there the first time."

They did as Russell suggested, Rachel moving as though hypnotized. When they came back into the living room, she sat on the sofa, Russell sat next to her.

Although the play-acting had worked to this point, now even Penelope was nervous as to what would come next.

Algernon leaned back, "Let's just relax, Penelope, and talk. Let's mentally travel somewhere, other than Nepal. Where else would you most like to go?"

Visibly relieved, Penelope leaned back and said, "St. Petersburg."

"Why, St. Pete?"

"I guess because I read a book that made a deep impression on me— *Nicholas and Alexandra*. It was the story of the last Tsar of Russia and his family. It was so morbidly tragic, yet so well written you felt you were living with them at the time. I'd love to walk in those same streets and try to envision their life."

From this book they explored others each had liked, which lead to their best movies, then to favorite experiences, then to significant people in their lives, to places they had enjoyed and even to politics were they found they were not far apart. Finally, they just lay back and let a satisfied silence fall.

Russell had long-since forgotten the time until, in this silence, he heard a clock chime three. Startled, he checked his watch; it was three o'clock!

Laughing, he sat up, "I'm supposed to be shopping for something, I'm not sure what and I still haven't found it. Or have I?"

Rachel came out of her own reverie.

"Russell-Algy, I have so enjoyed this, *child's play*, it has been wonderful. I apologize for only providing a banana and milk, you must be starved?"

They stood up, the spell broken.

"I feel like we have had plenty of nourishment, enough to digest for a long time." He moved toward her and put his arms around her waist, drawing her closer. Her body, was rigid at first, then she did not resist. "I am very fond of Penelope, you should know that."

Uncertain where she was headed, looking up at him, she said, "Algy, I need to go slowly." But she did not pull away from him, then he kissed her. When they parted, she said, her voice quaking, "That was nice, but it was just over the speed limit, don't you think?"

Russell laughed, "Remember, I'm a lot older then you are, time is more valuable to me."

"I'm hardly an authority on kissing but you do nicely for an elderly man."

They were both laughing by then. Russell held her tightly for a minute, then stepped away.

"I've got to go, that's enough excitement for the elderly, you teaser."

Rachel reached for his hand, "Russell, thank you for being so nice. You make me feel like a normal person. I like you very much, but...."

He had put his hand over her lips.

"No buts! I think I understand where you are in your journey and I respect that, just don't try to define our relationship yet. I still have a few years left in me." He winked at her and left.

CHAPTER FIVE

The day before the wedding dawned cold and overcast. Caroline, up early and ready for the day, looked out at the thermometer. She cringed, it read ten degrees. "Is that necessary?" She asked the thin glass tube. There was a heavy frost glazing the front lawn. "That means tricky driving."

"Who are you talking to, Mom?" Russell had wakened early and had driven over to his mother's, leaving Allison at the Canvasback, curled in an embryonic ball fast asleep.

"Good morning, Russell. How did you sleep over there?"

"Oh, fine, Mother." In fact, he had not slept well at all. He had rehearsed the day with Rachel to a point where he met himself coming and going. Was he just playing with her, or did he really feel something special for her? It was not his normal, blasé reaction to a girl. "How are you doing on this semi-auspicious day?"

"Good, but I will be glad to get it going. How was the drive over?"

"A bit greasy, but not too bad."

"Eggs and bacon?"

"Please."

"Where did you eat yesterday? I had expected you back for lunch. I never asked you whether you found what you were shopping for."

"I just grabbed something to eat. As far as the shopping went, I'd have to say it was exploratory, but very rewarding."

"You make it sound mysterious. Is it something for Allison?"

"No, Mom, I doubt she would think of this as a present."

"Oh? I can't deal with mysteries today. Good luck with whatever it is."

"I may need it."

"Here, sit down and eat your eggs and stop trying to confuse me."

"When is Uncle Leigh arriving?"

"Sometime between now and dinner. He was being his usual obscure self, saying only he'd be here for dinner."

"You said he had gotten married again; will his wife be with him?"

"I'm not sure, Russ, I would guess not, however. I may have chilled that idea."

"The Bishop and his wife?"

"One-thirty. We are gong to have a short run-through when they get here; Sam feels he needs it."

"So, the only other people are Sam's Senior Warden?"

"The Browns, Nancy and Dwight, and, of course, Rachel."

"Oh, she's coming, too?" Russell knew very well that she was invited.

"Well, don't say it that way, Russ. She's a lovely person. I hope you will do what you can to make it easy for her—this is a very difficult time for her."

"Well, I could try. Why don't you seat me next to her?"

"I could do that, that would be nice. Thanks, Russ."

* * * *

After the Bishop and Nancy arrived, they all went to the church for the rehearsal. Caroline alerted Rachel they were leaving.

The rehearsal went smoothly as Caroline was sure it would—Sam seemed able to master the rudimentary layman's movements he was required to make. The Bishop and Rachel discussed their roles and the organist ran through the first verses of the hymns she would play. Caroline had asked that two pieces be played just before the service, *Jesu Joy of Man's Desiring*, and *Sheep May Safely Graze*.

When everyone was sure of his role, they moved toward the doors to leave; as they did, the Bishop touched Rachel on the arm, "Rachel, would you stay with me a moment?"

"Yes, of course, Bishop."

"Sam, you folks go ahead, Rachel and I will be along in a minute."

"Fine, sir. See you back at Caroline's."

They sat quietly until they were alone in the church, then the Bishop said, very quietly, "Rachel, I have wanted to talk to you since Sam told me of your desire to leave St. James. I believe I understand your reasons: you have been through a great deal. You have lost two people dear to you, both in ways that severely challenge us to understand. But you have kept your head up and continued to serve this church faithfully, and with grace. I want you to know that your rector believes you are an exceptional person—one who has so much to give to your work. Neither he nor I want you to leave thinking you have not served Him well. If, indeed, it is something you feel you must do, we will support your decision. If you do leave, know that I will welcome you back when you are ready to return. Are you still convinced you will be doing the right thing, Rachel?"

Rachel had to fight her emotions as the Bishop's words pricked her unhealed wounds. His eyes, sad, gentle, yet penetrating so deeply, she felt he could read her every thought.

"Bishop Phillips, I wish I could stay. St. James has been my first real home. No one has been kinder to me and at the same time given me the inspiration to know how to serve God. Sam has been dear to me in so many ways." Rachel's voice was uneven, on the verge of breaking. "I want to return here, if I can, but something deep inside me tells me I must stand back and listen. I have been truly shaken, I confess to you. I need to find that one clear voice that I had heard before all this happened. I know how selfish and dramatic I sound, but I have to trust myself in this or I may become someone else, someone not truly me. I'm doing a terrible job trying to explain, I know. Can you forgive me?"

The Bishop extended his hand and grasped both of hers, tightly knotted by her effort to explain herself.

"Rachel, it isn't up to me to forgive you. It is He, whose forgiveness you already have. He will be with you always. You cannot be alone in your search. Might we kneel together for a moment, Rachel?"

Rachel's face was streaked with tears as she knelt beside the Bishop, his hand on hers.

After a few minutes, he sat up in the pew and she followed.

"Rachel, I have something else I need to tell you."

Her emotions already unsteady, she braced herself for what this could be.

"I have a friend, an Archbishop if that matters, in Singapore who has started a health clinic for Tibetans in Nepal. I took the liberty of writing him a note about you and your desire to go to Nepal. I got his reply yesterday. He would be very eager to have you join his staff. I have no idea what your plans are, but if such a contact would be useful to you, he seems most receptive."

"That is so nice of you, Bishop. I shall certainly contact him. I don't know how I may be able to help him, but it sounds very appealing."

"Good! I have brought the information with me and will leave it with you. Shall we join the others? I will need to thumb a ride with you, if you'll pick me up?"

"I'm sort of ashamed of my ancient Civic, Bishop, but if you can curl up enough to get in, I'll try to get you there."

* * * *

Back at Caroline's, Rachel dropped the Bishop at the front door and then parked her car away from the main entry.

Before she could open the front door, Russell opened it.

"Hi!"

"Hello, Algy," she smiled, but the emotional session with the Bishop showed.

"Anything wrong, Pen?"

"Could we find a place to—talk?"

"Sure, Mom's den, come on."

Once in the den, he closed the door

"I need to talk to you, Russell."

Seeing she was struggling, he came up to her. She put her arms around his neck and clung to him.

She didn't make a sound, but he could feel her body tremble as she drew in deep, choked breaths.

"Rachel, what is it," he whispered?

"Hold me, please!"

After some minutes, her breathing became more normal and she relaxed her grip on him.

When she leaned back from him, he saw the tears on her cheeks.

"Let's sit down, Rachel." He led her to a small sofa in the corner of the room. "Now, don't tell me anything I don't need to know; it's enough for me, just this."

"Oh, Russell, I am making such a colossal mess of things! I hate myself right now. How could I have ever thought I could be mature enough to help other people?"

"Easy does it. Let's sort of go back a bit. What happened at the church?"

"It isn't what happened at the church, it's what happened when I went to Divinity School, when I went to college, when I thought I could help Ben the first time, when I *knew* I had to go to Nepal—anything and everything!"

"Rachel, look at me."

When she was finally able to, he saw eyes that were brimming with tears, frightened, defiant, beseeching.

He kissed her trembling lips; this time he felt a passion in her he had not felt before.

Unconscious of anything around them, they did not hear Caroline peer in, and then quickly and silently close the door.

Rachel finally broke away and sat back. She reached for his hand, "Russell, I have to talk to you."

He leaned back, sensing she had reached some sort of decision.

"Russell, I think I could love you, or I already do, but I can't! I won't! You deserve more than that." She put her hand over his mouth. "No, no, let me finish. You don't have to be a psychologist to know I'm one mixed up adolescent. I was bad enough after Ben's death, but then—then, for goodness sake, then you appeared. You play the sympathetic male and I fall all over you like you are the first man I ever met. I let you kiss me, then I think it's love—maybe it is, maybe it isn't. The point is, I'm a mess and I hate myself. The Bishop told me just now of a position I could have in

Nepal. Isn't that wonderful? Except as soon as he told me, I didn't want to go, because of you. If I'm not crazy, I'm awful close!"

Russell listened, watching her face contort with her confused, conflicting emotions. He pulled her to him.

"Rachel, Rachel, you are so normal it is boring. Everything you say makes perfect sense. I pray to God what you feel for me *is* love, but even if you find out it isn't, that is perfectly normal, too. Look at me." She turned toward him. "I may be a half a step ahead of you, but I am not sure I love you enough to "forsake all others," etc. I think I do, but we both need to use this time to our advantage.

I'm going to say something I may regret: it's that I think you should go to Nepal; stay there until you find some calm in your life, then, let what you feel for me happen or not. If you don't call me off, I will come to Nepal in six months, then we'll see where we are. No promises made, no promises broken. I will miss you terribly, but I think we both need this."

Rachel looked up at him, her eyes bright, without a tear. "It must be your advanced age, but I know you are right. Russell, I'm sorry...."

"No. No 'I'm sorrys'"

She smiled, "I knew Scott about three days—I thought that was love because I had never known what it was before—I'm learning. I think I know, but I will do what you say and I will pray." She nestled against him, her eyes closed, truly at peace for the first time since Ben's death.

* * * *

The Browns arrived at five, but still no Leigh. Caroline was preoccupied with seeing that everyone was comfortable and had something to sip on. Finally, she began to apologize for her brother, then decided that was a waste of time. Shuttling back and forth to the kitchen, she bumped into her son.

Taking his arm, she pulled him back behind the kitchen door.

"I didn't really mean for you to go *that* far entertaining Rachel!"

Unaware that they had been observed, he stared back blankly, "I'm sorry? What does that mean?"

"I opened the door to the den by mistake, Russ, sorry. You and Rachel seemed, shall I say, engrossed. Don't hurt that girl, my son. It would seem that you have your hands, or should I be so crude as to say, your bed, full at the moment."

Dawning on him that his mother must have seen them kissing, he replied, defensively, "It's nothing like that, Mom, believe me."

"Good! That young lady has enough on he mind right now."

"I promise, I will do nothing to upset her."

"Don't forget Allison. I really like her."

* * * *

Just before six there was a commotion as the front door burst open and Leigh appeared. Throwing his bag ahead of him, he came into the living room catching everyone, except his sister, by surprise.

"Ciao, my friends! Leigh Barlow for those of you unfortunate enough not to recognize me. Sis, hello—how's this for timing?"

Looming before the Bishop and Nancy, he continued, "This is, of course, the Very Reverend Bishop and his fair lady." He bent and kissed Nancy's hand.

"I do not know this beautiful lady and her Lincolnesque companion?"

Dwight rose and offered his hand, "Dwight Brown and Nancy, Leigh. Pleased to make your acquaintance."

"And then there are these two devastating beauties! Boy, am I glad Patrice stayed home."

Caroline, never able to keep up with her glib brother, had risen and clamping a firm grip on his arm, hissed, "Leigh, for goodness sake, this isn't a grand opening!" Then turning to Allison and Rachel, introduced them, "This is Allison Thomason and this is *The Reverend* Rachel Mason. Now please sit down and be good!"

Leigh greeted Allison with a wink and then bent over Rachel's hand to bestow a kiss, and, in a stage whisper, "I pray you are not wed, fair lady?"

Rachel, whose emotions had been on a roller coaster for the last few hours, responded with downcast eyes, "No, kind sir, but I am about to hie me to a nunnery."

The Bishop roared in appreciation, Russell gave her a thumbs-up.

"Egad! There may still be time!" Leigh turned to Sam.

"Reverend Sir, I am a miserable sinner as, I'm sure, my loving sister has implied. Slander, nothing but slander, nonetheless, I throw myself on your mercy. Redeem me if you can."

"Leigh, everything I have ever heard of you is fulfilled this evening. Greetings, I am sincerely glad to meet you." He pulled the reluctant actor into his arms and embraced him.

Flustered, Leigh muttered, as an aside, "Now, I don't think that was in the script?"

The embrace seemed to quiet Leigh's agitation much as a straight jacket might for a mentally disturbed patient, but only temporarily disconcerted, Leigh spotted Russell.

"That leaves, not least, but last, my handsome nephew! Russell, it *is* good to see you again! You are still making obscene money connecting dots and coms in the ether, or ether out of dots, or whatever it is you do?" He shook Russell's hand and put his arm around his shoulder. "Here, ladies and gentlemen, is a young, well not so young anymore, man who could have put Jason Robards in the shade. I will never forget his role as Nana, the dog, in Peter Pan. Absolutely spellbinding!"

"Excuse me—hello—Leigh—hello!" Caroline was trying desperately to curtail her brother's performance.

"Oh, yes, Sis? I missed a cue?"

"Leigh, I wonder if it might be a good idea to take your bag upstairs to your room, wash your hands, or whatever, and freshen up for dinner. We are hoping to sit down at seven. So, if I may draw the curtain on Act One, we will look forward to more of this tragedy, a little later on! Russ, would you show your Uncle to his room?"

"This is a small house, but even for that size audience, the applause was deafening! Tally-ho, my friends, we will meet again."

After Leigh had followed Russell upstairs everyone sat in stunned silence. Finally, Sam cleared his throat, "Yes, well, Leigh has been acting for what, Caroline, maybe thirty years? He does bring a certain enthusiasm to his roles, although that may not have come across. It is possible, I suppose, that those were some of his lines in his new play?"

Caroline, who had retreated to the kitchen, stuck her head out and suggested that if anyone wanted another drink, now would be a good time. Everyone raised his hand.

* * * *

Dinner went more smoothly. Leigh, apparently hungry, busied himself with his food. As his hunger was assuaged, he discovered the young lady on his right to be very attractive. Allison, mesmerized by this larger-than-life celebrity, was totally beguiled by his reference to the great theater names he had worked with, the glamorous actresses he had played with, he, of course, rolled his eyes when he said "played with." Interspersed with his magical tales, he made Allison to understand that, with her beauty, she had a lock on fame and fortune in the theater.

Sitting next to Allison, Russell was only vaguely aware of the exotica Leigh was unveiling to his starry-eyed companion, he was totally engrossed in probing Rachel's opinion of the widely publicized changes that were happening in the Anglican Communion. Russell, hardly a regular churchgoer, had, however, followed the turmoil in the papers. Rachel and Russell were in fact, earnestly discussing the subject, but it also served another purpose than the pursuit of an ecclesiastical update. Russell had been able to whisper to her that his mother had apparently seen them "engrossed" in the den when the door had been closed. Not certain at which point of their tête-à-tête she had observed them, they both assumed it might have been when they were kissing. Thus, appearing academically consumed seemed to them to contradict any more sensational interpretation. Even beyond this observable truth, the extremely serious nature of their discussion allowed them to covertly hold hands under the table, nicely camouflaged from unwelcome eyes by the length of the tablecloth.

Something Russell had been overheard to say about the insurgent rise of faith-based politics during the last election prompted Leigh to break into his session with Allison to say, "Faith-based politics: oxymoron, in its purest form!"

Keenly aware of Allison's father's position in the movement, Russell turned to his Uncle.

"Uncle Leigh, you should know that Allison's father is a very influential figure in the Church's political involvement. He is pastor of a huge church in Naples. She could tell you a lot more than I."

Satisfied that he had shielded Allison from any inadvertent aspersions his Uncle might have authored, he turned back to Rachel.

The Bishop, however, over-hearing Russell's comment looked across the table at Allison, thankful for Russell's forewarning.

"That is very interesting, Allison. Of what denomination is your father's church", the Bishop asked?

"I don't know that he's affiliated with any denomination, sir. I know he thinks powerfully highly of Mr. Robertson, in Virginia, whatever church he may be."

"Pat Robertson, I see. He is an influential spokesperson for the more aggressive wing of Christendom."

"You like him, too, Bishop Phillips," she asked?

"I'm sure he is a very nice person, Allison. I would probably take issue with some of his positions. Perhaps the church needs outspoken crusaders like Mr. Robertson, but I am more comfortable treading softly and listening rather than tramping so loudly and shouting. It's just a difference in approach, my dear. Hopefully, we are both heading in the same direction?"

"Bravo, Reverend Sir! Well, said, but confronted, as it were, by a herd of stampeding elephants, I select that word advisedly, one had better have an unshakable faith!"

"Touché, Leigh, touché. Unshakable faith with a madman's gun at one's head might well lead to an awful headache!" Dwight threw in with considerable feeling.

Caroline, uneasy with the direction the conversation was heading, broke in before anyone else could offer an opinion.

"Folks, why not move into the living room? We can enjoy our coffee in a little more comfort." She rose to emphasize her suggestion.

The rest of the evening was a delight; Leigh, center stage as always, entertained everyone with anecdotes of his lengthy stage career. He enacted scenes that had gone awry and the comical rescue efforts the actors used that had made the scenes even more hilarious. He recited Rex

Harrison's lines from *My Fair Lady*, mimicking Elisa's cockney responses until everyone was laughing so hard he could not be heard. He was at his best as an entertainer, and once everyone had been able to adjust to his in-your-face style, they thoroughly appreciated his unique personality.

The hands of the clock circled the dial several times before Caroline gracefully suggested that because of tomorrow's events, everyone might welcome an early night.

It was eleven before Caroline and Rachel, who had volunteered to help, had brought the house back to the order Caroline wanted.

They sat down briefly to relax. Rachel, a bit uneasy about what Russell had whispered to her at the table, was wary. Caroline, on her part, was quite naturally intrigued by what she had seen.

Thinking to control the conversation, Rachel asked, "Caroline, nosy as I am, can you hint at where you and Sam might go on your wedding trip?"

"Oh, that isn't a secret, although we haven't advertised it. We are going to the Caymans for two weeks. We'll stay in Miami tomorrow night, then fly there on Sunday."

"That sounds idyllic! Well, I should run along. Thanks for everything, Caroline!"

Caroline was slow to respond as she studied Rachel's face. The pause was long enough to provoke more uneasiness in the younger woman.

"Things are alright with you, Rachel?"

"Yes, yes. Why do you ask?"

"No reason. I just need to know you are going to be easy with yourself."

"That is so nice of you to be concerned. I do feel better about Ben, I really do, but I would have to confess to you that my life seems to be in some sort of fast-forward mode right now."

Caroline took her hand as Rachel got up to leave.

"You know how much you mean to me, Rachel. I've always felt that one step at time was a lot better than break-neck speed."

Knowing exactly why the warning was given, she replied, "I want to think I have learned *something* in the last six months, Caroline. I will be careful."

The phone rang just as Rachel was leaving. Caroline seldom got calls after ten o'clock and unless the caller tried twice after eleven o'clock, she never answered. This time she had an inkling as to who the caller might be.

"Hello."

It was a husky, female voice with a broken accent that answered; she almost hung up.

"Missy Piker—run, dis iss a fren de padre you iss—"

Caroline might have been fooled on any other night, but knowing her prospective groom as she did, she knew immediately whose voice it was.

"Sam Adams! You are certifiably deranged. You're lucky I didn't hang up on you. Why are you calling at this hour, may I ask?"

"Why am I calling? A question like that makes me question your ardor. I am calling to tell you how much I love you. Why else would I be calling?"

"Oh, well that's different. That's nice, Sam, thank you. I love you very, very much, too!"

"I didn't get a chance to kiss you goodnight with that horde of guests around. Know that I am kissing you now."

"Oh, Sam, you are so crazy—I love you so!"

"Then tomorrow's a go?"

"Why not."

"OK, just checking, then I'll be there."

"Good."

"Goodnight, my darling Caroline."

"Goodnight, my dearest Sam."

* * * *

Although the next morning turned into a series of five breakfasts, it made the day speed by. Lunch was a gesture and then, suddenly, it was two o'clock, time to bathe and dress.

Caroline had ordered her dress in Baltimore—a light gray dress with very simple lines. She did not like anything ostentatious, preferring understated clothing, but she did insist on the subtle touch of quality. As she looked at herself in the mirror, she hoped the dress appropriately suggested her role as the Rector's second wife to those who had known and loved Beth, yet implied her own confidence in becoming his wife in her own right.

Leigh had volunteered to drive his sister to the church and with his typical panache, he had rented a white, extended Cadillac limousine.

"Good heavens, Leigh, I will feel like an aged Cinderella in this Hollywood chariot!" But she was very pleased he had given this much thought to her comfort.

"Not only that, Princess, but I have a black jacket and cap which I will don and act as your chauffer and drive you to the airport."

"Oh, Leigh, you are something! How utterly silly and nice of you to do that. Thank you."

The Church was at capacity by three-thirty. Xavier ran back and forth to the Parish House carrying extra chairs until the aisles and entry were completely filled. He made as accurate a count as he could and came up with two hundred and seventy-five, fifty more than capacity.

Caroline arrived promptly at four. The organist was just finishing, *Jesu, Joy of Man's Desiring*, as she entered the vestibule.

Bishop Phillips was standing at the chancel steps, magnificently robed, his Bishop's miter making his normal six-foot-six height appear to be at least eight feet. Behind him, in contrast, Rachel's vestments reflected the simpler feeling of the parish. The ceremony was a brief, moving, and joyous celebration. As Caroline and Sam moved back down the aisle, he touched as many hands of old friends as he could reach, his eyes veiled with emotion.

* * * *

The reception was a modified melee; too many people in too small a space, but everyone had a chance to greet the new couple. As the line of well wishers dwindled, Lance Bosley clapped for attention. Finally gaining some measure of silence he, announced the parish gift to Caroline and Sam.

Dwight had forewarned them about the gift, knowing it would come as a shock. They both were uncomfortable with the expense of the gift, but could do nothing but accept it with feigned enthusiasm, gracefully. Dwight had told Sam that Lance was the primary donor.

After the announcement, there was a moment of startled silence, then polite applause. Most of the guests were dumb-founded at the cost of the gift and wondered how it had been paid for? Had Dwight Brown paid for it out his own pocket?

After almost two hours of mingling with their guests, Caroline and Sam prepared to leave. Leigh brought the limousine around to the front door, their suitcases already in the trunk so, in a hail of rice, they waved goodbye to their guests.

The remaining guests were slow to disperse, but the Bishop and Nancy soon followed Sam and Caroline. Dwight, Nancy and Lisa had sneaked away before Lance had made his announcement. Russell knew he had an obligation to stay with Allison which he did, obligingly, but not without making furtive glances in Rachel's direction. She, knowing his plight, taunted him by feigning anguished love. They were both aware, however, that Russell would be leaving early the next morning and that any further contact would be extremely unlikely. Strangely enough, though both felt a great attraction, neither of them knew how to handle the situation.

As Sam was leaving, he had asked Russell if he would move his car into the garage, apologizing that there could be "stuff" that might have to be moved to accommodate it.

Finding Allison in the dwindling crowd, he told her about the car and that he'd be back in a minute. He then made an exaggerated circle of the room in order to appear to run into Rachel.

"I'm going to put Sam's car in the garage, I would be eternally grateful to you if you would show me where it is, Miss Mason."

"The last time I saw it, it was attached to the Rectory, but one never really knows about attachments, does one?"

"That little bit of innuendo is unworthy of a priest, Miss Mason," he laughed. Come and show me." He took her arm and pushed her out the back door.

Pointing at the car that he considered an antique, he said, "There she is! Boy, you clergy live high off the hog!"

He unlocked the passenger door and helped her in. Groping with the unfamiliar instruments, he found the ignition.

"I shall miss you, Miss Mason."

"Don't, please, Russell. I'm a little fragile right now."

He moved the car very slowly toward the garage—as he did so, he reached in his pocket.

"Rachel, I found this thing yesterday—it's nothing—but it's something. I wanted to give you something." He reached over and handed her a small package."

"Oh, no, you don't need to give me anything, Russell. We've—I've—You've given me more than you know already." But she fumbled open the simple wrapping and held up a small, brown image. "Oh, how darling! What is it?"

"He's a Buddha—a comical Buddha, if you will. He will protect you in my absence. He has a great sense of humor."

The little pot-bellied man, squatting, his stomach ballooning over his legs, smiled wickedly at Rachel.

Russell had gotten out of the car to open the garage door. He pushed aside several tools and a large trashcan, then got back in the car. He looked over at Rachel.

"He's not meant to replace me, you understand, just act as a temporary substitute." He pulled the car into the garage.

When he had turned off the engine, Rachel moved over on the seat.

"Russell, you have got to go *home*! The longer you stay, the harder it is for me to understand why I'm going halfway around the world." She put her head on his shoulder.

"We sort of dealt with that yesterday. You have to go, Rachel." He turned and put his arms around her. Just as he was about to kiss her they heard a female voice.

"Russell!"

"Allison," Russell whispered.

They separated as she came into the garage.

"What are you doing, Russy?"

He opened the door and stepped out.

"Rachel, had never seen an antique car before; I was just showing it to her."

Rachel stepped out on the other side of the car. "Hi, Allison."

Allison had never felt Russell was her private property, but in the last few days she sensed she had gained Mrs. Pickering's support and was now more optimistic about landing her son. She did not see the lady preacher as any sort of challenge, so she accepted what Russell told her.

"It is cold, though, Russy. Maybe we should go back to your mother's. What do you think?"

"I guess you're right, we should. Miss Mason do you need a ride to your house?"

"No, thank you, Russell, I have a car."

"Then, it's goodbye, Miss Mason. I have enjoyed knowing you." He extended his hand and they exchanged a long, firm handshake. His last glimpse of Rachel's face was of a happy, if tentative, smile, her lips trembling, perhaps from the cold?

* * * *

The flight from Baltimore to Miami was "delayed because of equipment problems," which, translated to Sam, meant there was a heavy snowstorm in Chicago that had grounded all flights. The airline "hoped" to find other equipment, but no time had been established.

Caroline and Sam found seats in a remote area of the terminal. Every half hour or so, Sam would walk to the monitor to see if any progress had been made. He returned from his fifth trip with the news that the flight was tentatively scheduled for midnight. It being nine o'clock meant three more hours of studying the faces of other frustrated passengers as they ebbed and flowed in front of the wedding couple. Their major topic of conversation, quite naturally, was the parish gift of the European trip. Caroline thought it was a wonderful idea until Sam tempered her enthusiasm with a categorical, "Impossible!"

"Caroline, there is no way I can leave this parish for two months. It would be completely negligent of me to leave for that length of time—two weeks, sure, even three weeks maybe, but never two months, eight weeks!"

"I tend to suspect you feel that eight weeks is a few days too long?" Caroline was not without an owlish sense of humor.

"Yes, Mrs. Adams, I do," Sam laughed, aware he had perhaps come on a bit strong.

"If only I had married into wealth, then the ugly reality of work would never have reared its head."

"You are lucky I am still compos mentis at my age so I *can* work."

"Seriously, Sam, it is something of a problem. It is such a generous gift that we will have to be careful about our response."

Having been told by Dwight that Lance had been the largest donor, Sam was not overly concerned about offending the parish if it had to be modified.

"I will depend on Dwight to handle the details; I know he will do it gracefully."

"Would you consider a two-week trip, Sam?"

"Yes, I'd like that. I can get a substitute for that length of time."

"Good. It should really be fun."

"I'll just go and check the monitor again. Look expectant when I return."

CHAPTER SIX

Sunday after the wedding was much like a day after Christmas, quiet, reflective and very slow to inspire anyone. Russell and Allison had left at nine for the airport,

Russell using all his self control, did not attempt to call Rachel one last time.

The Parish House was in an unusual state of chaos; several ladies of the Guild had come in the afternoon to wash up the coffee pots and serving dishes that had been used. Xavier appeared and began returning the chairs from the church to the Sunday school rooms. Fortunately few people came to the Sunday services so the rather disorganized state of the church did not seem to matter. Taking a break, he was peeking into the rectory garage to see the car that, hopefully, would soon be his when he heard the thrumming of a powerful engine pull up behind him.

"Hi!" Lisa called.

"Hello, Lisa." He was glad to see her, but he worried about the ladies in the Parish House who might be watching.

"I came early."

"Early?"

"Yes, in case you could go today. You do remember you said Sunday?"

"Si, I remember, but I can't go today, I have to help clean up the church."

"What are you doing? Can I help?"

"No, I can do it, thanks."

She got out of the car and came over to him. She was really a cool looking girl, he thought, but she made him nervous. He didn't understand what she wanted of him.

"Why can't I help?"

"Well, because, you know, I mean, it's my job."

"Xavier, if we are going to go steady, we've got to share."

"Miss...."

"Lisa!"

"Lisa, I don't want you to get dirty, that's all."

"Come on, let's just do it!"

"Alright, I've got to straighten up the Sunday school rooms." He felt trapped, she wouldn't take no for an answer and that meant he had to go inside where the women were working.

Entering the Parish house, the women greeted Lisa.

"Hello, Lisa, you looked lovely yesterday."

"Thank you."

"Beautiful dress, Lisa!"

"Thanks."

"That color looked just perfect on you with your blonde hair and blue eyes."

"Do you think so?"

Xavier worked as fast as he could in order to get Lisa out of the building.

"You are going to help, Xavier? How nice. He's a nice boy."

The tone was not condescending, but it did suggest a raised eyebrow.

Lisa worked as hard as Xavier, straightening the chairs, picking up crumbled napkins, half-filled cups of coffee and then stooping down with a dustpan when Xavier had swept the floor.

"I wish you wouldn't do this, Lisa. I mean, you know, you get all dirty."

"Looks pretty clean to me, Xavier. What's next?" Her hair had gotten tousled; she casually swiped at it and blew at an errant strand, her face flushed.

Xavier was struck with how pretty she really was.

"That's all here. I need to check the church."

"OK, let's go."

As soon as they had left the building, the ladies exchanged knowing looks and began an excited conversation of "*can you believe this, Lisa Brown and Xavier, whatever his last name is!*"

At the church, Xavier made sure the thermostat was set back to sixty-five, the rear door locked, all the leaflets were picked up and hymnals back in their racks. Lisa watched him work quickly and efficiently.

"That do it," she asked?

"Just about."

"Want to go for a drive?"

"Maybe tomorrow would be better. Think?"

"Sure, but we could go today, too."

It was the slight pleading tone that unnerved him. She really sounded as though she would be hurt if he said no.

"Well, we could, I guess, but you drive, the roads are a little snowy."

"All right, come on!" She sounded delighted that she had finally gotten him to go.

Walking to the car, she said, "I'm a little pushy, aren't I?"

"No, it's just, you know, I mean, you're nice, but you must have lots of friends….", his voice trailed off, but the unsaid question was, "why me?"

"I don't have a lot friends, actually. I thought we could be friends. I bother you, don't I?"

"No, you don't, I—like you, it's just that…."

"Xavier, for goodness sake, 'just' what? Because I have a Jag? Because my Dad has money? Because my Grandfather is somebody in the church, what? 'Just' what?'" She had stopped in front of him, her hands on her hips, demanding an answer, her eyes pleading with him to like her for herself.

Xavier had never been on a formal date—sure he had been with lots of girls in groups, but, unless they "shot up" as he used to do, they all just rammed around aimlessly, no one coupled with anyone else.

"I like you, but…."

"You already said that before. Do you like me or not?"

"Yes." It was a relief to say it looking at her and not having to qualify it.

"Wow! OK! We have all that settled. Come on, get in!" She threw herself into the driver's seat, pulled on her seat belt and put the car in gear. Smiling at him, she said, "You said you liked me, right? Then you are my boyfriend, right?"

Xavier blushed, "I guess so."

"Why don't you say it this way? 'Lisa, you are my girl friend!'"

"I don't even know you, I mean, we've seen each other twice."

"How long does it take for you to like or dislike someone?" She was speeding down the church lane to the street.

"Oh, I guess, some time."

"Do you not like me?"

"No, of course I don't."

"Then you like me—say it!"

"I'm not going to say it just because you want me to. I'll say it when I'm ready."

"Fine! I'll wait." She slowed the car and stopped, turned off the engine and sat there with her arms crossed.

"I can get out and walk home, you know?"

"I thought you wanted to take a ride?"

"I did, but you are making it, you know, complicated."

"How complicated is it to say you like me?"

Exasperated, yet very conscious that he could like her—a lot, he said, "Lisa Brown, I really like you! How's that?"

"Do you mean it?"

"Yes."

She let out a shriek that temporarily deafened him.

"You are my boyfriend, Xavier! What is your last name?"

"Mendoza," he replied, studying her face for any reaction.

"Awesome! I like it! Let's go!" She started the engine and swung into the right lane just ahead of a Cadillac Escalade that blasted her with its horn, then it swung out to pass her. Lisa hit the gas pedal; the Jaguar shot away from the lumbering SUV as the super charger kicked in, leaving the Cadillac far behind. She did not tell Xavier about the gesture she saw in her rearview mirror.

Xavier was impressed and just a little nervous.

"You sure drive fast!"

"The car goes fast, I just steer." She slowed as they neared the Interstate.

"Want to drive?"

"No, no, you go ahead. I'll drive tomorrow."

"Have you ever driven a hundred?"

"No, and you better be careful, I mean, they have State cops on this road."

"Let's take a chance, want to?"

Embarrassed to say no, he nodded. It was dusk and the skies were overcast so the visibility was not ideal. He didn't really like the idea.

She depressed the accelerator and the car responded smoothly. There was little traffic ahead so she put the pedal to the floor. Xavier watched in awe as the needle moved quickly past ninety, then ninety-five, then one hundred.

"She'll do much better, want to?"

He was afraid of using his voice so he simply nodded.

Pressing harder on the pedal and increasing the speed, the car effortlessly moved up to one hundred and ten, then settled on one hundred and twenty. As carefully engineered as the car was, at that speed, it was light on its wheels almost as though it were airborne. She shot past a line of trucks, then had to slow for what appeared to be a double line of cars ahead.

"Well, that's as fast as I've gone, so far. Fun?"

"Yeah! Awesome!"

When the speed had finally dropped to seventy-five, she touched the brakes, easing the car to forty-five, then she cut across the median and headed back to Afton.

"See, the car drives itself, Xavier. You'll like driving it. Do you do drugs?"

"I did, you know, I mean a couple of months ago. Since I began with Father Sam, I stopped."

"What did you do?"

"Mostly Ecstasy."

"That's cool, want to?"

"I can't, I mean, Father Sam and all."

"Oh." She sounded disappointed.

"How long will you be with Mr. Brown?"

"I don't know. My family is a mess." Her voice flat, hurt, and disinterested.

"Oh?"

"I can't talk about it, Xavier, don't ask me, please."

"I'm sorry."

"I'll be here at least until the summer."

"Cool."

"You will be my friend, won't you, Xavier?"

"I said I would."

She had turned off the Interstate by now.

"Take you home?"

"No, that's OK, Lisa, I, you know, should get back to the church."

"For what?"

"Just, well, I mean, that's where I work."

"You finished working. Are you ashamed of where you live?"

"No, that's not it. I...."

"You are ashamed!"

"No, I'm not! Alright, turn left at the next intersection." He directed her to the trailer court and to his mother's trailer.

"See! That's my mother's home! Like it," he said defiantly.

"Why are you ashamed of it, Xavier? It looks great to me—like it would be cozy, homey-like."

"It's OK, I guess." He opened the door to leave.

"Wait a minute. You forgot something."

"What? I didn't bring anything."

"Are you my boy friend?

"I already said I was."

"Boy friends kiss their girl friends goodnight, I think."

"Lisa, you are something else!"

"You don't want to kiss me?"

"Yes, well, I mean, but...."

She reached across the seat and kissed him full on the mouth.

"There!" She said softly. "I like you, Xavier. Please like me."

Completely at a loss for words, he backed out of the car and closed the door. She turned the car around and shot out of the trailer park.

* * * *

Rachel's one bedroom apartment did not provide generous extra space; everything had been planned in the most economical manner. What had turned out to be a luxury, however, was the small but separate dining room. She had never used it for its designated purpose, preferring to sit at the breakfast bar, or take her meals into the living room. The space had been converted to her "Nepal Room." Strewn with books, maps, with pictures scotch-taped to the walls, and a bulging notebook, she had learned more about Nepal in a month than she knew about Canada. She was smart enough to understand that her knowledge was book-deep; that the actual country could not be understood from reading words on a page. In fact, the more she studied this unique country, the more inadequate she felt. The mixture of Hindu and Buddhist religions superimposed on pre-historic tradition defied Western comprehension. The heady Himalayan mystic that had hypnotized Scott and so many other climbers, was a world away from life in Kathmandu and the countryside. Yet, a far distant Everest could be visible from Kathmandu and it cast the same mind-stopping shadow of awe on those who dared to look.

The more she studied Nepal, the more she was conscious of a flickering fear that danced dangerously close to destroying her desire to go there—malaria, Maoist insurrection, primitive violence in a male dominated society. After all, it was only the tragic romance with Scott that had brought Nepal to her mind at all. She wasn't gong there to assault Everest, then why? What could she hope to do there—to find?

Then there was Russell: "go to Nepal—stay there until you find some calm in your life—then we'll see where we are." These words and the still small voice from deep inside her that called out, "go and listen," gave her the courage to continue her journey.

CHAPTER SEVEN

Xavier spent a little more time in the shower on Monday; he even shaved the dark fuzz from his upper lip. Searching for something other than his mother's perfume, he found an old bottle of her last boyfriend's shaving lotion. Smelling it, he wrinkled his nose, but assuming it must have some secret powers of seduction, he slathered it on his cheeks. Assessing himself in the cracked mirror on the back of the door, he patted down his black cowlick and decided it was the best he could do.

He had finished most of his work around the church yesterday, thanks to Lisa's help, so there was little else to do by lunchtime. Checking his watch every ten minutes or so, he urged the hands around the dial. He wished Lisa had said she would come earlier than three. He wondered what she was doing that would keep her busy until three? Maybe she had other friends, although she said she didn't? Maybe she had another boyfriend? By quarter of three Xavier was exhausted by anticipation. Fidgeting, he went to the Men's Room in the Parish House at least three times to check his hair.

Three o'clock passed, then three-fifteen. By three-thirty, he had adjusted himself to the only conclusion there was: that she had forgotten. Crestfallen and angry at himself for believing he was someone special to her, he started down the lane to go home.

He had no sooner started than the sleek green Jag roared up the lane.

Traveling so fast she passed him before she saw him, she braked violently and backed down toward him.

"Xavier! I'm sorry! Get in and I'll turn around up at the church." She opened the passenger door.

Xavier got into the car, his expression a mixture of embarrassment at his own doubts and a manly resentment that she had tested him.

"Hi! I'm sorry. I had to do something that took longer than I thought." She drove up to the church parking lot, turned around and then got out.

He hadn't replied.

"Are you mad at me, or what?"

"No."

"Don't be mad at me, Xavier." There was that soft pleading tone, perhaps this time even more urgent.

He wasn't mad at her, but at himself.

"I'm not mad, Lisa. I just thought you had forgotten. No big deal." He came around the car and climbed into the driver's seat.

She instructed him on how to adjust the driver's seat and the outside mirrors.

He settled in, adjusted the steering wheel and started the car. The deep hum of the engine made his heart beat a little faster. He eased the car forward and turned down the lane.

"Why don't we get on the Interstate; that's as good as anyplace."

As the miles ticked by, Xavier felt more and more at ease with the car. He fought the desire to floor the gas pedal as she had done the other night, but he did ease it past eighty before slowing it down to the speed limit.

"How do you like it," she asked?

"Awesome!" He looked over at her smiling, and instead of seeing her normal happy expression, she looked detached, staring straight ahead.

"You OK, Lisa?"

"Oh, yes, I guess."

He drove another thirty miles in silence. Noticing a billboard advertising a bunch of fast-food places at the next exit, he asked her if she'd like a coke or shake.

"Sure, OK."—again the flat, preoccupied tone.

Pulling into the drive-up at the Burger Chef, he ordered two hamburgers and a coke and a chocolate shake; then he pulled around to a parking place as far from the store as possible.

They ate in silence, Xavier more and more puzzled by her strange behavior. Finally, summoning up his courage, he asked, "Lisa, you gotta be thinking about something. We'll go back to Afton."

As though startled, she seemed to re-focus on him.

"Oh, no, I'm—I guess I'm thinking. Sorry, no don't go back, Xavier."

The way she looked over at him made him certain there was something wrong.

"What is it, Lisa, you don't look right?"

"It's too stupid, that's all!" She spit out bitterly.

"Is it something that happened with your grandparents?" He groped for some inkling as to her anger.

"No, no. It's nothing to do with the Browns. Xavier, do you have to be back for dinner?"

"No, I guess not, why?"

"You know what? I'd just like to drive for a while; see how far we can get in a couple of hours, then head back. Want to?"

"That's cool with me. Want to drive?"

"No, you drive. If I'm quiet for a while, is that OK?"

"No, problem." He wheeled the car back onto the Interstate and concentrated on the increasingly heavy traffic around Wilmington.

Around five, as it was getting dark, she stirred; he wasn't sure she hadn't been asleep.

"Where are we," she asked?

"I'm not sure. The last sign I saw said Norristown twenty miles."

"Why not look for a place to eat, then we can decide where to go, want to?"

"That's cool."

They passed several exits that didn't tempt them, then turned off at a sign that read Newtown Square. Without any particular reason, they turned into a restaurant parking lot that advertised home cooking.

Lisa had said nothing for at least an hour and a half. By now, Xavier was both worried and annoyed. What kind of weirdo had this girl turned into; or was she sick, or something?

After they were seated, they ordered cokes and studied the menu. When the cokes arrived, Lisa opened her purse.

"I need a shot, want one?"

Xavier had been no stranger to booze or drugs, but her producing a pint of liquor startled him.

"That's cool." He pushed his coke toward her.

She poured a generous amount into his glass and as much in her own. She raised her glass to him, but did not say anything, then drank half the coke.

Xavier followed her example and felt the familiar burning sensation as it coursed down his throat.

After a few minutes, she looked up from studying her glass, her face blank of any expression.

"I got a problem, Xavier, and I need somebody to talk to. Would you listen?"

The girl had been a total puzzle to him ever since he met her. He had been unable to predict what she would do or say next. Yet he liked her and she had labeled him as her boyfriend. He wasn't sure what he could do to help her, but he wanted to try.

"Sure."

"You ever do it, you know, with a girl, I mean?"

Xavier was not prepared for that question.

"What do you mean?"

"I mean, you know—with a girl, in bed."

"Yeah, why do you need to know that?"

"Just 'cause."

"Because why?" He was getting a little angry.

"Don't get mad, please."

"I'm not mad, but I don't understand."

"I was late because I had to drive to Bel Air for a drugstore."

"Why Bel Air?"

"Because I needed to get—I needed to get one of those kits that tells you if your pregnant." She said the sentence as though it was one word; it had came out so fast.

Xavier was stunned and embarrassed by her admission.

When he didn't reply, she continued, "I am."

"You're pregnant!" Xavier used the words, but hey had no meaning. "Yes."

"Maybe the kit is wrong?"

"Maybe."

"What are you going to do?" Xavier was still trying to deal with the enormity of what she had said.

"I don't know."

"How is it possible? You've been here a couple of months."

"I missed my second period yesterday. It was when I was living in Connecticut."

Xavier could not deal with what was happening; he just stared at her.

They finished their cokes and Xavier asked for a refill. She emptied the remains of the bottle in their glasses, then ordered the first item on the menu, neither caring what it was.

The alcohol had little effect on them; the reality of Lisa's admission dampening whatever impact it might have had.

After a moment or two, Lisa said, "Xavier, I'm sorry! I really am. I was worried about this, but I hoped I was wrong. It ruins us. I'm sorry." Her eyes were brimming with tears.

Only a natural, caring instinct prompted his automatic response. "Don't cry, Lisa, maybe the thing is wrong, anyway there are ways, you know." He didn't really know what he was talking about.

She made an angry swipe at her eyes, "I won't cry, that would be stupid! I'm just so mad at myself I could scream! I don't want this food we ordered, let's just leave, want to?" She had pulled several bills from her purse and placed them under her napkin. "That's more than enough."

"Let's go." Xavier got up.

As they passed the waitress, he said, "The lady isn't feeling too good, we gotta leave. The money's on the table, thanks."

Lisa got in the driver's seat and they took off. Back on the Interstate she concentrated on observing the speed limit knowing she had had too much alcohol. What conversation there was was disjointed and sporadic, each consumed with the ominous problem she faced.

Approaching the Maryland line, Xavier felt her speed increase and saw that she had hit ninety.

"Better watch the speed, Lisa—the cops will be out."

He had no sooner said this, than she spotted a flashing red light in the rear view mirror.

"Uh,oh! Hang on Xavier!"

Lisa had long since reached the end of her ability to find a way out of her personal dilemma so the challenge of out-racing the police presented a much more do-able solution to being arrested for speeding and testing positive for alcohol. When the car began to shudder, she eased off on the gas. They shot by cars as though they were parked.

"There's a toll gate just before you go back into Maryland, Lisa," Xavier yelled.

The police car was far behind but still there.

"I'll just have to run through it."

"No, don't do that! If you drop down on Route One to Route Forty, you can avoid the toll booths."

Immediately they saw the sign for Route One and she slowed barely enough to negotiate the turn, then raced down the short stretch of One to Route Forty. Increasing her speed again, she crossed the State line into Maryland. Still at high speed, she no longer saw the flashing red light.

"I'd slow down or we'll pick up another cop," Xavier said, looking back at the highway.

She slowed to eighty and made it to the turn-off for Afton without any further threat.

When she turned into the trailer court and stopped at Xavier's trailer, she was exhausted and totally sober.

They both sat there for a full minute, unable to say anything, then she spoke in a low, muffled voice, "I'm so sorry, Xavier. I hoped we could be friends—you be my boyfriend. I'm sorry."

"I *am* your boyfriend," he replied self-consciously. "I'm sorry you've, you know, got a problem, but I like you, Lisa, and I want to help, I mean, you know, be around. Maybe we can figure out some way?"

When he said "we", Lisa's heart rose out of the frightened, black shadows that had swallowed it.

"Would you still be my boyfriend, Xavier? I want you to be. I like you very much."

"I will. We can find some way, I'm sure." His brave assurance did not include any idea as to what they could do, but it gave Lisa the hope that it might be the end of a very lonely road.

She reached over and kissed him and, this time, he kissed her back

* * * *

Rachel had conducted the services Sunday after the wedding. She had noticed that the attendance was down. Normally they would count three hundred and fifty to four hundred at the three services, but this Sunday there were only two hundred. She did not give it any thought, believing it perfectly natural for the parishioners to take a breather after the wedding and because of Sam's absence, until Marcy spoke to her after the eleven o'clock service.

"Wonderful sermon, Rachel! I particularly liked the way you used the anthem, *Sheep May Safely Graze* that was played at the wedding. I only hope we sheep are safe to graze with some of the shenanigans that are going on?"

"Shenanigans? I'm not sure what you mean, Marcy?"

"Bosley and his group, you know."

Sam had not thought it necessary to relate Marcy's earlier warning about Lance.

Marcy rarely let restraint of any kind temper her vocal chords, but it was obvious that the girl did not know what she was referring to so she decided to let it go.

"Oh, well, just an old lady's imagination, I suppose. Anyway, you did a great job today, I'm proud of you."

"Thank you, Marcy, I appreciate that."

"Have a great day, Rachel, see you next Sunday." She walked away after a friendly squeeze of Rachel's arm.

Rachel walked back to the vesting room, pondering Marcy's remark about Lance Bosley. Would the fact that Marcy wouldn't describe what his "shenanigans" were, mean they had been directed at her. She had mentioned to Sam that she felt a subtle cooling toward her on the part of some in the parish after Ben's death. He had pooh-poohed it, attributing her feeling to a natural sensitivity at this particular time; on the other hand, the smaller congregations might be a further sign. It was an awkward situation for everyone, she realized; something she'd just have to live with and pretend it wasn't happening.

She had sent off her letter of interest to Bishop Gurung in Singapore yesterday, but she had difficulty letting go of the letter at the mail slot, her memories of Russell so recent and unnerving. It seemed so final—definitive, like burning all her bridges. Then she remembered his own admission that he, too, was not sure he could commit himself—they needed time. How *ridiculous* of her! They had only just *met*!

Giving the letter a final push, she repeated several times, "I *know* what I'm doing! I know what I'm *doing*! *I know what I'm doing*!

* * * *

Wednesday, Sam called Rachel from the Caymans. She reassured him that all was well, that she had written the Archbishop in Singapore offering her services and that she had had dinner with Nancy and Dwight Brown on Monday night. She said she had met Lisa Brown for the first time and thought she was a charming young lady, if perhaps a little shy and withdrawn. Sam had laughed, saying she must have Lisa confused with someone else; the only Lisa Brown he knew was about as shy as a used car salesman.

Sam told her that he and Caroline were having wonderful weather—in the mid-eighties and that they had been scuba diving twice and that Caroline had turned into a mahogany nymph he no longer recognized; in other words they were having an idyllic time.

CHAPTER EIGHT

The day after Sam and Caroline returned from the Caymans, Sam sunburned and five pounds heavier, and Caroline, tanned and looking ten years younger, began to play catch-up. The first order of business was a message from Bishop Phillips asking Sam to call at his convenience. Sam interpreted that to mean, "sooner."

Dialing the Bishop's number, he bet himself he knew what the call was about; a new curate candidate.

"Hi, Karen! How are you? Not half as good as I am, I'm positive!"

"Do I hear the lilt of the Caribbean in your voice, Reverend Sir?" Karen laughed.

"Would you believe I danced almost every night? Astounding what a fool you can make of yourself if you half try."

"Oh, come now, you loved it, I can tell."

"Yes, honestly, we had such a fabulous time I flirted with the idea of opening a sarong shop down there."

Karen was charmed by Sam's exuberance. Although he had always been friendly and funny, she had missed the special note of happiness that had so characterized him when Beth was alive.

"Well, sir, things have fallen apart in your absence, so we are thankful you are back. Will you hold a minute, Sam, while I chase up the Bishop?"

"Yes, of course, Karen. Nice to be back."

Shortly Chauncey came on the line, "Samuel! Welcome back. It certainly demonstrates the power of your dedication that you came back at all. You had a good time, I'm sure?"

"Yes, thank you, Bishop. I'd like to lunch with you soon and recount some of my Neptune adventures; I was really quite Cousteau-y."

"Oh, I'm sure you were. I will look forward to our lunch. Sam, time passes and I want you to have an assistant as soon as possible. We don't know when Rachel will leave, so we need to move along. I have a young man I'd like you to talk to. His name is Farley, Tom Farley. Nice lad. He's come up the hard way; had to drop out of college a couple of times for money reasons. He did a hitch in the Navy, and then took several years before deciding on the ministry. All that adds up to thirty-six years. Would you consider talking to him, Sam?"

"I'd like to very much, Bishop. He sounds like an interesting man."

"He has a family—wife and two small ones. He's serving, on a temporary basis, in a church in Shephardstown, West Virginia. I have the Bishop's permission to talk to him."

"Great! I appreciate your help, Bishop, thank you."

"Karen will call you after I've talked to him. Great to have you back. My best to Caroline."

After he had recounted the conversation to Caroline, he pretty well decided that Mr. Farley would be his new assistant; he sounded just right for St. James.

He, Caroline and Xavier spent most of the first afternoon that they were back carrying Caroline's clothes, and personal belongings to the Rectory. Sam encouraged her to bring anything and everything that meant anything to her, including books, pictures, dishes, pans, whatever. She took him literally so poor Xavier made any number of trips back and forth until around six when everything seemed to be done.

Xavier had been using Sam's car to transport Caroline's things. When they had finished, Sam said, "Xavier, why don't you take the car home tonight. What do you think?"

"I'd like that, Father Sam, if you trust me?"

"My friend, I have long-since trusted you; you are like one of the family. Here are the keys."

Xavier received the keys as thought they were the most fragile crystal. His obvious delight was so touching that Caroline felt a lump in her throat.

"Thank you, Father Sam, I will take care of it for you.

"You are most welcome, Xavier. Good night."

* * * *

Caroline had invited Rachel to dinner, knowing that Sam would want to be brought up to date on parish activities, but Rachel waited 'til after dinner to report the persistent rumors of Larry Bosley's activities.

"Well, it sounds like Mr. Bosley is going to be our reformer. That should be interesting, Rachel." Sam did not appear overly concerned.

"Sam, I think it could be serious. Assuming these rumors are right, Lance seems to have some rather grandiose plans."

"We need leaven, Rachel. If Mr. Bosley has his head on right, he may be able to instill a new spirit here. I know I'm old and stodgy; maybe he can help us all?"

"What about the abortion issue and same-sex marriage, Sam? He will be on a collision course with lots of us."

"Well, yes, but those things will have to be confronted. As long as rational argument can prevail, reasonable people will prevail."

"Excuse me, Sam, but I don't hear too much reasonable talk from anyone on these subjects; it's either or."

"Well, if reason won't prevail, maybe prayer will. We can't avoid the issues; they are there. I am not unaware of the highly charged debate going on—I can't stop it, but maybe we can temper it—try to lessen the hysteria and violence. I am not afraid of Lance Bosley, nor should you be. Let's see if we can work with him."

"Oh, Sam, I hope you can. I will be of little help to you, I'm afraid, especially if I leave fairly soon."

"Well, let's see how it all develops. We may be making a mountain out of a molehill. Incidentally, Miss Mason, the Bishop called me about a replacement for you, a Mr. Farley. I would expect to talk with him in the near future and I would appreciate it if you would have your own conversation with him and give me your opinion."

"I'd be happy to, Sam, for whatever it's worth."

"Rachel, your opinion means a great deal to me; remember that!"

"Sam, how I shall miss you," she said softly.

* * * *

Sam had arranged to talk with Tom Farley on the Monday after his return from the Caymans. On the Sunday before Farley's arrival, Xavier had asked to speak with Rachel after the services. When she had taken off her vestments, she went looking for him and found him sitting on the steps of the Parish House.

"A little cold for that, Xavier. What would you think about going inside?"

"Could we sit in your car, Miss Mason?"

"Sure, that would be fine."

It was obvious from the start that Xavier was nervous which surprised her because they had always had an easy relationship.

"This old timer may not be a Jaguar, but it's pretty good transportation, Xavier." She patted the faded dash.

Xavier shot her a glance she couldn't interpret: suspicious, defensive, alarmed?

"Why would you say Jaguar, Miss Mason?"

"I don't know? Jaguars always seemed like cool cars to me, don't you think?"

'Yeah, I guess so. Miss Mason, I need to ask you something."

"Anything, Xavier."

"Lisa Brown and I are friends," he said, falteringly.

"That's nice. She's a very pretty girl." Rachel masked her surprise at his announcement, not realizing they had met.

"We need to talk to you, if we can, I mean, you know, see you alone some time, maybe soon." He was searching Rachel's face for any sign of suspicion.

"Why of course. I'd like that. When do you want to talk?"

"Would this afternoon be OK, I mean, we'd like to do it as soon….," his voice trailed off.

Rachel's mind was leaping ahead from one possibility to another, but her face did not reflect anything but friendly interest.

"This afternoon is fine. How about two o'clock?"

"That's cool. I appreciate it, thanks."

"You know where my apartment is. I'll see you at two, Xavier." She watched as Xavier stepped out of the car; intrigued with what she guessed might be a totally unexpected romantic relationship.

* * * *

Promptly at two, she heard a knock on her front door.

"Come in Lisa—Xavier. Nice to see you again, Lisa."

"Hi, Miss Mason."

"May I offer you a coke or something?"

They both declined and sat together on the sofa. They looked small and very young and, was it her imagination, rather grim? She had thought about them over lunch and guessed that possibly Dwight or Nancy had learned of their friendship and had counseled Lisa to reconsider.

"Miss Mason, I'm pregnant," Lisa spoke up clearly and without apology.

Rachel was, obviously, unprepared for such an announcement. How could she be pregnant, she had only been in Afton for a few weeks?

"Lisa, how, may I ask, do you know already?"

"I missed my second period and I took one of those kit tests."

Rachel began to figure hurriedly; two months ago Lisa was living with her parents in Greenwich, Connecticut, as far as she knew. If so, it was a boy there. It didn't make the situation any better, but she was relieved for Xavier's sake.

"Do you plan to have the baby, Lisa?" Rachel was trying hard to recover an outward calm.

"I don't know, probably not, but I don't know how you do it."

"If you mean, how *you* do it, you *don't*. That is terribly important for you to understand."

"I've known girls who did."

"Lisa, please listen to me, I want to help you, but I simply can't if you were to try to injure yourself. It is very dangerous!"

"Well, probably I won't, but I don't know how you get it done?"

"Maybe we've rushed to the idea of abortion. Have you given any thought to having a child, Lisa?"

"I'm too young, Miss Mason. I made a mistake and I know it, but I won't have a baby now!"

"You know who the father is, Lisa?"

The girl laughed, sardonically, "Oh, yes, I know Todd very well."

"Have you told him?"

"No, and I don't intend to."

"Let me say, first of all, I appreciate your coming to me. I can imagine how you must feel and I want you to trust me enough that you will come to me any time you want to. I am going to repeat my earlier question, however; have you really given yourself enough time to think through the alternatives: having a child and raising it? Having a child and giving it up for adoption? Millions of couples would want to adopt a baby. Then, of course, there is abortion."

"We have talked about it, Miss Mason, and Lisa doesn't want to have the baby."

"Xavier, you and Lisa are good friends, I gather, do you feel as she does?"

"I would be willing to be the father, Miss Mason, but I guess Lisa has to decide."

"All right, let's do this: you two talk about this more; try to think of it in several different ways, then let's meet again on Wednesday at this same time. We'll see how you feel then and we'll go from there. Depending on what you do decide, you will have to tell Mr. and Mrs. Brown and I will need to let Father Sam know. Other than that no one needs to know anything at the moment. Now let's have a coke; I'd like one."

After Lisa and Xavier had left, Rachel lay down on the sofa, not through exhaustion, but more to collect her thoughts. She had been shocked at Lisa's news, but, at the same time, she was well aware that millions of girls go through the same trial every day. What help could she be? Where were her parents? She knew the Browns would be devastated. Morally, what should her role be? If Lisa insisted on an abortion, what advice should she give? The strident screaming of anti-abortionists offended her, but could she advise the termination of a prospective life?

So, suddenly her own quandaries seemed insignificant. Here was a seventeen-year old girl, confronted with questions that no one had the wisdom to answer.

She knelt down at the sofa, put her head in her hands and asked for guidance.

* * * *

The week went by too quickly, so that he suddenly realized Tom Farley was scheduled for tomorrow, Monday. They had arranged to meet at the Burger Chef where he had met Rachel for the first time seven short months ago. He had no difficulty spotting Farley as soon as he came in the door. He was tall, over six feet, solidly built, with a broad forehead hinting at early baldness. He was pulling off his sun glasses when their eyes met. Farley's face instantly lit up with a broad grin.

"Father Sam Adams, Tom Farley. I am really pleased to meet you."

His voice was a deep baritone with just the touch of what Sam guessed was a near-Boston accent.

"Tom, very nice to meet you. I could buy you a cup of coffee here, or we could get one back at the church?"

"I'm all set, sir, unless you want one?"

"Let's go along then. I normally drive the Rolls when I come to Burger Chef, but one of the servants is using it, so I'm forced to use the Olds." Then as an aside, "I get delusions of grandeur, I warn you." He winked at Farley.

Back in Sam's study, they spent several hours in a rambling, easy-going conversation, touching on family, sports, books and places they had lived. They compared notes on Service life, Farley had been a Gunners Mate on a cruiser, and, finally, Farley's experience in Shephardstown.

Sam heard the voice of a modest, hardworking, not elegantly educated man who had found himself only when he had entered the ministry.

Toward noon, Sam said, "I'd like you to spend some time with my assistant, Rachel Mason, after lunch. As I'm sure Bishop Phillips has told you, she will be leaving shortly to go to Nepal. First, let's get some lunch. I am a very recent bridegroom and I'm eager to show off my bride. I have a wicked weakness for young women, so don't be shocked at how much younger she seems than I."

Farley was startled and a bit disappointed that his man, with whom he had felt so compatible, should have this....? He settled on "peculiarity."

When he was greeted by Caroline, he was momentarily disconcerted; was this the girl's mother?

"Tom I can see a question written all over your face. Please meet my lovely young wife, Caroline. At my age, even three years seems very young to me."

Farley began to laugh as he shook Caroline's hand.

"Mr. Farley, I am very pleased to meet you. I can only guess what this old man has told you. I warn you, he has a sense of humor that cannot be categorized, nor should it be."

After a light lunch, Sam called Rachel and arranged to meet her at the Parish House in half an hour.

"After you've chatted with Rachel, Tom, I'd like you to meet my Senior Warden, who is also a dear friend. I'll try to wind this up by four so you can get started back home."

"It's not a long trip, sir, so the time doesn't matter."

"Tom, call me Sam, if you will, I am uncomfortable with 'sir'."

"Yes, of course," Farley replied, but it was obvious he was not comfortable with the familiarity. "I guess it's a hang-over from Navy days, sorry."

Rachel spent an hour with Farley. Their talk ranged over a wide number of subjects. She spent some time probing Farley's academic background and although she believed he had a sound foundation, she could sense he was a little defensive about the grades he had received. Knowing how little her outstanding academic record had prepared her for actual parish ministry, she wisely overlooked it.

Then, after a brief visit with Dwight, Sam drove him back to his car.

"Tom, I need an assistant. This parish is growing too fast for one man.

We have lots of young couples as well as a cadre of oldsters. We also have aggressive young families that are eager for change.

I am old enough not to feel the need for new wine in old wineskins, but I will not stand in the way of intelligent change. The man, or person, I should say, I want is someone who has horse sense; who doesn't respond to every fad that comes along. I am particularly cautious when it comes to those who feel religion should be an integral element of politics, or vice-versa. I don't care a fig whether you are a Democrat or a Republican as long as you recognize that those are political labels, not religious one. I like you very much and I would like you to join me here. It will not be an easy job, but if it isn't fulfilling, I'm stupider than I think I am. You certainly can mull it over for a couple of days and let me know later."

"No, Sam, I would be honored to assist you. I made up my mind hours ago. I would like to come here, and thank you for asking me, sir."

"Tch, tch! You do have a flaw, but we can make that a project. Let's talk timing, housing, salary, etc, on the phone tomorrow after you've gotten home and discussed things with your wife. I think we can make you comfortable here."

Sam watched Tom drive off in his Beetle, very pleased with the prospect of working with a man like Tom. The fact that he was black added a dimension the parish needed.

* * * *

Wednesday, when Lisa and Xavier sat down with Rachel, it quickly became apparent that Lisa was determined to have an abortion. Rachel felt obligated to challenge her position.

"Lisa, tell me, if you were thirty-five, single and became pregnant by a well educated man, would you still want an abortion?"

"Yes, I would," was her immediate answer.

"What would be your reason?"

"It would have been a mistake."

"But you would have known the risks."

"It still would have been a mistake. Does making a mistake make it right to bring a baby into the world?"

"Making a "mistake" when the consequences are known, does seem to put the burden on you, don't you think?"

"It's still a mistake baby. The world is full enough of mistake babies."

"Is it embarrassment, or people's opinion that would make you not want an illegitimate child?"

"I don't give a damn—excuse me—darn, what people think."

"What about ending a human life?"

"It isn't human yet."

"If you were to discover you were not pregnant, would you still indulge yourself as you did with the boy in Connecticut?"

"You mean sleep with someone before I was married?"

"Yes."

"Probably, but only if I loved him."

"You would want to keep the baby?"

"It would make a difference."

Rachel's questions were entirely academic, her life had been so isolated from this kind of reality, but she felt she had exhausted every avenue she could think of.

"Lisa, do you really want an abortion, knowing you will be ending a life?"

"Yes, I do!"

"I think, then, that you need to talk to your grandfather."

"All right, I will."

"Can you accept his opinion, his decision?"

"I will have an abortion anyway." When she said this, she reached for Xavier's hand.

* * * *

Rachel told Sam the entire story.

"Do you think there is any possibility of changing Lisa's mind? What if her parents forbid it?"

"I am convinced she will have an abortion, Sam. This is a very strong-minded young lady."

"Oh, me, oh, my, the tangled web we weave. I am so sorry. This will hurt the Browns. You have to wonder whether Lisa's parents' problems triggered this?"

"I would repeat, this is a very strong-willed gal, who appears to know her own mind."

"Life doesn't give us easy decisions, does it, Miss Mason?"

Rachel did not respond to this, but rather said, "I admire Xavier, Sam. She seems to rely on him very much and he is there for her."

"Wonderful! I love that boy!"

CHAPTER NINE

All of a sudden, life at St. James seemed to be moving to a new, discordant tempo. In some ways, the change might have been traced to Ben Stoddard's suicide, triggering Rachel's decision to leave, but the change was more pervasive than that. Like an imperceptible vapor it permeated otherwise random events, giving them the appearance of a common taint.

Sam was keenly aware of the change. His ear picked up a nuance as casual as the sound of apprehension in Marcy's tale of Lance's activities with their barely disguised hint of aggressive and intractable Christian rectitude.

Like a sailor many years at sea whose eye scans a threatening horizon, Sam first checked his own seamanship. He had been reminded of a body's frailty when he fell from the pulpit with a heart attack last year. But physical impairment was not a primary concern. Of greater importance was the resilience of his spirit after the many years of testing. Was his spirit more a muscle that strengthened through use, or was it like a bone embrittled by age? He had the pulse of a caring man. Unconsciously it responded to the cries for help from the minutely reported ills of the world: aware of the pathetically simple needs of a starving child in Africa, his inability to respond, tested his spirit.

He was not given to depression, but it could be argued he might have benefited from it. It would have blurred the starkness of pain, requiring less of the man. The face of good humor he wore was not a mask, rather it conveyed his spiritual energy. To those who suggested he was too sensitive to grapple with reality, he could reply that he had survived three years in Viet Nam, two years as a missionary in Kenya and unnumbered tragedies that had crippled the lives of those in his parishes.

Only in his most private world, did he admit his battle with an exhaustion he fought against defining. Looking, he could no longer clearly see down the passageway of his life, but rather saw only a door. That he could not see past the door, he accepted, not morbidly, but as a sign of his mortality; not with fear, but rather with the calm acceptance of a race all but run.

One of the most personal problems that had developed was Lisa's pregnancy and abortion. The Browns were emotionally shattered. Although her pregnancy had occurred before she came to live with them, they condemned themselves for not having acted sooner when they knew their son was having marital problems. Fruitlessly rehearsing what might have been, they condemned themselves to a psychological prison.

Dwight became almost inaccessible for parish affairs as well as a reluctant adviser to Sam, embarrassed by an act he illogically blamed himself for. In his emotional confusion, he focused his frustration on Xavier. He knew without question that Xavier could not have been the father, but yet, the boy was indelibly linked to the pregnancy by the unfathomable friendship he shared with Lisa. Xavier suffered the anger that rightfully should have been directed at the absent father.

Beyond that an unanticipated turmoil erupted from Sam's choice of a "non-white" curate. Naively, Sam had assumed that the Civil War mentality, harbored by some, had matured enough to allow the acceptance of a fellow Christian, black or white. But he had been wrong; ages old genetic prejudices emerged to fuel whispered objections. Hearing of the whispers from Marcy, Sam was deeply saddened, but now more determined to follow a voice more certain than that of the insecure.

On top of these uncertainties, the first Parish Meeting to discuss the enlargement of the church had demonstrated stronger than anticipated support for starting over in a new location. It had been an increasingly heated meeting that Sam wisely decided should be adjourned pending further thought and prayer. Lance had made an impassioned plea for "a new beginning." Sprinkled throughout was the innuendo that certain recent decisions were not in the mainstream of the congregation's wishes.

* * * *

In the midst of these symptoms of change, Rachel had received a reply from the Archbishop in Singapore. He welcomed her to his work in Nepal, and urged her to come as soon as it was convenient. After consulting with Sam and the Bishop, she was given leave to make her travel plans.

Now anxious to act, rather than dwell in uncertain limbo any longer, she booked her flight for March tenth; this gave her little time for second thoughts.

Normally, she and Russell exchanged e-mails at least once a day, but the day she made her travel plans, she had received no acknowledgement from him, nor did she receive any messages for the week before she was to leave. She tried calling his apartment, but got no answer. In desperation, she asked Caroline to try to reach him, but she had no better luck. In an attempt to comfort her, Caroline said he sometimes went on long business trips that would take him away for a week or two. She was concerned herself that he had seemingly disappeared and at such a critical time for Rachel. There was nothing to be done about it, but it left Rachel badly shaken.

* * * *

Sam had asked Rachel to preach on her last Sunday at St. James. It was a courtesy she deserved. He would have strenuously denied an ulterior motive, but well aware of her more liberal beliefs on social issues, he waited with interest to see if she might touch on any of those sensitive areas.

He did not have long to wait. She began by thanking those who had welcomed her to the parish and, especially, those who had been so kind and understanding to Ben. She stressed the word "understanding", and paused after saying it.

"Understanding is an interesting, if not curious word. The archaic use would imply *tolerate*, to *be sympathetic*. It is a word that is not frequently used in these days of hardened points of view. To tolerate, or to be sympathetic to one's fellow man is a Christian principle. Christ demonstrated this by forgiving Peter for his three denials. He forgave Thomas for his lack of faith that He had risen from the dead.

There is a virulent poison in our Christian bloodstream that tries to separate faithful Christians from "People of Faith." The People of Faith have formed a Roman legion to combat the faithful Christian; the one who gropes his way through life trying desperately to interpret God's will, but who is unwilling to seize the pulpit of categorical certainty.

Tolerance, sympathy, and understanding are Christian virtues, not owned by any group and especially they are virtues not to be castigated for political gain.

I will pray for this parish when I am in far off Nepal, that it may find a middle path through the divisions that could destroy its Christian purpose.

Thank you and goodbye."

Rachel's voice throughout the sermon was soft; her words distinctly enunciated and said with deep conviction. For those close enough to the pulpit to see, her eyes blazed with an inner fire that few had seen since her arrival.

After the service, in the privacy of the sacristy, Sam came up to her and held her without a word for a long moment. The gesture did not need words, it was her farewell to St. James.

* * * *

Xavier appeared at her apartment the afternoon before Rachel was to leave. She had asked him to come to see her.

"Please come in, Xavier. It is so nice of you to come. Thank you. Would you have a coke or something?"

"No, thanks, Miss Mason." He was polite, but she could see he had other things on his mind.

"Please, sit down, Xavier. Can you stay for just a minute?"

"Sure. I got plenty of time." He sat down on the edge of the sofa, stiff and ill at ease.

Rachel knew it was going to be difficult, but she needed to reach out to him somehow.

"Xavier, you know how proud I am of how you handled the situation with Lisa. I just need to know that you are all right, you know, deep inside?"

"It's cool, Miss Mason. No problem." His voice, flat and low, denied his words.

"No, Xavier, it isn't cool. We both know that, don't we?"

He squirmed self consciously.

"Have you talked to Lisa?"

"They won't let me."

"Is she still resting, do you know?"

"I guess so, but I don't know. Mr. Brown won't tell me nothing. He says they are going away for a while."

Rachel walked over to her purse and found her cell phone.

"Xavier, I know you won't understand this, I'm sure I wouldn't, but Mr. Brown doesn't dislike you. He is so upset about Lisa that he isn't thinking clearly. I know how much you helped Lisa. I'm gong to call the Browns and ask to speak to Lisa, to say goodbye. When I get her on the phone, I'll give it to you, OK?"

Xavier's eyes brightened and a cautious smile appeared.

"Would you, Miss Mason? I'd sure think that was cool if I could just talk to her."

Rachel dialed the Browns' number. Nancy answered. Rachel explained that she hoped to say goodbye to Lisa if it were convenient.

Nancy apologized for not coming around to say goodbye, but things were difficult, as Rachel could appreciate. After they had talked a bit more, Nancy said she would go up and tell Lisa that she was on the phone. A few minutes later, she heard Lisa's voice.

"Hi, Miss Mason. Thanks for calling."

Rachel listened intently to hear the click of the receiver of the downstairs phone. In the meantime, Rachel asked how she was feeling and told her about her flight tomorrow, but until she finally heard a distinctive click, she said nothing about Xavier.

Satisfied they were alone on the line, Rachel said, "Lisa, I have done a naughty thing. I wanted to say goodbye to you, but I also wanted Xavier to be able to talk to you. Your grandfather is understandably upset and thinks it would be better if you two didn't see each other for a while, or, for that matter talk."

"What a jerk! Xavier had nothing to do with me being pregnant, but he can't seem to get that through his fat head!" Her anger and resentment made her spit out the words.

"Lisa, please, this is very hard on your grandparents."

"Bull crap! They think it's easy for me?"

"Lisa, please. I want you to talk to Xavier in a minute, but first, try to think of the shock this is to your grandparents. You, at least, had forewarning that this was a possibility. Be as kind as you can to them, for my sake, Lisa."

"Alright, I'll try, but I feel like a prisoner up here."

"Goodbye, my dear Lisa. I will think of you often."

"Goodbye, Miss Mason. Thanks for being a friend." Lisa's voice had softened, her anger spent.

"Here's Xavier."

"Hi, Lisa!"

"Hi, Xavier. I'm sorry about my grandfather."

"Let's not talk about him. How do you feel?"

"I'm OK, sore, I guess."

"When will you be able to get out?"

"I don't know. My grandfather has taken the keys to the Jag so I don't have any wheels. I heard them talking about going up to Connecticut to my parents' house for a while. I'm like a prisoner."

"I wish I could see you, Lisa."

"Do you still like me a little?"

"I'm your boyfriend, you said, Lisa."

"I wish you would be. I like you so much."

Xavier heard Lisa's voice break and then a quick intake of breath.

"Lisa, I like you more. Don't cry. I'll wait 'til you get out."

"Promise?"

"I promise. I should get off the phone in case they pick it up. Bye, Lisa."

"Bye, Xavier."

He handed the phone back to Rachel who had come back into the room as she heard Xavier say goodbye.

"Thanks, Miss Mason. That was really cool. You're a nice lady. I wish you weren't going away." He stood, ready to leave.

"Xavier, two things: could you call me Rachel, and could I hug you once?"

She didn't wait for him to come to her, but walked to him and hugged him until she felt his arms come, tentatively, around her.

Thoroughly embarrassed, he backed away.

"Thanks for all you did for us,......Rachel." Then his face broke into a wide smile and Rachel felt she had accomplished just a little.

* * * *

Rachel's flight left Baltimore at 8:55 PM, with two stops; one in London, and one in Doha, Qatar. It was a twenty-five hour trip that arrived in Kathmandu at 4:15 PM a day later. Arrangements had been made for a British nurse to meet her at the airport.

Caroline and Sam planned to take her to the airport, and had made a reservation for dinner at the Chesapeake House. It was a sentimental time. Both Sam and Rachel struggled to keep the solemnity of the occasion from getting too emotional. Sam knowing something about Far Eastern customs from his days in Viet Nam, could only hope that Rachel would be strong enough to deal with such a radically different lifestyle. Rachel, knowing Sam's age and the history of his heart attack could only pray that she would find him in good health when she returned.

When their sinfully indulgent chocolate covered, strawberry topped, New York cheesecake was served, Sam put a package by Rachel's place.

"Sam, I'm having a difficult enough time as it is—you shouldn't."

"It is the same gift I was given many years ago when I started out. It became my good friend as I hope this will be yours."

She slowly opened the wrapping and picked up a red leather-bound Prayer Book and Hymnal. Its pages were tissue-thin so that its size was easily held. Sam had found a reproduction of a painting by an unknown artist entitled, *The Holy Family at Work*, that he had pasted on the reverse side of the first page. The painting showed Joseph as a working carpenter, Mary, with young Jesus at her side, teaching. The significance of the everyday working scene was not lost on Rachel. She excused herself and walked rapidly to the Ladies' Room.

When she returned, her eyes were reddened, but she was able to smile apologetically. She encircled Sam's neck and kissed him, then did the same to Caroline.

"I promised myself I wouldn't cry, so I won't, anymore. Thank you, thank you, my dearest friends."

It had been agreed that Sam would drop Rachel at the airport and not go in with her because of the lengthy security checks.

Caroline gave Rachel a goodbye kiss and whispered, "Don't worry about Russell, something quite ordinary will explain his silence, I'm sure." She hoped what she said would prove to be true.

Rachel nodded, but, nonetheless, she felt hollow inside, as though her experience with Russell had been an illusion, a figment of her imagination.

* * * *

Friday evening was the one day in the week when Sam allowed himself to enjoy two martinis. It had been a tradition in his marriage to Beth and now was carried over with Caroline. This particular Friday evening, following the bittersweet loss of Rachel, had been a particularly testing week. Caroline, aware of the tensions that seemed to be building, gave their cocktails just a shade more vodka than usual. She reasoned that it was not to encourage inebriation, but rather to loosen the neck muscles she suspected had been the cause of Sam's headache.

"Do you know what I think has caused this sudden tumult in our otherwise placid existence, Mrs. Adams?" He toasted her and sipped.

"Let me guess. You ran out of black shoe polish?"

"My, you are perceptive. No."

"The air in the left front tire is low?"

"That's not even close."

"I give up as I know you want me to."

"Your brother! In his innocent exuberance, he has upset the normal vectors in Afton. They are out of alignment, like jackstraws."

"It hurts me that you would impugn dear old Leigh. I confess to never having thought of him in terms of jackstraws. How can you be so certain?"

"There is no other logical reason. At the reception, I saw him talking to Lance Bosley. I knew then that there would be trouble in River City." Half finished with his martini, he turned pensive. "Caroline, I am concerned about a number of things that just don't seem headed in the right direction."

"I talked to Nancy Brown today and that situation is certainly going in the wrong direction. Poor Dwight doesn't seem able to accept Lisa's abortion. I certainly can understand how demoralizing it must be, but he is hurting Lisa and, even Xavier, as I understand it. I'm worried about both Dwight and Nancy." Caroline picked up their glasses and retreated to the kitchen.

"Yes, I am too. I've talked to Dwight, but the whole thing is just too personal for him to open up about. I haven't tried to talk to Lisa, but I know Rachel had a couple of sessions with both Lisa and Xavier. She was a better fit than I would have been anyway." Sam had waited until Caroline had put his glass down.

"Poor Xavier. I hope he won't be tempted to revert to his old, bad habits."

"I am watching him very closely, Caroline. I think he has closed that door permanently. The other thing that is really beginning to fester is this controversy over the church expansion. Lance has, apparently, convinced a number of people that we can handle a heavy debt, in fact, he argues that we should—that it is humbling and makes us "work harder." How's that for spiritual reasoning?"

"How do you really feel about the church question, Sam?"

"I can understand the allure of building a beautiful new temple. Why not? To the glory of God! It would be heresy to debunk that purpose. But, you are also tempting the devil by thinking that a glorious new church is truly an affirmation of faith. Remember the stable where He was born.

I'm getting heavy and I'll stop in a second, but remember, you asked. It is not a decision I should have a strong voice in. As long as the discussion doesn't deteriorate into a bitter division of opinion, I should keep myself out of it. Unfortunately, I sense Lance is making this his mission and that, in the process, he will ride roughshod over quieter, less verbal folk. Without Dwight's diplomatic involvement, I can foresee Lance prevailing. I should be sorry if that were to happen.

It's funny, but when someone professes to speak for "the people of faith," I feel my skin crawl. It evokes the image of a secret society, a Skull and Bones of true believers. Those of us who continue to struggle with the eternal truths are, apparently, unwashed and can't be admitted to the fraternity.

By the way, I thought that Rachel said it very well.

Well, enough of that. Let's enjoy our second libation and think of azure Cayman waters."

* * * *

To one who was thought missing, he didn't know he was. Russell had written a long letter to Rachel just before he left. Knowing that computer communication from Finland would be problematical, he had written the letter and left his laptop at home.

Denise's father had called him on the phone late one night, telling him that Denise was dying of tongue cancer. She had asked about Russell several times so her father, reluctantly, had felt he should call.

Russell, moved by the fact that she still thought of him, decided instantly to go to her and be of whatever comfort he could be. Her health, according to her father, was extremely poor; they did not expect her to live out the week.

Canceling several business appointments and penning a long explanatory letter to Rachel, he flew out of Miami the following day.

Denise was heavily sedated when he arrived and did not seem to know him during her brief periods of consciousness. Then, as apparently sometimes happens, her mind cleared. She was ecstatic when she saw Russell. They began a long reminiscence of their year together in Europe;

the playful joy they had found in every new town and the romantic excitement of their never to be forgotten experiences. Denise seemed to glow with good health during these talks, even appeared to mend under the doctor's skeptical eyes, but, too soon, she relapsed and disappeared again into the morphine fog of a land Russell could not visit. Yet, unconscious as she seemed, she sensed Russell's presence and would reach out for his hand.

Knowing Rachel might be leaving at any moment, he was torn by his desire to leave, and yet, he was deeply touched by Denise's seeming need for him; he could not leave.

Ten days after he arrived, she died. She was cremated and the funeral was held two days after her death. Denise's father, surly when Russell first arrived, grew to appreciate, if not fully understand, the intimate bond his daughter had forged with this American.

The long train trip to the airport and then the flight back to Miami, consumed almost two days. When he called Rachel's phone, he was told it had been disconnected. Fearing the worst, he called his mother and confirmed that she had left three days ago. His mother had said that they had no way of contacting her and would not have until she wrote to them. Apparently Rachel had been told that it might take two to three weeks before she was located in a place where normal communication might be expected.

Rachel had been able to rush off a brief note to Caroline and Sam telling them of her safe arrival in Kathmandu. In the meantime, Russell's letter explaining his sudden departure sat in the Afton post office awaiting forwarding instructions.

* * * *

Caroline's brother, Leigh called shortly after Russell's call.

"Hi, Sis! Should have called earlier or, better still, written to thank you for the hospitality at your wedding. I had a great time. How'd you like the Caymans?"

"We had a very nice time, thank you. It is a lovely place, just enough off the beaten track to be peaceful. Thank you for coming to the wedding,

Leigh, and thank you for the thoughtful transportation. How is the play going?"

"Closed last week. It was a dog! I got a decent notice out of it. I've signed on with a tour company to take *The Music Man* to the four corners of our kingdom. Actually, we play Baltimore in early May."

"Should I ask what part?"

"You insult me—underestimate me—embarrass me! Tin-horn Harold, who would you think?"

"Oh, that's wonderful, Leigh! You don't think it will be too much for you?"

"I'm fit as a tuba, Babe. No, it'll be a challenge, and it's such a great part. Why don't I send you a couple of tickets for Baltimore? Maybe you would want to take that couple who was at your dinner, Sam's Warden?"

"Hmm, well maybe not this time, Leigh. It's too long a story to go into."

"Whatever."

"How is Patrice doing?"

"She got a part in *The Unsinkable MB*. Bit part, but it gives her credits."

"How does that fit with your tour?"

"Doesn't, but if her show folds, she can join me, or something else may turn up for her."

"You don't think you're seeing too much of her, do you?"

His sister's sarcasm was not lost on Leigh.

"Oh, Sis, it's the life we live. It works, sometimes. How's old Sam?"

"He's fine. We are into a sort of unsettling time, however. There seems to be an effort being made to change the church here and in the process wrest some of Sam's authority away. It's too complicated to go into on the phone, but it does worry Sam."

"Time to retire, Sis. How's that little cutie of a curate?"

"I assume the person you are referring to is The Reverend Miss Rachel Mason? If so, she left for Nepal a week ago."

"No kidding? Bully for her! That takes chutzpa what with all that Chinese crap going on. What's she going to do, lead a charge of the white brigade against them?"

116

"She's going to work in a Tibetan refugee camp, I think, although she had not been assigned to one for certain when she left."

"Gutsy broad! I'll have to get to know her when she gets back."

"No, you won't! You look for your eighth. or will it be your tenth, wife in Bozeman, Montana, not here."

"There really is no controlling my virile blood, Sister-mio. I and most women are helpless before it."

"Leigh, it was wonderful to talk to you. We would like to see you when you get to Baltimore, so let us know dates and details."

"I will. Happy Days, Vicar's wife!"

* * * *

It was a Thursday afternoon when Sam had just returned to his office from making parish calls that he ran into Xavier doing his normal straightening up routine in the Parish House.

"Xavier, how are you, my friend? Do you have a minute for a chat?"

"Yes, sir, I'll be right in." Xavier put down his dust rag and ran a comb through his hair.

"Sit down and talk to me. We haven't had a good talk for some time. This is March, school is over, when, late May?"

"Yes, sir, May twenty-eighth, I think."

"How will you do, as far as marks are concerned?"

"Pretty good, I guess."

"Could you translate that into grades?"

"I should get three A's and one B, Father Sam."

"Xavier, that is wonderful! I didn't do that well. What are you planning to do in the fall?"

"Get a job. It isn't I don't like this job, I do, but I guess I need to earn more."

"No college plans?"

"I can't afford college, Father Sam."

"Would you want to go if you could afford it?"

"I guess so. I haven't thought a lot about it, I guess."

"If you went to college what would you want to study? You know, what would you want to be?"

"I really don't know, maybe a teacher?"

"You have a lot of ability, Xavier, and what's more, you take on responsibilities seriously."

"I like working for you."

"Well, thank you, my friend. You really work for St. James, you know."

"You are St. James, Father."

Sam felt a lump in his throat and did not reply immediately. Then, much as he had when he proposed the sexton's job to Xavier to wean him from his drug gang, he had another inspiration.

"Xavier, I think you should go to college. We could do it the same way we did the car, except this time instead of hours worked here at St. James, you'd have to maintain a B average."

"I don't understand, Father?"

"I don't blame you. It just occurs to me that you should go to college and the money can be arranged."

"How?"

"I'm not sure, but that part is easy. First of all, I want you to think seriously whether you would want to go. If you decide you do, then we'll see where you should go. Talk to your mother, then we'll sit down together and talk about it. Will you do that?"

"I.... I could think about it, but I can't understand how it will work. It costs a lot of money, doesn't it?"

"No, let's do first things first; you decide whether you would really want to go, then we'll talk money. Can you do that?"

"I guess I can, but I haven't thought about it much. Where would I go?"

"I'm not sure, but it probably would be good to stay fairly close by, probably stay in Maryland. I'm going to change the subject, but let's get together, this is Thursday, say next Monday at your Mom's house, after school. Is that alright?"

"Yes, I guess so." It was obvious that Xavier was totally overwhelmed by this new, unbelievable idea.

"Now Lisa. I know Mr. Brown has been difficult, Xavier. Have you been able to talk to Lisa at all?"

"Only once when Miss Mason called her." He could not use her first name as Rachel had asked.

118

"I'm going to talk to Dwight, Mr. Brown, and I'm going to see if he will let her have a little more freedom. I believe she's well over her operation. It would be nice if you could talk to Lisa about college." Sam was far more devious than most people thought. He suspected that if he could put Lisa and Xavier together to talk college, she would be the ultimate influence.

"I wish I could see her, Father Sam."

"Well, we'll see. You think about college right now. There will be a time for Lisa soon, I hope. You might even talk about college with her."

"She needs a friend, Father Sam," he barely whispered.

"She's lucky to have you."

* * * *

Sam had thought about Xavier's future a number of times, but had not discussed the idea of college with Caroline. He had intended to, but had simply put it off. Now, having broached the idea to Xavier, he knew it was time.

That evening he began talking about Xavier, artfully, or so he thought.

"Caroline, I had a chat with Xavier this afternoon. That is one bright boy! He is getting all A's and one B."

"Really?" Her voice suggested she was preoccupied.

"Yes. He is a real student. I really like that boy."

"I believe you've said that before, as I remember."

"You don't agree from the sound of your voice."

"No, no, he's a fine boy."

"But, I mean, he is a very good student."

"A's and B's are good grades."

"Caroline, I don't believe I am fully engaging you in this conversation."

"Really? I didn't know it was a conversation. I thought you were simply extolling Xavier's virtues, again."

Sam studied his new bride, trying to determine whether she was even vaguely interested in his subject. Trying another tack, he said, "It seems unfortunate that some kids can't go beyond high school for lack of money."

119

"That's true."

"Some colleges are somewhat reasonable. I'm not talking Yale and Princeton, you understand."

"No, not Yale or Princeton."

"Some of these kids deserve to get some help."

"I'm sure they do."

"Caroline, are you paying attention at all?" Sam had finally gotten provoked by her seeming lack of interest.

"Yes, my darling, I am paying attention, but I have suspected from the first sentence of your little play-let that you want to send Xavier to college. I agree, we, you should do that. He deserves to go to college. There, see, I was paying attention." She had come over and sat down next to Sam and put her arms around his neck. "You are such an old softy, you're mushy. I love you mush-pot."

Embarrassed, relieved to have his idea out in the open and agreed to, yet having to realize she had been several steps ahead of him, provoked him into a long, humbling laugh.

"If I have failed to say it ever before, I find a woman's mind a wondrous thing."

BOOK TWO

CHAPTER TEN

The flight from Doha, Qatar, to Kathmandu, was late to take off. The weather had closed in just before Rachel's flight from London was in its final descent. In attempting to land, the pilot had to pull up and go around on his first effort. The second attempt ended with a jarring landing, but no one on the plane complained, just relieved to be on the ground. Poor Rachel, who had flown only once before when she had gone to Ben's trial, had been petrified. Fortunately, her seatmate, a middle-aged man from Karachi, was the sole of tranquility. She had difficulty understanding him, but the tonal serenity of whatever he was saying, helped to control her panic.

As the pilot revved the engines for the take-off for Kathmandu, Rachel reached for her companion's hand.

"Would you let me hold your hand, please, sir?"

The man, undoubtedly a Muslim, looked at this strange woman with half-lidded eyes, glazed with disbelief. Realizing she must have run afoul of another far-Eastern custom, she quickly withdrew her hand. The plane lumbered down the runway through blinding snow, Rachel consigning her soul to the Almighty.

Interminable hours later, her peace of mind totally shattered, she began bargaining with the devil, gambling that the shuddering, diving plane might hold together until they reached Kathmandu. Finally, well into the twenty-fifth hour of her trip, she fell asleep, totally exhausted.

The next thing she knew, it couldn't have been five minute later, she thought, the Karachi gentleman touched her arm.

"Nepal airdrome, madam." He pointed downward.

At this, Rachel awoke, but still drugged from two days of sleeplessness, she momentarily panicked, unable to recall why she was going to Nepal. Her ears hurt terribly as the plane seemed to dive toward the airport. Then, beyond belief, the wheels touched the landing strip and she had arrived in Kathmandu. She vowed to spend the rest of her life in Nepal, never to fly again.

Ironically, Rachel's landing in Kathmandu was just minutes from Russell's landing in Miami, returning from his trip to Finland. When she later learned what had taken him away, she thought of Finland as close enough to Nepal for them to have gotten together. She would look back on her limited knowledge of the world with great glee, but only after she had finished the hard course ahead of her.

* * * *

Rachel, weary and bedraggled, stepped cautiously down the stairs from the plane, her carry-on tugging heavily on her shoulder. The steward had explained that the passengers would have a short walk from the plane to the terminal, as there were no jet ways. Snow was still falling in tight, hard kernels that stung her face. Down on the tarmac, she followed the other passengers to the lighted door of the terminal. Once inside, she looked in vain for the person who was to meet her, as she was being led into a walled-off section of the terminal for a security check.

Rachel knew she should be excited at finally being in Nepal, but she was so tired she had to keep reminding herself that she was there. The security check was very thorough; a polite, but insistent female guard examined her very closely. Finding the Happy Buddha Russell had given her, she tapped it several times trying to determine if it were hollow, hiding some sort of drug. Finally allowed to proceed, she walked toward the baggage claim area.

"Reverend Mason!"

Startled, Rachel looked toward the voice. Standing ram-rod stiff, holding a sign with Rachel's name on it, was a tall, thin, middle-aged woman with thick, black-rimmed glasses. Rachel walked toward the woman, trying very hard to smile.

"I am Rachel Mason." She extended her hand.

"Veddy, veddy glad to make your acquaintance, Reverend. I am Penelope Heathcote, RN. Welcome to Nepal."

As soon as the woman had said her name was Penelope, Rachel thought she would burst out laughing, tired as she was. She made an exaggerated effort to put down her carry-on, then, barely able to control her expression, she managed a surprisingly exuberant, "Penelope, I am so happy to meet you!"

"Let us go toward the baggage area in order to reclaim your valise, shall we, what?"

"Yes, let's. It is so nice of you to meet me. What time is it? I'm afraid I am no longer sure."

"It is two thousand hours. Your plane was four hours late in arriving. I would judge your weather to have been inclement?"

"We had all the weathers there are, I believe," Rachel said, the memories still affecting her peace of mind.

"Yes, not uncommon across the steppes, I believe. It relates to the terrain."

Rachel found her bag and wheeled it through a detection device to a customs area. Her newfound friend said she would meet her at the exit area.

Again, the inspector took great pains to examine her bag, lifting, squeezing, and in some cases, smelling everything in the bag. Finally, she was free to leave.

Penelope took the suitcase from her, lifting it as though it were empty.

"I certainly can take that, Miss.... Penelope." She made a half-hearted attempt to reclaim the bag.

"No, in deedy! I shall carry it effortlessly. Let us proceed to the public conveyances."

Once seated in the taxi, Rachel fought the need to sleep, but she was only partially successful; she kept drifting off, her head dropping, then jerking up as she fought to stay awake. She thought she heard, as if from a long way off, that she was to stay at the Shangri La Hotel.

She was able to walk, unsteadily, into the hotel. Miss Heathcote took care of her registration and bid her goodnight, saying she would call at a convenient hour tomorrow. Mercifully, Rachel was led to her room where she locked the door and fell onto the bed, fully clothed, and did not wake until noon the next day.

Something woke her, possibly a cleaning woman in the hall. She dragged herself to the bathroom and into the shower where all she could coax from the rusty showerhead was a weak trickle of tepid water. Partially clean, but not refreshed, she burrowed in her suitcase for clean clothes.

The phone rang while she was brushing her hair.

"Hello?"

"Cheerio! Heathcote here. Hope your rest was restorative? Were it convenient, I would stop by in an hour? The local refugee coordinator seems anxious to meet you. Will an hour be convenient?"

"Oh, yes. I will be ready, thank you." For the first time since she had landed, she was conscious of a feeling of excitement. She was actually beginning her new work!

* * * *

Ms. Heathcote led Rachel to a low, one-story, ugly brick building in downtown Kathmandu. A modest sign hung precariously over the door stating, *All Faiths Union of Tibetan Relief Aid.* Inside, a skeleton staff of Tibetans bent over desks piled high with files. They were ushered to an office in the corner,

A Mr. Dorji greeted Rachel formally, his head bobbing up and down as he expressed his appreciation for her service. His English was very good, his phrasing more formal than she was used to.

"The Archbishop has requested of you that you consider an assignment in one of our larger settlements. It is located near Pokhara about 200 kilometers from Kathmandu. It is one of the oldest Tibetan settlements and is located in a charming valley setting. The Archbishop believes you will like it there. Do you care to comment at this juncture?"

"Well, no. I am totally ignorant about Nepal; I am ashamed to admit.

I will be very happy to serve wherever you or the Archbishop believe I may be of service."

"How nice of you to reply in that way. Good! Will you be able to leave in the morning?"

"Yes, I guess so." Rachel suddenly felt that the world was rotating at a very rapid rate.

"Good! I would ask you to spend a short time with one of your countrymen. He likes to meet the new members of our group."

"I will be happy to."

Mr. Dorji led her to his front door and pointed across the street to a six-story building across the street.

"That is your government's building. You will find Mr. Durgan on the sixth floor. Welcome to Nepal and thank you again for offering your services, Miss Mason." Rachel nodded to Mr. Dorji and crossed the street. Taking an elevator to the sixth floor she was directed to Mr. Durgan's office down a long hallway.

As she entered, a secretary greeted her, "I would guess that you are Miss Mason. Welcome to Kathmandu, Miss Mason. Please go on in, Mr. Durgan is expecting you."

Durgan's office was a large, corner room that commanded a sweeping view of Kathmandu looking northeast. She could not be sure, but in the brief glance she had, she thought she saw an immense peak in the far distance. Could that be Everest? A chill ran down her spine when she realized how near she was to where Scott had spent his last days.

"Come in Miss Mason." A voice came from the corner of the room; the lighting was such that she did not see anyone at first.

"Why not sit over here?" He pointed to a chair across from him. "It gives a pretty good view of the Himalayas. I assume that's the reason you came to Nepal."

Rachel had reached the designated chair, but before sitting down she looked more closely at the man. He had not risen and sat leaning back, his jacket off, his vest unbuttoned. From the little she could see, he had a high forehead and affected a bushy, black mustache. He sat studying her, slowly twirling horn-rimmed glasses. She sat and waited for him to speak, still not having any idea who he was or why she was seeing him.

127

He shifted his scrutiny of her to something he must have seen on the ceiling.

"Tell me who you are, Miss Mason?" He could not have sounded more bored.

Rachel, who was still tired from the long journey, took an immediate dislike to this person. The contrast between Mr. Dorji, who was as gracious as he could be, and this loutish man about whom she knew nothing, was jolting.

"Excuse me, sir. I confess to being a little tired from my trip, but could you tell me who you are and why I am here?"

"Name is Durgan, that's about all you need to know. I work for our mother country. But you, I understand will be working for an international church group. I repeat, who are you and why are you here?"

"I do not understand that question, Mr. Durgan. You seem to know my name and who I will be working for which is more than I know at the moment."

"Then why did you come?"

Rachel was getting angry, but, uncertain as to who this man was, she restrained herself.

"I believe you answered your own question, I will work for a church group."

"To what end, why?" His words were slow, almost ominous.

"When I am assigned, I will tell you 'to what end." Her irritation showed through her reply.

"You seem rather aggressive. I wonder why? You gave testimony for a killer, I read. Why would you do that?"

Rachel felt dizzy. It might have been the stagnant air in this office, or simply her lack of sleep, but she knew it was her reaction to something far more personal than those things. How could he know this?

"I.... I.... because I knew he was innocent," she stammered.

"He wasn't though, was he?"

"He was innocent in my eyes, Mr. Durgan," Rachel blazed!

"I don't think you need to get emotional, Miss Mason. Do you? Do you know where he got his drugs?"

"I absolutely refuse to answer any more questions, Mr. Durgan. What has this got to do with my work here in Nepal?"

"People who may have done irrational things in the past are not unlikely to do them again. We have an untidy little war going on here, Miss Mason. One of my jobs is to see that irrational people are not here in sympathy with the insurgents. You seem a little up tight, Miss Mason. I think we'll call it a day. I hope you enjoy your little stay here. I will keep in touch. Goodbye." He walked to his desk, picked up the phone and dialed. The interview was over.

Rachel stared at the man's back, then walked out, leaving the door open. She could not swear it, but it seemed that the secretary had an amused, if not sympathetic, expression on her face as she passed.

* * * *

Making a stop at an outfitter's on the way back to the hotel, Rachel bought several pairs of khaki trousers and shirts at Miss Heathcote's recommendation. She told Rachel that the laundry facilities at the camps were notoriously unreliable. Several times, Rachel had raised leading questions about Mr. Durgan, but she had deftly avoided any comment, dismissing him as just one of the Americans who acted as advisors to the Nepal government. Still festering from his rudeness, Rachel was left with no real understanding of the interview.

She had seen very little of Kathmandu, but the wild bicycle traffic gave her some insight into its teeming population. Deposited at the hotel, she was content to eat an early dinner and write a hurried letter to Sam and Caroline. Where was Russell?

Falling into bed at seven o'clock, she had no idea what time it was in Afton, knowing only that the effect of the higher altitude of Kathmandu made her very sleepy.

Up at dawn, she tortured herself again with the shower, then repacked her bags and went down to breakfast. As she entered the dining room, she saw her seatmate on the flight from Qatar. He was seated with a wild-haired, fully bearded man who was obviously in the midst of telling some exciting story, his arms flailing, his voice carrying over the other conversations in the dining room. To punctuate the end of his yarn, he slapped the table with all his strength and let out a roar of self-appreciation.

Rachel indicated to the young man who was guiding her to her seat that she would prefer something in the corner, away from the two men. She had no sooner sat down, however, than she was conscious of her Karachi friend looming over her.

"Good morning, madam. I trust you have rested well after our flight from Doha?" His silken voice evoked the terror of the flight.

"Yes, thank you."

"I trust you have made connections with your agency?"

"Yes, thank you." She was conscious that the wild-haired story-teller had come up to the table.

"And have they assigned you to one of their camps, may I presume to ask?"

"Yes, I will go to Pokhara this morning."

"That is a most delightful city, though Prachandra has recently caused some difficulties."

"Oh, I am not aware of any difficulties."

"May I introduce Mr. Reginald Toomey. Mr. Toomey flies supplies to some of the more remote Tibetan facilities. Mr. Toomey, Miss Mason."

"Cheerio, lass. Happy to have you join our intimate little group. I heard you say you are gong to Pokhara. I'm flying there me-self at noon. Give you a lift?"

"Oh, thank you no. They have arranged a car, I believe."

"Safer in my wee plane. The Maoies have hit that road a couple of times lately."

"I'm sorry, but I feel I must follow their instructions, thank you." Rachel had been inspecting the pilot more closely and she could see that he was far younger than he first appeared. He may have affected the hair to make him appear older, she guessed. He was still not a reassuring sight.

"I'll be with Durgan if you change your mind. Glad to have the company."

"Thank you so much. I will keep that in mind."

"Very pleased to have seen you again, Miss Mason. Have a safe journey." The older gentleman bowed and excused himself.

"I can show you the Annies like you've never seen 'em. They is the Annapurnas, you know. You'll be sorry to miss 'em. Looks like a bully day!"

Rachel suddenly found herself tempted, as irrational as that could be. Here was an opportunity to get a special view of some of the mountains that had so hypnotized Scott—maybe her only chance. Yet, this weird looking man represented the antithesis of her concept of an airline pilot.

"On second thought, I'd like to ride with you, Mr. Toomey." The words were out of her mouth before she could stop them. It must have been the thinner air or, possibly, an element of her personality she had never known to exist. "I would need to talk to Mr. Dorji first, however. May I call you at Mr. Durgan's?"

"Rightie-o, lass. See you at noon at the field. Everyone knows me there." He gave her a mock bow and followed his older companion out of the dining room.

Rachel was left with her own amazement. *What in the world possessed me to say that—you idiot!* But she savored enough of her bizarre agreement to make her smile. Though she felt the palms of her hands sweating, she looked forward to her first real adventure in Nepal.

* * * *

It had been two weeks since Lisa's operation, as she chose to call it. She and Xavier had not seen each other in that time. Finally, her grandfather gave back the keys to her car, but with restrictions.

"Lisa, I want you to have your car, but I must insist that you stay in the immediate Afton area and, though I shan't forbid it, I would prefer it if you and Xavier did not see a great deal of each other for the time being. I think this should be a period of reflection for all to us. I know you understand."

Lisa, who had been extremely unhappy with her grandfather's restrictions, could only mumble words that hinted at concurrence, she did not want to concur at all.

Finally free, she went immediately to the church. Xavier was not there so she went to his house. His mother answered the door.

"Mrs. Mendoza, is Xavier here?"

"Please to come in, Miss. No, I am afraid he is not. School is just over. He would have gone to Father's church from there." She did not know who the girl was, but she seemed a pretty one and very polite. She was pleased that her son had a friend like this. "May I have your name? I will tell him you came here."

"I'm sorry. I'm Lisa, Mrs. Mendoza. I am Mr. Brown's granddaughter."

Xavier's mother had never met Mr. Brown, but she knew that he was an important man. This made her even more self-conscious about her home.

"I'm sorry Xavier is not here. I would ask you to sit down here and wait for him, but it is not much—you can see."

"It is very cozy, Mrs. Mendoza, much more than my house is."

Mrs. Mendoza could not know what Lisa's words meant, she only assumed the girl was just being polite."

"Oh, I don't think so, but you are kind to say so, Miss Lisa."

"I'll run along and see if I can catch Xavier at the church. It's nice to meet you, Mrs. Mendoza. I think your son is really cool!" She backed out of the door and walked over to her car.

Mrs. Mendoza watched as Lisa got into her car. She didn't know anything about cars, but this one had the look of being expensive.

"Such a fine girl for my son to have as a friend, but Mr. Brown's granddaughter?" She closed the door and went to her kitchen shaking her head, talking to herself in Spanish.

* * * *

On her second attempt at the church, Lisa found Xavier. He was carrying a vacuum cleaner over to the church.

"Hey, Xavier," she yelled excitedly!

He turned as she pulled to a stop.

"Hi, Lisa! Am I glad to see you!"

"Get in," she urged him.

As soon as he had closed the door, she grabbed his hand.

"Oh, Xavier! How terrible! I hated my grandfather for not letting me see you. How are you? Are you still my friend?"

"Yes, of course."

"My boyfriend, even after all that nasty business?"

"Yes, Lisa, I am."

She leaned over and kissed him on the mouth.

"Father Sam is in his office—better be careful"

"Who cares? I'm so happy!"

They caught up with things that had happened, mostly with Xavier since Lisa had little to report. Xavier mentioned the conversation he had had with Father Sam about college.

"He thinks I may be able to go, Lisa." His eyes sparkled as he told her.

"That's awesome! Where would you go?"

"I don't know, somewhere, you know, in Maryland, I guess."

"Then I will go there, too. I'll get my parents to let me skip twelfth. I have enough credits and good marks."

"You could do that?"

"Sure, it's easy. Oh, won't that be cool! We could see each other every day and nobody to mess around with us." She reached across the seat and kissed him again.

"Well, it's not, you know, for sure, but he thinks he can."

"That's just too cool! You kiss me now." She offered him her face.

"Lisa, I can't, not here—Father Sam."

"Oh, bother Father Sam! Is he against kissing?"

"No, of course not. I mean, you know, here in the parking lot."

"But I'm so glad to see you."

Xavier moved quickly, kissed Lisa and then sat back, looking out the window for any sign of Father Sam.

"That was nice. OK, I've got to go. I'll see you here tomorrow?"

"Yes, I'll be here. Bye, Lisa."

He watched her drive away with the feeling of wonderment that she still wanted to be his girlfriend.

CHAPTER ELEVEN

Sam had met with the Bishop several times since returning from the Caymans. It was his obligation to keep the Bishop up to date on the increasing agitation for change at St. James. The second and more definitive meeting on the church building was set for March fifteenth. It had become obvious that some forty or so parishioners supported Lance's effort to build a new church building and press for en entirely new format of the service. Implicit in these more radical plans was the expectation that Sam would see this as an invitation to retire.

Lance had made the keystone of his appeal the urgency to fight what he termed, the three cardinal sins of the Episcopal Church: abortion, same-sex marriage, and homosexual clergy, especially Bishops.

Early in their discussions, the Bishop had asked Sam to tell him where he stood on these issues and how that might affect his attitude toward a new church building. He knew of Sam's affection for Dwight and he needed to know that this allegiance would not, of itself, preclude a realistic analysis of a new church building.

"Bishop, I have rather normal loyalties. Dwight has been a very loyal lieutenant to me, and his family has contributed much to this parish. That said, I am prepared to accept the philosophy for a new church building if the reasoning is sound. But at this point, reasoning is at a premium—instead of reasoning, we are getting cant. One shortcoming I readily admit to is that I automatically oppose categorical, dogmatic positions regardless of the subject. I would not have been an ideal priest in John Paul II's hierarchy, nor, I gather, in Pope Benedict's.

Sure I have difficulty with some of the Episcopal Church's positions, or lack of them, but I am not ashamed to pray for guidance rather than presuming to *know* the truth.

To me, those who march in the People of Faith army would better be called People of Truth. Their *Faith* is really *the* Truth, unchallengeable, unvarnished *fact*. I am just not comfortable with that.

Entangled in all of these trumpet sounds is some sentiment for helping me into retirement. I will say only that I will retire when you ask me to, or when my spiritual and physical health tells me it is time, not before. Obviously, I will observe the mandatory retirement age, if I get that far. Beyond that, I will assure you that on these issues I will make myself known to friend or foe alike, rationally and without rancor and with a hopeful heart.

So, Bishop, that is where I stand, if that does not profane Brother Martin."

The Bishop did not respond immediately, then looked at his watch, "Samuel, it is almost two o'clock, we've been at it for a couple of hours and you need to get on your horse and go home, but I want to toast you first. I will have a pony of brandy and you may have a fresh cup of coffee when I do so."

After the waiter had brought the brandy and coffee, the Bishop raised his glass, fixed Sam with his penetrating eyes and said, simply, "I am proud to know a man like you, Sam. May God give us guidance."

* * * *

During Rachel's final orientation with Mr. Dorji, she asked if Mr. Toomey's offer to fly her to Pokhara would be possible and, if so, wise. Surprisingly, Dorji welcomed the idea and, though discounting the threats to a road trip, reasoned that flying would be more "efficient", although he left the final decision up to her.

On the way back to her hotel, a heavy, wet snow was falling. Though the sky was dark, the morning forecast had not indicated a serious weather problem.

She arrived at the airport at eleven o'clock. She had not seen it the night she landed but now saw that it was called *The Tribhuvan International Airport*. Grand though the title was, it reminded her of the airport in Salina, Kansas, even to the extent of having stray cows and chickens wandering aimlessly near the landing strips.

The snow still fell in fits and starts, one moment it was a blizzard, the next a diminishing spring flurry. The first official she asked where to find Mr. Toomey's whereabouts, amiably walked her to the far end of the terminal and through a glass door to a small, messy room that appeared to have been the main waiting room at an earlier stage of the airport. There was a chest-high counter facing the door and several dozen seats beyond. A large double door led to a walkway outside. The room was cluttered with lunch bags, old newspapers, and several pairs of soiled trousers. The floor looked as though it had not been swept in weeks.

Her guide waved toward the empty seats and said something like, "Captain Toomey soon, Memsab. Rest."

Rachel thanked him and put her bags near the outside door. She peered out into the erratic storm, but could not see any planes. Her bravado of yesterday was suffering second thoughts, but how could she change her plans now?

Shortly before noon, the door burst open and Toomey appeared. He had done nothing to enhance his appearance of yesterday, perhaps appearing even more disheveled, but his confident stride and hearty greeting gave Rachel renewed hope that she might not be pursuing a death wish.

"Ah! Miss Mason, I believe! Marvelous to see you again! Very wise decision. We'll be off tout de suit! Perfect flying weather! Snow won't last. Need to rub off the wings with glycol—just take a minute. You may stay, or go with me, as you wish."

"I'll go with you, I guess. The weather will clear up, you think?"

"Very low overhead, but visibility over a thousand feet is endless. Perfect day for sightseeing!" He darted outside so fast that the returning swing of the doors nearly hit Rachel as she hurried to follow.

It was probably a hundred yards to Toomey's plane so that each of them was covered with snow by time they reached it. Toomey scrambled up on the wing and unlocked the passenger door, as he did so the snow stopped completely.

"Ah, you see! Nepal weather. Here's my little beauty!" He came down the wing and gestured grandly at the plane. "She's one of the great Cessna's your fellow countrymen created—a magnificent 310, hardy, sensual and as close to a wife as I will ever have. Step aboard whilst I massage her graceful arms. Leave your bags, I'll stow them in the rear."

He had brought a large container of liquid from the plane and then proceeded to pour its contents into what appeared to be a bath towel.

Rachel tentatively climbed up onto the wing and then lowered herself awkwardly into the passenger seat.

Toomey worked on the wings for a few minutes, then stowed the bags and climbed into the pilot's seat. As soon as he was seated, he switched on the starter for the port engine. It turned over very reluctantly, the starter groaning over and over again. Then, prompted by words that Rachel did not know, he coaxed the engine to fire, the propeller spinning slowly at first, then as a blur. Toomey repeated the procedure with the starboard engine, but this time the engine responded promptly. The plane began to quiver with restrained power.

Toomey talked to the tower in what Rachel assumed was Nepalese and almost immediately she felt the brakes release and the plane move forward. The sun had burned a large hole in the overcast giving Rachel renewed confidence; her excitement now overcame her anxiety.

Toomey had been given clearance to take off so that when he reached the end of the runway he wheeled the plane sharply into the wind and eased the throttle forward until it reached full power. When he released the brakes, Rachel, was suddenly compressed into her seat as the plane sped down the runway; then she felt the exhilaration when the plane rose sharply into the clouds.

Toomey concentrated on the instruments, talking briefly to the tower. Soon, she felt the plane level off as he cut back the power. After a few minutes, he relaxed and sat back with a chuckle.

"Have you ever known a sweeter plane than my darlin'?"

"It is exciting to feel all that power, I must confess." Rachel was peering out the window studying Kathmandu as they rapidly pulled away to the west. There were miles and miles of tiny houses all tightly packed together, then, suddenly, there was nothing beneath them but miles and miles of neatly cultivated farm land.

"Your resort lies west of Pokhara, which is northwest of Kat. We'll fly north of Pok to within ten miles of the Anna Range. It'll knock your eyes out!"

When the plane had reached the cruising altitude of six thousand feet, Toomey glanced over at Rachel.

"What possessed you to come to this crazy place, Miss Mason, if you don't mind me askin'?"

"It's a fair question, but I haven't done well answering it yet. I hope to find out in the next few months. How about you?"

"Just for thrills. I didn't even know where Nepal was growing up. Took up flying after admitting school was too hard for me, or too slow, whichever. An old man taught me to fly. He died and left me this little beauty. I heard they was hiring pilots here, so I flew out and they took me on. Short history, I'm afraid."

"How long have you been here?"

"Let's see, five, no, almost six years."

"You must like it then?"

"Oh, there's good and bad, like everywhere, but the pay's good and I do like the old mountains."

"Have you every climbed?"

"What me? You have to be daft! They's not enough money in the Queen's exchequer to tempt me to climb them babies. No, I prefer being an eagle, not an ant. By the way, in a couple of minutes we'll be closing in on the big one, so keep your eyes bright."

"I had always thought that Annapurna was one mountain, but you keep referring to it as several."

"The big daddy is Annapurna Four, but there's a string of 'em, just some shorter."

Toomey corrected course to the north and, breaking out of a patch of clouds was 26,000 foot Annapurna, looming over them.

Rachel gasped. The only image that came to mind was a gnat approaching a gigantic elephant.

"I can't believe it!" she whispered. "Frighteningly awesome!"

Toomey did not comment, having the wisdom to know the mountains would speak more elegantly than he ever could.

They flew in silence, Rachel entranced, totally hypnotized by the power of the mountain. Scott's fate became ultimately real as she tried to imagine a human being attempting to conquer such a challenge.

The plane loafed along giving both of them a feeling of detached reality. Toomey, as many times as he had experienced the majesty of the Himalayas, was always overcome, as if drugged, by the terrifying silence that seemed to envelope them.

Suddenly the plane lurched violently to the left as though hit by a projectile.

Toomey, instantly alert, instinctively dropped his altitude a thousand feet and studied the gauges. The plane seemed to fly normally, so, assuming at worst they had hit a bird, he regained his normal altitude and continued on course. Giving Rachel a raised shoulder shrug, "You got me?" expression.

"Sorry about that Miss Mason. Must have been a humming bird hit—happens all the time." He laughed, but, unsettled in his own mind, he ran through a check list of what might have been damaged. He sensed a drag on the port side; propeller?, wing? As the minutes went by there were no further signs of damage so he had to assume whatever it had been had caused little harm to the aerodynamics of the plane.

Settling back, he was greeted by another "Whoop!"

Again the plane shuddered. This time Toomey was concerned. He dropped down to three thousand feet and veered sharply to the southwest toward the Pokhara airfield. The plane was behaving erratically as though bucking a fierce headwind. He grabbed the headset and broadcast, "*May-Day, May-Day.*" Receiving no response, he repeated it several more times with the same result.

Rachel gripped the seat bottom to steady herself against the erratic motion.

"Look out your side at the wing surface, lass. Tell me if you see anything, *anything* that looks odd." His voice was commanding, but his tone conveyed no anxiety.

She looked out and examined the wing surface, but saw nothing indicating damage of any kind.

"I don't see anything," she said in a small voice.

"Good!" Toomey was having to strain hard to hold the controls steady. He again yelled into the mouthpiece, "*May-Day, May-Day, you bastards!*" But again there was no response.

As hard as he tried he could not keep his altitude and the plane was bucking wildly as it descended.

Rachel, terrified and helpless, was afraid to ask the one question.

"We've got a problem, Mason, no doubt about it. This little beauty is hurt. I think I can get us down all right if we can make it to the airport, but I'm losing airspeed. Can't figure out what happened. It's possible some of Mao's cuties took some pot shots at us, but I don't see any damage." His voice was hoarse from yelling over the wind.

"Mao? Why Mao?"

"In case no one bothered to tell you, this country is filthy with unhappy Chinese, Miss. They...." He had to stop as he fought the wheel for control. Sweat broke out on his face. "I think I'm going to have to set her down. If you see a break in the trees—any flat place, yell out!"

The plane continued its stubborn descent.

At 500 feet, Toomey knew he had a desperate situation. He was getting no lift although both engines were operating at full power.

At the last minute, Toomey spotted a small clearing and jerked the controls in that direction.

"Be sure your seatbelt is tight!" he yelled. "Here, put this blanket around your head!" He had, somehow, pulled a blanket from the back seat and pushed it at Rachel. "This will be bumpy, but I think I can do it. Sorry, lass, for the rude flight."

Rachel was beyond being able to speak. She took the blanket and buried her face in it so that the final few moments passed in black terror.

The plane clipped the tree tops, reducing its speed, and ripping away the left wheel. Beyond the first impact, Rachel felt nothing.

* * * *

Back at the Tribhuvan Airport, they had read the May-Day signal and knew it was Toomey's plane, but they had, for unknown reasons, been unable to respond and, therefore, had no fix on his location. They knew his destination and normal route, but they also knew his independent character which many times had confounded them.

There was interference on the phone line to Pokhara, so that they could not verify whether he had landed there. Knowing Toomey's skills, the assumption was that he would make Pokhara. It was not until several hours later, when communication with Pokhara was reestablished, that they found out he had not arrived. It was assumed, his passenger not having been listed, that he was flying alone.

* * * *

Russell had been restless all day. Normally, he met each day on even terms and usually came out ahead, cheerfully and having felt he had accomplished something. It was rare that he felt an undefined disequilibrium. Today had not worked out in any of several ways, so that toward evening he was irritable.

Still upset because he had received no word from Rachel, he decided to call his mother one more time.

"No, Russ. But I think we need to give her more time. I think it's perfectly normal and natural that she hasn't written. She's in a strange new world. I think we need to give her a week or two to finally settle down a bit. I most certainly will call you if we hear anything."

Russell's only response was a disgruntled, "Hrumph!"

Even after he had convinced himself that what his mother had said made sense, he was acutely conscious of a feeling of apprehension. He did not like the feeling, nor could he find any logical reason for it, which irritated him even more.

"Why did I encourage her to make this hair-brained trip in the first place? On the other hand, what sense does this make, me acting like a new mother over a grown woman's decision? She's old enough to take care of herself—or is she? She's so naïve about so many things. Didn't I just read something about a fracas over there somewhere? I sound like a gibbering idiot! Boy! You need help." He ended his monologue no more at peace with himself than he had been all day. He had a strong impulse to call Allison, and even walked to the phone, then turned away, lecturing himself on his weak moral character. On that high plain, he even resisted having a drink. Finally, completely frustrated by the unknown cause of his dis-ease, he went to bed, only to have a nightmare sometime during the night.

* * * *

Despite the growing tensions in the parish over the coming meeting to decide the fate of the church building, Sam continued his normal routine. He had always placed home visits high on his to-do list. Although he was not rigid on any fixed numbers, he generally ended the week with ten to fifteen calls. Naturally, the older parishioners and those whose health was unstable claimed his first attention. But he made a point of calling on younger families where the mother was at home. These visits did not always evoke soul-searching discussions, but he usually was able to strike a common note that he felt brought "the church" unofficially into the home. Many children got to know him on these visits as someone other than a strangely gowned figure, remote and, if not frightening, certainly unrelated to their normal lives.

Interestingly, those families where both the husband and wife worked and he was unable to make periodic calls apparently were those who sided with Lance's agenda. It was frustrating to Sam to have so little personal contact with these families. Calling on Saturdays, he reasoned, was an imposition on a family with so little free family time, so this group pretty much lay beyond his personal touch.

Caroline attempted to persuade him to ease up a bit on his calls, but he held to them. For one reason, he really enjoyed making the calls, plus he felt it very necessary to move himself out of the church building and be a living presence in the community. If his role was that of a functionary of the Episcopal Church, he felt it mandatory that he play that role in the community, not just on Sundays or at Guild Meetings.

* * * *

The pain of their injuries was so severe that it left Rachel and Toomey in a state of semi-consciousness. How long they lay in the clearing, they would only understand later. At some point they had been lifted onto handmade stretchers and carried a painful distance to some camp. Here, a man whose only medical training had been to administer morphine to the critically wounded, completed a perfunctory examination of their injuries, and gave them a heavy dose of morphine.

At some point, one of the rescuing officers concluded, after studying their passports, that these were people of value to the insurgency and that extra care should be taken with them. He called for a helicopter to be dispatched from headquarters. When it arrived, Rachel and Toomey were loaded on board and flown a hundred miles west to one of the Maoist's hidden camps.

There was no reality to anything that was happening to Rachel, especially after the heavy doses of morphine. Her life was a series of brilliant colors, intensely red when her pain broke through the drug and various shades of yellow and green when the drug gave her temporary relief. Time no longer existed, in fact, before either Toomey or Rachel became fully conscious of their surroundings, three days had vanished. They had been kept alive with intravenous feeding.

The camp doctor concluded that Rachel's injuries were not life threatening. Her breathing was labored and she regularly coughed up blood. Until he could communicate with her, he was unable to make even a rudimentary diagnosis.

* * * *

After the Pokhara airport had reported that Toomey's plane had not arrived, officials in Kathmandu waited another six hours in the hope that some communication might be received from him. The plane had been due at 2:05 in the afternoon; the inability to communicate with Pokhara had taken two more hours, so it was ten o'clock in the evening that the King's Guard was officially notified of the missing plane. A military search party was organized in Pokhara and dispatched at daybreak. Unable to isolate a specific search area made the effort futile. Several single-engine planes were provided for low-level searches, but the forests were dense enough to hide any evidence of the crash.

The Nepalese army consisted of something approaching seventy thousand troops, split into eastern, central and western zones. As the violence and resulting success of the Maoists increased, their deployment to the embattled western and central divisions had necessarily been cut back.

The Maoist insurgents could number as many as fifteen thousand troops, though this number included young boys who had no formal military training. The Nepalese army, on the other hand, benefited from United States army training, as well as millions of dollars worth of combat equipment. The Maoist's armies preferred sudden, brutal strikes in isolated districts where only local police opposed them and in this way they had carried out violent activities in seventy-four of the seventy-five districts of Nepal. Their campaigns were characterized by lawlessness, violence, intimidation and destruction.

When neither the small cohort, nor the planes, had discovered Toomey's wreckage after three days of searching; the Pokhara garrison commander then called off the search.

In the confusion that had resulted from Tribhuvan's inability to respond to Toomey's May Day call, and the furor resulting from the loss of the plane, little attention had been paid to Rachel's whereabouts. Mr. Dorji had assumed she had decided to travel by bus to Pokhara and that she was already working in the relief camp. It was not until ten days later that Mr. Saugha from the Pokhara facility idly inquired of Dorji when they could expect the American aid worker. Following normal procedure, Dorji contacted the Pokhara police to whom he had directed Rachel. Consumed by the constant urgencies of the moment, the police had not responded for three or four days that no Rachel Mason was known to have arrived in Pokhara. Now, alarmed, Dorji contacted Durgan.

"Mr. Durgan, Dorji here. I have distressing news."

"So?"

"The young lady, Miss Mason, who was to work at our refugee camp in Pokhara is reported missing. That is, the police do not know of her whereabouts."

"Oh, shit!"

Dorji waited.

"All right, I hear ya," Durgan spit, and slammed down the phone.

CHAPTER TWELVE

Two weeks had passed since Rachel' departure; as the third week was beginning, Sam became extremely concerned. Certainly Rachel would have written by this time. Caroline tried to explain it as a poor mail system, but she, too, was beginning to doubt her own explanations.

"Sam, when you think it's the right time, I wonder whether you should call Chauncey. He might be able to learn something from the man he originally talked to about Rachel?"

"I was thinking of the same thing, Caroline. I will wait three more days, through Monday's mail. If nothing comes, I'll call Chauncey."

Monday's mail produced no letter, so Sam dialed Baltimore.

"Karen, good afternoon. How are you?"

"Good afternoon, Sam. I'm fine, thank you. How may I help you?"

"I'd like to speak to the Bishop, if he's free, Karen?"

"Sam, I'm sorry. He and Nancy are at Warm Springs for the week. He has an annual check-up down there every year at this time."

"Oh, yes, of course, I had forgotten. Well, I will try him next Monday. He will be back by then, Karen?"

"Yes, he will. I will make a note that you called."

"Thanks. Have a great Monday evening!"

"How did you know? My mother and I are going to the opera tonight. I'm really excited!"

"Wonderful! I envy you. What is the opera?"

"Faust."

"Oh, Karen, Faust has the most transporting aria in all opera, in my opinion—Marguerite's final aria as she ascends to heaven!"

"I know it and I agree!"

"Wonderful! Enjoy yourself, Karen!"

"Thank you, Sam. I will think of you during that aria."

After he had hung up, he told Caroline of the Bishop's absence for the week.

"Well, hopefully by the time he returns we will have heard something."

Russell called on Wednesday to raise the same questions, although he was a lot more agitated. He was certain, now, that something had happened to Rachel.

* * * *

Among the letters that had accumulated on the Bishop's desk was a cable from Singapore marked, *Personal and Confidential: To Be Opened By Addressee Only.*

Before Sam called, the Bishop had read, with dismay, what his colleague had written.

> *My Dear Bishop Phillips,*
>
> *In your absence, I am forced to write what would better be said over the phone lines. Unfortunately, I am scheduled to make extensive visitations to Thailand and Vietnam which will take me out of my office for several weeks.*
>
> *This morning I was informed by the authorities in Nepal that Miss Rachel Mason is missing and presumed lost in a heart-rending aircraft accident. There are no details to be had at the present, only that the small plane in which she was being transported to her assigned refugee camp went down. The wreckage has not been found, nor, of course, have either Miss Mason, nor the pilot's remains been found.*
>
> *I grieve for these young people as I grieve for you and Miss Mason's*

host of friends. Rest assured the instant I may hear anything further, I
shall immediately call you.
    Your Brother in Christ,
    Archbishop Gerund

"Karen, would you come in please?" When she appeared in the doorway, the Bishop continued, "Would you please call Washington and Lee University in Lexington, Virginia. Ask for the Alumni Secretary, I can't remember his name, and let me know when you have him on the line. There is some urgency to this, Karen, thank you."

She disappeared, and moments later stepped to the Bishop's door to tell him a Mr. Mattingly was on the line.

"Mr. Mattingly, Chauncey Phillips. How are you? Mr. Mattingly, I am an old graduate of W&L, Class of '73, Kappa Sig, etc. I wonder if you would do me a tremendous favor, sir?"

"I will try my best, Bishop Phillips."

The Bishop was reassured that the man knew of him.

"An old classmate of mine, Stuart Hawley, is in the State Department. Would your records possibly have a contact for him, preferably at State, but, if not, his home phone number?"

"Give me a minute, Bishop. I'm going to put you on hold, sir."

"Fine, fine."

A few minutes later, Mattingly came back on the line.

"I do have a phone number for Mr. Hawley, but it is his home phone, I'm afraid."

"Perfectly understandable, sir. Would you give me the number, please?"

"Certainly. It is: 571-732-3055."

"Thank you, Mr. Mattingly, I appreciate it." The Bishop hung up, frustrated in his hope to talk to "Digger" Hawley right away. He briefly debated not calling Sam until he had talked with his friend, but quickly decided he was morally obligated to share what information he did have."

"Karen, please get Sam Adams on the phone, if you can."

Shortly, Sam was on the line.

"Sam, good morning. How are you?"

"Fine, Bishop, you? I called the other day to talk to you about Rachel."

"Sam, let me interrupt, if I may. Something has come up that will bring me close to Afton today and I wondered whether you and Caroline could break away and have lunch with me?"

The Bishop had decided this rouse would be better than trying to handle the ugly news on the phone.

"Well, yes, of course, we would enjoy that, Bishop. What time would be convenient?"

"Let's say I arrive at the Rectory at eleven-thirty, that work?"

"Fine. We will look forward to seeing you."

"Bye, Sam."

* * * *

Arriving promptly at eleven-thirty, the Bishop suggested they sit down before leaving for lunch, he wanted to tell them something, then he told them all that had happened and showed them the cable.

Neither Sam nor Caroline moved, sitting stunned, trying to understand the icy words.

"But….?" Sam began, and then raised his hands in a gesture of futility.

"May God give us the grace to understand this. My heart goes out to you two."

Caroline's voice was hoarse, her words labored, "But if they haven't found the plane or the bodies, they can't be positive, can they?"

"No, but I gather that it is rugged terrain and might not yield the final answer easily, Caroline. I'm going to add one more thing that may or may not produce more information. I have an old friend from college who works in the State Department. I will talk to him to see if their people know anything about this, or may be able to find out more detail. Obviously, I will let you know anything I find out."

"Please, Bishop, please do!" Sam grasped at this straw, pathetically.

"The only other matter, which is entirely yours to decide, is how and when you let your people know. It is obvious that the press has not picked it up yet, but who knows when they might."

"I think I would prefer to wait a bit, Bishop. It is conceivable we will learn more from your friend," Sam responded quietly.

"Fine, I agree. Now, as far as lunch is concerned, I only used lunch as an excuse to come here and give you the sad news personally. I don't believe any of us feels like eating. I don't. I think, if you will excuse me, I'll just run back to Baltimore. Would you join me at the church for a quiet moment before I go?"

"That would help us all, Bishop. Shall we?" Sam got up, offering his hand to Caroline.

After the Bishop had left, Sam and Caroline sat quietly together in the sun room. They were enough in tune with each other's thoughts that words were not necessary.

Sam reached for Caroline's hand, "Caroline, my dear, we must call Russell. I will be glad to call if you would like me to?"

"No, Sam, I should. His relationship with Rachel was not easy for me to understand, however. I really don't know how deeply he, or she, for that matter, feel about each other. It will be a tremendous shock in any case."

"Suggestion: let's wait until we hear back from Chauncey, in case there is any further information. Think?"

"I guess that's wise. Take me out to dinner tonight, Rector, I really don't feel like doing anything in the kitchen."

* * * *

The Bishop dialed Stuart Hawley's number at seven-thirty, thinking they would have finished dinner by then.

"Hello?" A familiar voice answered.

"Digger, you Dog, how are you?"

"The voice is familiar and there are very few who can get away with calling me Digger Dog. How are you, Your Holiness?"

"Wonderful.... Well, I'd have to qualify that; my health is good, they tell me. Dig, I have a serious question to ask you."

"It sounds serious."

"It is...."

"If so, CP, I'll ask you to forgive me. We have guests and I should get back to them. Call me tomorrow, could you?"

"I'd be happy to, of course. Sorry I didn't want to interrupt your evening."

"No problem. Tomorrow then?"

Hawley hung up leaving the Bishop staring at the phone. That was very peculiar, he thought. He didn't even ask me what the problem was—not at all like the Digger I knew. Shrugging his shoulders, he picked up where he had left off in his New Yorker article.

Possibly ten minutes later, the phone rang.

"CP, my apologies. I am more comfortable at a pay phone these days when people sound like they want answers. We are running a Gulag at State these days and you can't be too careful. What can I do for you, Chaunce?"

"My goodness, is it that bad?"

"Badder than that, my friend."

"Well, I doubt my question would have interested any silent ears, but anyway…. the curate in the church of a friend of mine just went to Nepal on a mission with a Tibetan relief agency."

"Let me stop you right there, CP. You are asking about the hottest topic in super-secret Washington. The young lady's name is Rachel Mason and the pilot's name is Reginald Toomey. Am I close?"

The Bishop was stunned. "Yes, of course, that is who I was asking about."

"OK, just to give you some parameters: this little mess is sitting on the President's desk as we speak. I'll make it short and sweet: the Maoies have her. She's damaged but alive. They know they've got a live one and are smart enough to want big money for her release. *Underline this:* our government has designated the insurgent armies, officially the Communist Party of Nepal, as a terrorist organization. Therefore, our exalted leader says *we don't deal with terrorists.* So, Miss Mason is left high and dry."

"What a blessing, she's still alive"

"I guess so?"

"Interpret that for me, Dig."

"Well, if we don't come up with the money.... I'd rather not finish."

"What about the man?"

"They only want $50,000 from the English, but Tony-boy sniffs along with the Evil Empire, so he's dead meat, too."

"Stuart, this is impossible! That girl has to be freed!"

"I agree, CP, but I'm a couple of chairs short of the big desk."

"Is it a dead issue, then?"

"No, possibly not. It is a really smarmy situation. There is a lot of unrest in Nepal against the King, trying to restore some form of democracy and in the process try to negotiate a political settlement with the Maoist rebels. It's too complicated to give you all the nuances, but it's possible that Miss Mason could sneak through a crack during these negotiations. I would be doing you a disservice if I implied I felt positively about this, CP."

"At least she's alive! If she's alive, there is hope."

"Yes, Bishop."

"Well, I can't keep you any long, Digger. I am much obliged to you. May I ask, if there is anything you think I should know, that you call me?"

"Chauncey, hear me loud and clear: you know what very few, very few, are supposed to know. Everything is buttoned down tight as a tick. It may leak, but I don't think you want to get involved in that. To make this even more an Inspector Clouseau comedy, your call to me will trigger a check on who you are and what political affiliations you may have. If they don't like what they find, your phones will be tapped. That's what we call "National Security." One more thing, when you call me next time, use a pay phone and use, "The General" as your identity. I'm sorry, CP, but that's life in the Waste Land."

"How do you suggest I proceed, Dig?"

"If you really need to relate what I have told you to someone else, caution them as I have you."

"Well, my friend, you have given me some hope. I have to tell Sam Adams, it is his curate we've been talking about. Thank you, Digger, very much!"

"I'd like us to get together with you and Nancy, but this may be an awkward time. Please give her our love, CP"

When Chauncey hung up, he looked over at Nancy, his face a study in absolute bewilderment.

"What did Digger tell you?"

"If I understood any of it, I could explain it better, Nance. First of all and most important, Rachel is alive. She is a captive of that Chinese insurgent group and they want money for her release. That said, everything else about it is cloaked in the deepest secrecy. Digger warned me to be extremely careful how I handle the information he gave me. I have no choice but to tell Sam. It really sounds nasty, Nance."

When the Bishop called Sam he asked that Caroline get on the other phone, then he repeated, as close to verbatim as he could, his conversation with Hawley. He reiterated how extremely sensitive the information was and how it might affect negotiations for her release.

"I will leave to your discretion how you will handle this information. As far as my friend is concerned, we need to be sure we protect his role. It is very awkward, as I'm sure you can understand. My personal feeling would be, let's wait a bit to see whether the negotiations can produce anything."

* * * *

"Russell, Mom. How are you?"

"Good, Mom, just back from L.A., as a matter of fact, just stepped through the door. How are you?"

"I'm fine, Russ. We have had news of Rachel, indirectly."

"Oh, why indirectly?"

"It was through a friend of Bishop Phillips who works in the State Department." Caroline was working very hard to prepare her son for the news.

"Gosh! Rachel ranks up there, doesn't she! What does our Ambassador to Nepal say?"

"Russ, Rachel has gotten into a little trouble over there."

"Ah! Caught driving her rickshaw too fast, I'll bet."

"Unfortunately, it isn't funny, Russ. She has been captured by Chinese Communists who are holding her hostage."

"What!"

"I'm sorry to break it to you this way, but you had to know."

"What!" Unable to adjust from what he had thought of as humorous to the unbelievable story his mother had just told, Russell's mind could not make the transition.

"It is true, unfortunately."

"Mother, tell me, slowly, all you know about this, please."

Caroline repeated the sequence of events, starting with the Archbishop's cable reporting Rachel's death, through Bishop Phillip's conversation with his friend at the State Department. She did her best to stress the sensitive nature of the negotiations.

Russell was silent when she had finished.

"Russell?"

"Yes, I'm here. I'm having a hard time with this, Mother."

"I know, as are we, Russ."

"I'm going over there!"

"Russ, slow down! What reason would you have for going to Nepal?"

"Climbing."

"Russell, be reasonable! What would you expect to accomplish?"

"Obviously I would expect to help, somehow."

"Russ, please! That's an admirable idea, but you would only complicate matters. Bishop Phillips friend said there might be intense negotiations going on right now. It's important that we not upset anything."

"I don't trust them. Why isn't it in the papers? Why is it a secret? I just don't trust all this secrecy!" His voice was rising as his frustration increased.

"Russ, please! This is a very difficult time for all of us. Sam is particularly shaken. You must be careful what you do or say so as not to bring more grief into this than we already have. Promise me you won't do anything, *anything*, without first talking to Sam or me. Will you do that?"

"All right, I will talk to you or Sam later. Right now I'm in no mood to talk to anyone. Goodbye, Mother, I do appreciate how this would affect you and Sam. I'm sorry."

"Thank you, my son. We love you."

* * * *

The Communist insurgents in Nepal were notorious for abandoning their soldiers considered too gravely wounded to be of future service. Only those wounded who had had military training, essential to the cause, were transported back to the medical camps. These camps were widely scattered as the Maoists roamed the country and gradually moved eastward toward Kathmandu. The largest medical camp and the one staffed by the best doctor was one well to the west, safe from any government attack.

The doctor at the camp was a Pietre Botta who had been captured by the Communists during a raid on the Pokhara Tibetan refugee camp four years ago. Botta had been the principle target of the raid because the Moaists needed skilled medical personnel, and Botta had become widely known in Nepal since his arrival in 1995.

He had practiced general medicine in Zermatt for thirty years before coming to Nepal at the age of sixty-one. A widower for a dozen years, he had established a relationship with a younger Tibetan woman who had been captured with him. It was to Botta's camp that Rachel and Toomey had been air-lifted.

Rachel had recovered enough awareness by the second week after the crash to understand that she had been left virtually blind. She fought the terror silently and with Botta's help. He had found no external reason for the blindness; there were no external injuries to her eyes or head. Forced to diagnose without either CAT Scan or MRI equipment, Botta could not make a definitive diagnosis. He chose to believe that it could simply be shock, that time might correct. His gentle counseling along these lines, helped Rachel deal with her blindness. Botta had put Rachel and Toomey in beds next to each other so that Toomey could act as Rachel's eyes.

Toomey had suffered two broken legs and severe facial abrasions, but he was otherwise alert to Rachel's needs and was a diverting humorist. Botta had removed most of Toomey's head and facial hair in order to make the medication more effective. Had Rachel been able to see, she would hardly have recognized him.

For the first few days, Toomey, still confounded as to why his plane had crashed, rehearsed the sequence of the flight a number of times. He was quite sure that it had not been a projectile or simply a bird, but what else would have caused it, he could not seem to determine.

At one point, Rachel called out to him, "Reggie, are you there?"

"Yes, Lassie. Flat on my arse."

"What was it you rubbed on the wings before we took off?"

"It's an alcohol, glycol, why?"

"I just wondered if that could have been a factor in the crash?"

"No, no, Lassie. You use glycol to prevent freezing."

Rachel's naïve question, however, kept intruding on his more technical analysis. Unable to rid himself of her question, he rehearsed the entire routine, beginning with his rubbing down the wings with a heavy wet snow falling.... Toomey sat up in bed! Could it be possible that he had rubbed the wet snow down into the vent tubes in the wings, then as he climbed to a colder altitude, it froze, plugging the vent system. As the tip tanks emptied during the flight, they were sucked inward, deforming the flying surface and eventually causing erratic control and then the crash.

"That's it," he shouted!

* * * *

Rachel was living in a world she had never inhabited before. This dark world forced her to grapple with past events, not participate in the new world outside the darkness that she had so eagerly sought. The days, she no longer knew how many, since she had boarded the plane in Baltimore, lost their distinction and swirled in a meaningless cloud of confusion. She had always prided herself on her ability to think rationally, but how was it possible under these conditions? What meaning could she possibly find for what could only be described as ultimately bizarre! How could an otherwise naïve desire to help less fortunate people have turned into such a fiasco? How could her almost meaningless, but well-intentioned, life have suddenly become so futile? She would not let herself succumb to self-pity, but, nonetheless, she was appalled by the feelings of helplessness that engulfed her. She had no inkling as to what Toomey and her future would be. She had gleaned enough from the sporadic conversations she had heard, and could understand, that the Communists intended to guard them jealously. She did not dwell on how long and under what conditions she and Toomey might exist. She had, however, picked up enough in her short stay in Kathmandu to understand how bitter and violent the struggle between Maoists and the government was.

Through some incomprehensible twist of fate, Toomey's plane and been sucked into the vortex of this little known madness. Her well-ordered mind struggled without success to comprehend a meaning—a rational course of action—a belief system that would sustain her. In her darkened world, there was no light to be found, yet enough of what she had been had left the faintest spark of hope, but it flickered dangerously low in the gloom of her blindness.

* * * *

One day when Botta stopped by Rachel's bed, he saw tears on her cheeks.

"Miss Mason, Dr. Botta. May I disturb you?" Rachel blinked several times, ashamed she had cried.

"Yes, of course, Doctor."

"I would sit and talk with you for a bit, if that would be alright with you?"

"Please."

Perhaps it was her weakened condition, but she found Dr. Botta's voice hypnotic. It, first of all, was very deep and his words were accented unlike American English, nor was the cadence familiar, but it was the voice of one who spoke to her without words, of a life of deeply felt understanding.

"Miss Mason, you don't know me very well, nor I you, but I sense in you one who had made a decision much like mine. May I bore you with a bit of my history?"

"I would like it very much if you would, Doctor Botta."

"You see I, too, volunteered to come to Nepal to work in the Tibetan camps. I came here in 1995, full of hope in the belief that I could make a difference and that what I did, and others like me, could change conditions for the Tibetan people. As life has demonstrated, there is no short-term solution to the Chinese occupation of Tibet. The exodus of the beleaguered Tibetans will not stop, nor will their persecution.

The work itself at Pokhara had many satisfactions. I felt I was helping. Pathetic as that help was, it was only a finger in the dike, but in order to continue, one has to persevere in hope. I am not a religious man, Miss Mason, but I do believe mankind has a greater purpose than annihilation. But, to continue, you see I am old enough to have a senile wandering mind. Four years ago, Prachandra, the Maoist leader, raided the Pokhara refugee camp and carried me and Rinchen, who is not my wife by any official pronouncement, by the way, to this primitive outpost.

I was outraged for some time. I refused to help those who had been the very cause of the tragic cases I had tried to help. But, and this is important that you consider; the longer I have been here, the less I look at these unfortunate people as Communists, but rather I see them simply as the wounded of the world. I believe my work here is as important as it was in Pokhara. My work, in either camp, will not stop the madness, but I can hope to mend a stricken creature—to give him hope for at least some short time.

This will seem pathetic to you and perhaps even cast me as a Communist in your eyes, but I am not political, I am only a healer.

That will be the end of my little story, Miss Mason. The point is, that if your lot is to be imprisoned here with me, there is much good we can do. Neither of us will change the political blindness that is killing and wounding all these people whether they be Communist, Tibetan or Nepalese."

"Thank you from the depths of my heart, Dr. Botta. I am humbled by your God-given devotion," Rachel murmured, deeply moved.

* * * *

The phone restrictions the Bishop had imposed on contacting him, made it difficult to communicate, which, Sam understood, was the whole point of it. Monday afternoon before the "hoped for" final meeting on the church expansion, Sam had received a cryptic message, saying, "Call

Ted." Ted could only be Chauncey's son, Ted Phillips who lived in Towson. Sam didn't know him, but he quickly found his phone number and called.

"Ted, this is Sam Adams. I'm a friend…."

"Yes, Father Adams, I've been expecting your call. May I read what my Dad gave me?"

"Yes, by all means!"

"My writing is horrible, but here goes:

> *Sorry it has taken so long, but there has been nothing to report until this afternoon. The communists are still demanding a million dollars for Rachel's release, nor will they allow any of our Embassy people to see her. They claim she is well. The CIA is involved, for better or for worse. The Station Chief in Kathmandu, a man named Durgan, claims to have some sort of contact inside the Maoist hierarchy.*
>
> *The State Department and the President are stonewalling any information, and still deny there is any negotiation for her release, so it is hard to be optimistic. At least she seems to be alive and well. Sorry there is so little information, Sam.*
>
> *Yours, Chauncey*

"That's it, sir."

"Well, it is nice to hear something. Thank you, Ted."

Sam hung up, relieved that Rachel was well, but at the same time, very anxious about what her future might be.

CHAPTER THIRTEEN

By seven-thirty the church was packed with side chairs in the aisles and in every open space. Xavier had prepared for a large turnout, but even the chairs he had stacked in the vestibule were not enough. As Sam waited to start the meeting, he tried to estimate the number of people. Knowing that the conventional pew seating was two hundred and forty or so, he estimated the additional chairs might provide fifty or so more. He rounded up the number to three hundred. Very satisfying, he thought.

Finally, when he saw no new people entering, he stood up and raised his hands for quiet.

"Good evening, everyone! Thank you so much for coming. This is the participation we prayed for. If I may, I would like to say a prayer to begin our discussions. I think the Lord's Prayer is most meaningful for this occasion. I would like us to say it slowly, dwelling on each word. So many times, as familiar as it is, we speed through it. Let's try." Sam set the tempo and he paused on the phrase, 'Thy will be done.'

After the prayer had ended, Sam continued, "Ladies and gentlemen, we have much to go over so let's start. Up here on these tables, you will see artist renderings for the proposed new church building and a rendering of a proposed expansion of the current building. I think before you all come up to take a look, we should give you a rough idea of the relative cost of the two proposals. The new building is obviously subject to modification, either toward a larger more elaborate building, or a more compact structure. We do not have land costs at the moment, but our best guess is three-five thousand dollars an acre. Using this figure for the estimated 3-4 acres that would be required, we have come up with the figure of one hundred twenty-two thousand dollars for the land. The vestry has tentatively agreed that for the proposed new building that you will see up here, we have a total estimated cost of one million two hundred-fifty thousand dollars."

A gasp went up from the parishioners.

"I know that seems like a lot of money, and it is, but I think that should not be our ultimate reason for not considering this proposal.

The alternative proposal would be to remodel our present building. This, obviously, would be less costly. We have a pretty firm bid from a Baltimore architect of five hundred thousand dollars. The plans, as you will see, call for an extension of the roof on either side of the ridgepole with a consequent enlargement of the nave. We currently seat two hundred and this plan would add seating for one hundred and fifty more, or, if cathedral seating were planned, an extra two hundred, or double the size of our present church. The organ would be placed in a balcony at the rear of the church with seating for the choir. Those changes will be better understood when you look at the plans.

We have four sets of these two proposals and I would hope that everyone would come up and study them, after which we can discuss them in as much detail as anyone might want. Because Lance Bosley has advocated a new church in a new location, I would now defer to him for any comments he may care to make—Lance?"

"Thank you, Father Adams. You have done an excellent job of explaining the two proposals, especially as far as costs are concerned. What I would like to do is draw attention to the *meaning* a new church would have, not its cost, dollars to me are secondary to meaning.

A new church building with attendant facilities for a Sunday school, perhaps even a grade school casts St. James in a *new, active* and *aggressive* mode. *Here we are, people! This is what we believe!* What we believe should be clearly understood; that we hew to the traditional values. At the same time, we enjoy our religious services in a more modern, entertaining manner; new voices, new instruments, new format. All designed to draw people in who are seeking a God who believes in the old fundamental truths, not a god of changing, indecisive vacillations. And we need to shout these beliefs to the house-tops, if not to the Senate-tops." Lance paused for a smattering of laughter.

"Excuse me, Lance, I believe we need to move on so that all will have time to study the building plans, I know you agree." Sam's tone was polite, but left no doubt that he would not permit Lance to politize the meeting.

"As you will, Reverend."

"Let's divide into four lines and proceed to the plans. We have people here who are familiar with the two proposals so don't hesitate to raise any questions you may have." Sam gestured for the first rows to begin to line up.

The examination took more than two hours as the parishioners pored over the plans and asked questions, then returned to their seats and continued discussing the different ideas with their neighbors. Interestingly, or perhaps predictably, much of the discussion had not so much been the relative merits of the church buildings, but of the new direction that Lance was proposing.

It became apparent from raised voices, that there was going to be a significant number of people who wanted ritual change, modernization, but at the same time, a few vociferously, really did want an ultra conservative interpretation of the church's role in social behavior.

It was eleven o'clock before Sam called the meeting to order again.

"Well, friends, again, I congratulate you on digging into this thing whole-heartedly as you have. I think we could proceed toward a vote. We have prepared ballots for a silent vote, or, we can simply have a hand vote. Let's try the hand vote method for deciding how we will vote: those in favor of a secret ballot, please raise your hands. The Vestry will count the hands, please."

There was a pause as people considered the alternatives, then hands went up. The final count, favoring the secret ballot was seventy-five. Because there were close to two hundred and fifty people attending, it was concluded that the secret ballot method had failed.

"Alright, we made that decision, now let's vote on the two proposals. First, may I see a show of hands of those who favor a new church building in Afton?"

Again, there was a pause of indecision before the hands went up. The final count was one hundred and ten.

"Just to verify that number of one hundred and ten who voted for a new church, let me see a show of hands of those who favor an expansion of the existing building."

This count was one hundred and fifty, which seemed to mean that ten people had changed their vote from supporting the new building. There was a great deal of conversation when the final votes had been substantiated.

Sam ended the formal part of the meeting with a plea for unity. "My dear friends, you have expressed yourselves in the old-fashioned American town meeting manner. There are no winners or losers. We have simply agreed to disagree. We will, however, proceed to implement the plans for the renovation of our existing building. We will keep everyone informed of projected construction dates and, of course, how we may continue to worship together during this time. Thank you so much for your time and thoughtful consideration. To those who favored a new beginning, as I understand Lance's position, we will be sensitive to changes that may be appropriate. Thank you, again, and goodnight."

Not wanting to cut off any discussions, Sam let it be known that the meeting was formally over but everyone was welcome to stay as long as they chose.

Sam had suggested that because of the Brown's personal history with the church, Dwight play only a minor role in the meeting, so, though both Nancy and Dwight attended the meeting, he had not spoken.

Lisa had come with her grandparents, but she had only a fleeting interest in the questions being discussed. She had seen Xavier briefly when he brought in more chairs, but not to speak to.

After, the meeting when her grandparents were talking to a group of friends, she sneaked over to the parish house where she guessed she'd find Xavier, but he wasn't there.

On the way back to the church, she spotted Xavier's mother, "Hi, Mrs. Mendoza. I'm Lisa, remember me?"

"Si, of course, Miss Lisa. I am happy to see you."

"Have you seen Xavier, Mrs. Mendoza?"

"No, no. He was here, but then I don't see him."

"Gee, I wonder where he could be?"

Just then her grandparents walked out of the church.

"Lisa, is that you? Let's run along, shall we. It's getting late."

"OK, one minute." She dashed into the church and looked around hurriedly, but still no Xavier. "Damn!" she said through clenched teeth. Then, as suddenly, he appeared, pushing a cart with folding chairs.

"Hi, Lisa!"

"Oh, there you are! I was afraid I wouldn't see you, Xavier." She walked up to him and kissed him just as her grandfather came back into the church.

"Lisa! I asked you to come along! We want to leave. Come now, please." Dwight was not pleased with what he had seen.

"I'm coming, Gramper!" Lisa's voice betrayed her displeasure with her grandfather. "Sorry, Xavier, Grumpy's grumpy." She squeezed Xavier's arm and turned to leave.

"Bye, Lisa. See ya!"

In the car, Dwight expressed himself more forcefully. "Lisa, as I remember, I asked you not to see a great deal of the Mendoza boy."

"I don't see much of him at all!" Lisa responded crisply and quite truthfully.

"Kissing him in public like that would give the opposite impression, Lisa!"

"I'm not much for impressions, Gramper." It was a simple statement of her credo, but it had an insolent bite.

"Well, I am, Lisa. I'm afraid until you are more aware of the message impressions give, I will ask you to stop seeing that boy. Is that clear, Lisa?"

"Gramper, you shouldn't make me agree to that. It is not fair, and you know it isn't. I like Xavier. He is a good friend of mine. You should be happy that I know such a good person." Lisa was not pleading, she was simply telling her grandfather how wrong he was.

Nancy decided the discussion had gone on long enough. "Lisa, please! I know it must be lonely for you isolated with us and with few close friends, but you must agree to some of our rules. Your grandfather is

164

concerned about you, it has been a difficult time for all of us. Can't we just get along without hurting each other?"

"I don't want to hurt anyone, Grammy, but I have a right to see people I like. You are afraid I'll have another baby—well I won't! I know you were hurt and embarrassed by my baby problem. All I can say is, I made a mistake with that boy, but not in having an abortion. Xavier is not like that other boy, he is a very nice boy and I like him and I want to see him."

When Lisa had finished, her grandparents found nothing more to say. Lisa interpreted this as tacit approval of her relationship with Xavier.

* * * *

A month went by after Rachel's departure for Nepal and still neither Sam nor Russell had received any word about her. Russell was increasingly aggressive in his conversations with his mother, urging that something be done.

"The State Department people are the people who have to know what is happening with Americans abroad. I think we should demand information! Something is wrong, Mother, and you know it as well as I do. I would demand that they tell us something in twenty-four hours or we will go to the newspapers for help."

Finally, Sam and Caroline couldn't help but agree. It had been long enough!

Sam called the Bishop and told him what they planned to do. There would be no hint as to where their information had come from.

Sam began the inquiry the next day, not demanding a twenty-four hour response, but making it very plain that they sensed a tragedy had occurred. The reaction from the man at the State Department had been non-committal, but he promised that inquiries would be made.

Three days later, not having heard, Sam called again and this time stated that unless he heard within twenty-four hours, he would contact the *Baltimore Sun* and ask their help.

An hour later, Sam received a call from a Mr. Moody at the State Department, who identified himself as Public Relations Officer.

"Mr. Adams, sir, we have received your request for information on a

Miss Mason in Nepal. You must bear in mind, sir, that American citizens travel all over the world and at any time there could be ten thousand Americans abroad. We do our best..."

"Excuse me, Mr. Moody, but Miss Mason has been gone, almost five weeks without a word other than she had arrived. She would have written us several times in this length of time. I will have to insist that we get some word from your Department today, or I will have no alternative then to get help from journalists. I'm sorry!"

"Mr. Adams, I will be pleased to convey your concern to my superiors, but the newspapers are an unreliable source of fact, I would caution you."

"Thank you, Mr. Moody. I will await your call." Sam hung up.

The next call came one half hour later from a Mr. Starnz.

"Mr. Adams, sir, good morning. Starnz here. I understand you have some concern about a young lady in Nepal. First of all, let me reassure you that every American citizen is sacred to us and we do everything possible to provide protection for him or her. Miss Mason is no exception."

Sam noted that Mr. Starnz seemed to know that his Miss Mason was a *young* lady.

"Nepal, as few people understand, is in turmoil, which does not imply that we don't maintain excellent communication with their government. It does explain why we, conceivably, may not be able to respond to your rather stringent time limit, however."

"Mr. Starnz, first of all, thank you for calling. However, I must insist that I receive factual information regarding Miss Mason's health and well-being today, or I will seek other help."

"Do you, then, feel she is in jeopardy and, if so, why do you feel so?"

"Too much time has elapsed; she would have communicated with us several times by now."

"Well, Mr. Adams.... may I ask your profession?"

"I am an Episcopal priest."

"Well, Reverend sir, I can appreciate your concern. Let me do what I can here and try to get back to you as soon as possible."

"Thank you, Mr. Starnz, but please keep in mind the twenty-four hour period which will end tomorrow morning at nine."

"Well, we will do our utmost, Reverend."

Caroline came over and put her hands on Sam's shoulders. "You are a hard nose, Sam! Good for you! I'm sure they will have to admit the problem now."

"I'm not sure, Caroline, that a little old minister in Afton will move the President of the United States to admit he is subverting his own stated policy."

There were no further calls until eight-thirty the following morning.

"Reverend Adams, Tom Winship, I'm Assistant Secretary of State, Embassy Relations. Good morning to you, sir."

"Good morning, Mr. Winship."

"My people have told me of your concern for a young lady in Nepal. I want you to know we recognize your concern for this young person and we are moving heaven and earth to get you an answer—and we will get one! But, it is possible we may not be able to within the rather stringent time constraints you have imposed. Why not let us have a little more time, at least a week, in order to develop a full report for you. How would that be?"

"I'm sorry, Mr. Winship, enough time has gone by. I will have to insist on my original statement: if I haven't heard from her or about her by nine o'clock this morning, twenty minutes from now, I will seek other assistance."

"That may not be wise, Reverend Adams."

"I'm sorry? What do you imply?"

"Simply that were you to go to a newspaper, you would only create a greater problem."

"A greater problem than what, Mr. Winship?"

"I mean only, it might complicate our own investigations."

"Mr. Winship, at this stage, I want action and I'm not convinced there is any action, or that action has been forestalled for some reason."

"I'm not sure I understand what you are suggesting, Reverend Adams?"

"We are wasting words, Mr. Winship. I will hope to hear more positively from you in the next twenty minutes."

Sam hung up and called the Bishop. He told him of the whole sequence of calls and his decision to involve the *Baltimore Sun* in his quest.

The Bishop concurred and suggested the name of a reporter he knew, a Tad Andrews.

Sam waited until ten minutes after nine, and then dialed the reporter.

"Good morning, Sam Adams here. Bishop Phillips gave me your name. I have a story I want you to tell. I wonder if we might get together?"

"You are a friend of Bishop Phillips?"

"I am the Rector of St. James Episcopal Church in Afton."

"I see. How may I help you?"

"I wonder if we might get together so that I might tell you my story?"

"Of course, any time, any place."

"There is some urgency and it would undoubtedly be considered confrontational by our government."

"I will be where you are as soon as you tell me where that is."

"If you would be willing, I might ask you to come here at your convenience."

"It is nine-fifteen, I will be there by ten-thirty. I will come to the Rectory. I have been to your church before."

"Thank you, sir. I will look forward to meeting you."

As good as his word, Andrews pulled up in Sam's driveway at ten-thirty.

"You are nothing if not prompt, Mr. Andrews!" Sam greeted him.

"Tad, sir, if you will." They shook hands and Sam led him to the back room of the Rectory.

Sam's first impression of the reporter was that he was misplaced not playing inside linebacker for the Ravens. He was well over six feet tall and must have tipped the scales at more than two hundred thirty pounds, with no belly hanging over his belt. His tousled hair brushed the tops of large, brown eyes that never seemed to blink. His size would have been intimidating were it not for a very gentle, natural smile that was disarming and invited a feeling of good will.

Caroline brought coffee and joined them.

"Tad, the reason I wanted to talk to you is that the young lady, who had been my curate, left for Nepal thirty-seven days ago. She had gone to Nepal to work in a Tibetan refugee camp. The only word we have had from her was a brief note written the evening she arrived in Kathmandu.

Because we had become concerned when we did not hear further from her, I talked to several people, among whom was a person from the government. He told us her capture was being suppressed at the highest levels for, purportedly, reasons relating to negotiations for her release."

"Sir?"

"Yes, Tad?"

"I need this background, but I also need as many facts as you will give me. This has the smell of a major story and one that could involve many people, some of whom may be high-ranking officials. If you do not wish to tell me actual names, I can work around that for the time being, but I would warn you that names can be found out if the pressure builds."

"I understand. For the time being, I would like you not to use the gentleman's name who referred me to you, nor do I feel free to name the person in the government."

"Question: Who, then, would be the source of your information?"

Sam was stumped. How would he have any knowledge of Rachel's capture?

"Tad, I have a problem. I don't feel I can jeopardize a person's privacy by using his name, yet how do I establish the credibility of my information otherwise?"

"Well, I can use "unnamed sources" going in, but if it gets sticky, and I'm sure it will, they can make it ugly if I don't name names. You've seen the stories, I'm sure, on the *Time* and *New York Times* reporters one of whom was jailed for not divulging her sources? Let's wing it at first and see how many hornets fly out of the nest."

"Do not jeopardize your reputation, Tad! We will find a way, if necessary."

Sam then proceeded to tell Andrews all of the information this "high-ranking" State Department official had given the Bishop. The capture had been known hours after the plane had been assumed downed and that Rachel and the pilot were being held for ransom by the Chinese Maoists, who were asking a large amount of money for her release. The State Department, under orders from "high officials" in the White House, had refused to negotiate because the Maoists had been classified as terrorists. But in fact, someone was negotiating with them with the full knowledge of the White House. On top of everything else, the White House was prohibiting the release of any information as to Rachel's status.

When Sam had finished, Andrews whistled, "Wow! When you said 'it might be confrontational', you were the master of understatement. The first thing you should know is that your source at State will be flushed. How you knew of him will be found out or is already known.

My story need not be a condemnation of government action or lack thereof because we really don't know yet what they *have* done. What it should point out is the poison of secrecy. We don't know what steps are being taken to free Miss Mason, or, the worse case scenario, that there is simply a stalemate going on because our Administration refuses to deal with terrorists. If that were to be the case, usually the spooks at C.I.A. are the babies who deal with off the table deals like this. I will find out who the Station Chief in Kathmandu is and track his record. I do know a correspondent with the *Times* who is in Nepal and I'll contact her."

"Are you sure that the person who told us about Rachel in the first place will be exposed?"

"I would believe that the man at State's phone has been tapped and they have recorded all his calls. When this hits the fan, they'll comb every call and come across the Bishop's call and check it out. They may miss him, but they are pretty thorough. Before we get to that sticky wicket let me talk to Claire Tremont in Kathmandu to see if she's aware of this thing in any way. We have a code that she can use if she really does have some info."

"Wouldn't she file a story if she was aware of Rachel's capture?"

"In all probability, but the spooks can play pretty rough hardball if they want to sit on a story. Do you have a cell phone, Father?"

Proudly, for the first time, Sam said, "Yes, I do."

"Give me the number and I'll use it for the time being. Are you sure you will be all right with the possible repercussions of all this, Father?"

Sam looked over at Caroline, "Caroline, what do you think?"

"I say let's find out what's happened to Rachel and get it out in the open. I will not be intimidated."

"You have our answer, Tad."

"Great!" He got up to leave. "I think you have a legitimate right to know, so let's get started. I'll call you as soon as I talk to Claire. Thanks for the coffee."

"Thanks for coming, Tad, and for your help."

"It could get messy, but we'll get it out in the open where it belongs."

After Andrews had left, Sam called the Bishop and told him the complete story.

"I'm not at all concerned about myself, Sam, but I do need to talk to my friend. He's the one who will suffer whatever hell-fire our administration chooses to mete out."

"Well, Caroline, the fat's in the fire. I only hope we are doing the right thing. I believe we are."

"So do I. I guess I should call Russell this evening and tell him what is happening or about to."

She studied her husband after this latest flurry of activity. He really didn't need this kind of high-tension cat and mouse game on top of the still simmering church question. Marcy had reported that Lance had held a meeting of those who had voted for a new church building and there was a strong sentiment for breaking away to form a more compatible congregation. Were these troubling events to be her husband's reward for his years of gentle parish service?

Chapter Fourteen

During the fourth week of Rachel's recuperation, her vision slowly began to improve. At first everything was dim and gray, objects and faces indistinct, but after four or five days Toomey's face emerged more clearly and then she saw Dr. Botta's face for the first time. Both faces confounded the mental images she had created.

She had remembered the pilot as a heavily bearded, wild-haired man of indefinite years. What she now saw was a clean-shaven face and head, with over-large, brilliant emerald green eyes. His full-lipped mouth curved upward on one side and downward on the other, giving more the impression of a naughty boy caught with his hand in the cookie jar than that of a fearless, veteran bush pilot. In her exuberance at being able to see him again, she felt him endearingly precious as the one who had saved her life.

Dr. Botta was even more of a revelation. Rachel had envisioned him as a squat, bespectacled little man, gray-bearded and balding. What she began to see was a painfully spare man, well over six feet tall, hunched over at the shoulders, his neck extended so that his face, with its sharp aquiline nose, gave him the appearance of a giant bird, condor-like, as he peered down at her. She would not have been able to guess his age; the tightly stretched skin of his face showed no wrinkles.

"Miss Mason, I believe your vision is beginning to return. I can see expression in your eyes that I had not seen before."

"Yes, oh yes! It is so much better. I can almost see as well as before!" She was like a happy child, with no memory of the night's frightening nightmare. As her vision improved, Rachel was able to repress the final few seconds of the disastrous flight—there was only a before and an after.

"I am so pleased. Though I had hoped it was a temporary condition, I could not be sure. On to another subject, if you will permit me? The camp commander, Ramesh Lawa, has spoken to me to say that Prachandra who is the General Secretary of the Communist Party in Nepal, will be here later today. He has asked that you meet with him. I have concluded that some negotiations for your release have been conducted, but have not gone well. More than that, I do not know anything. I do not wish your hopes to rise prematurely, Miss Mason. I know the Communists to be arrogantly rigid in their demands. I would question their willingness to truly negotiate. Being an American, they understand that you give them the upper hand. I do not say this to discourage you, anything is possible, but only to forewarn you of possible disappointment."

Rachel's heart raced at the mention of release, but she heard very clearly the words of one who had been a captive for many years.

"Mr. Lawa has asked me to attend you at the meeting. I have not told him of your returned vision. I would advise that you feign blindness. Whether it will be an asset to your release, I cannot say, but let us try."

* * * *

Prachandra arrived in the late afternoon in a large helicopter. Rachel was summoned immediately. Dr. Botta led her by the arm to the central building of the complex. Comrade Prachandra, whose real name, Botta had told Rachel, was Pushpan Kamal Dahal, was seated at the end of a long table. He gestured Botta to seat Rachel at the far end of the table and sit next to her. Though Prachandra spoke fluent English, he demanded that native Nepalese be used.

"Physician, tell this woman that we, the Communist Party in Nepal, wish her to return to her homeland, but her government will not cooperate."

Botta translated for Rachel.

"Your accident has made you useless to our cause. I will permit you to write a letter to your family, describing the accident, your injuries and blindness, and ask for their help in returning you to your country."

Again, Botta translated.

Rachel turned to Botta, "Ask him how my family can gain my release if my government can't?"

Prachandra, having understood her question replied in Nepalese, "Because of the expense of rescuing you and your care since your rescue, we are asking for modest recompense, but your government refuses to pay. Perhaps your family will be willing to pay?"

After Botta had finished translating, Rachel asked the logical question, "How much do you want?"

"That is not important for you to know. I want you to write this letter. Comrade Lawa will read it and send it to your family. If they are willing to send the money, we will provide instructions as to how it must be done." He rose, nodded at Botta and left.

One of Lawa's aides pushed a piece of paper and ballpoint at Rachel.

Botta spoke to him in English, but he raised his shoulders as though to say he did not understand.

"He indicates he does not speak English, Miss Mason, but I would be careful what you say," he whispered.

Rachel took the pen and began to write, making every effort to convince the guard that she could barely see what she was writing.

> *"Dear Mummy and Daddy,*
>
> *I am writing you from a hospital camp in Nepal. The plane I was in crashed, and I was rescued by friendly Chinese. They have treated me very well, but I have trouble with my eyes so that they believe I would be better off in the United States. They have asked for some money to compensate for the expenses of my rescue and treatments. The U.S. Government has refused to pay so I wonder whether you might be able to pay them from my savings—you know how much that is. Please reply to the address that they will provide if you are willing to pay.*

Say hello to my brother, Russell, and let everyone know how nice these people are.

My dearest love, your daughter, Rachel.

(She addressed the envelope to: Mr. Samuel Adams, St. James Rectory, Afton, Maryland, USA)

Rachel folded the letter and pushed it toward the guard. Botta held her arm as she rose and led her out of the building.

Walking back to her tent, she told Botta how she had written the letter in ways that would indicate that it had been written under duress.

"One wonders what amount of money the Communists would have asked that the government refused to pay?"

"I would hazard a guess that it is more complicated than the amount of money, Miss Mason."

* * * *

"Xavier, I talked to my Mom last night about college next year. She didn't say I couldn't, so as far as I'm concerned, that's a 'yes.' She said she'd talk to my father when she saw him and see what he says."

"Good. Father Adams has sent a letter to the University of Maryland asking for an application. I can't believe I could be going to college! If you come, how cool it could be."

"If I go, I may sell the Jag."

"What! Why?"

"I'd want the money; we could use it."

"But how could you do that, Lisa, you're only seventeen, the car wouldn't be in your name, would it?"

"But it is, or it's a joint ownership with me and my Dad. I'll be eighteen the end of August and then I can get ownership."

"I wonder whether you should do this, Lisa?"

"I'm going to, though."

"Well, if you do, Father Adams will sell me his car in May for two thousand. I've saved almost that already. We could use that in college."

"Fantastic! I think we could get about forty-five thou for the Jag."

"But your father and mother gave it to you, isn't it really theirs?"

"My Dad makes lots of money, Xavier, he'll never miss it. I think money is one of the problems my parents have had."

"Too much money!"

"Yes, weird isn't it. What does your Dad do?"

"My Dad disappeared ten years ago."

"Oh, I'm sorry. I didn't know."

"No problem. I've had two 'Dads' since then."

"What do you mean?"

"Guys that have come to live with us."

"Oh."

"You wouldn't understand," Xavier said with a touch of bitterness.

"I understand loneliness, Xavier."

"Well, I guess that was it?"

"Do you have a 'Dad' now?"

"No, Mom decided it was a losing deal so, since she began coming to Father Sam's church she says she doesn't need a guy around."

"Will she be alright when you go to college?"

"Oh, I think so. She's really proud I may go."

"Does she work?"

"Yeah, she works at the Canvasback five days a week and works at the Bridge Diner at nights."

"Awesome! I feel sorry for her."

"Don't. She's always worked and wouldn't know what to do with herself if she didn't."

"My Mom has never worked."

"I guess she's lucky."

"Not so lucky, I guess. Whatever, let's get a coke."

* * * *

Sam was at the hospital calling on Charlie Bourne when his cell phone rang. Charlie had been brought in by ambulance that afternoon with chest pains and was awaiting the results of his tests. He had been partially sedated so that when the phone rang, Sam quietly stepped out into the hall to answer it.

"This is Sam Adams. May I help you?"

"Father Adams, Tad Andrews. How are you, sir?"

"Fine, Tad, you?"

"Great! I had a chat with Claire Tremont of the *Times* in Kathmandu. Can you talk, or should I call back?"

"No, this is fine, Tad."

"Well, the up-shot of it is that, without telling Claire exactly why I was calling, she volunteered the fact that 'something' was going on in Kathmandu, but neither she nor the other reporters had been able to find out what it was."

"That's interesting, isn't it?"

"Claire has spent a bunch of years overseas at hot spots—Somalia, Darfur, Iraq, and so on. She has run across the CIA man who is in Kathmandu before, name of Durgan. She has grown to distrust him and she believes there is something fishy going on. For one thing, he has put a censorship on all reporters' stories. Nothing goes out he doesn't approve.

I think we need to bust this thing wide open, sir. We wouldn't be gambling much. The fact that you haven't heard from Miss Mason in five or six weeks makes it a hundred to one that something has happened, but I will do as you wish."

Sam thought for a second, "Let's go, Tad. Do you have enough detail to write the story?"

"I think I do, but I'd want you to read it for accuracy so let me write it and then I'll come to Afton. I should be finished by five, so would seven be convenient for you? I'd like to catch the eleven o'clock deadline here at the paper, if possible."

"That would be fine, Tad. Go for it!"

"I'll call you if anything changes, sir."

Sam hung up with a feeling of excitement and prayerful hope that this would shine enough light on the situation that something might be done for Rachel. He went back into Charlie's room to await the doctor's determination.

* * * *

Promptly at seven, Andrews drove into the driveway. Sam ushered him in and called Caroline from the kitchen.

"Here are two copies of my story. Please don't hesitate to correct anything. I want it as accurate as we can make it.

Caroline and Sam sat down and studied Andrews' story.

MARYLAND CLERIC FEARED CAPTIVE OF NEPALESE COMMUNISTS, was the headline.

"The headline might change; we have a guy whose job it is to punch it as much as he can."

> *Miss Rachel Mason, until recently the Assistant Rector of St. James Episcopal Church in Afton, Maryland, has not been heard from in five weeks since arriving in Nepal where she had gone to work in a Tibetan refugee camp. She is known to have taken a plane to Pokhara in north central Nepal, which has been reported missing and is feared lost. Chinese Communists control much of the area of the crash site. There is speculation that she may have been taken captive by the Maoists. Efforts by her Rector and friends to verify this information with the State Department have been met by silence.*
>
> *Miss Mason, is a native of Kansas and a graduate of Kansas State University and Berkshire Divinity School in Massachusetts.*

Sam looked at Caroline for her comments.

"I don't write news stories. It looks alright to me."

"I agree. I don't see anything wrong with it," Sam agreed.

"It is the headline that will trigger the reaction, not the news story anyway. If you are OK with it, let's go with it. You realize your life will be changed when this hits the streets?"

"Our life is not an issue, Tad, it is Rachel's we are concerned about. Don't worry about us."

"OK. Thank you so much. Hopefully this will pry some info out of the government."

* * * *

Rachel's vision had almost stabilized, allowing her to see almost as well as before the accident. Restless to do something, anything, she asked Dr. Botta how she might help him. She had no nursing training, but she needed to get involved however minimal her assistance might be. Botta suggested that she simply follow him around for the first few days; in that way he could judge her tolerance to seeing the grievously wounded bodies, many of whom were boys as young as twelve.

The hospital tents were removed from Rachel and Toomey's area by several hundred yards so that only very rarely had she heard sounds that could have been cries of pain. As she and Botta approached the hospital area, however, Rachel felt the first signs of nausea as she heard the pitiful cries of those in agony.

"This will not be a pleasant experience, Miss Mason. I suggest you do not let your stare linger on the faces of some of these men—try only to watch as I dress the wound, and that only briefly. It will take you time to be able to tolerate this misery. When you feel you have had enough, simply walk back to your tent. I will understand."

Rachel swallowed hard, but followed the doctor into the first tent. There were twelve cots on either side, the first held a teen-age boy with half a leg. He lay apathetically staring up at the tent roof. He barely moved as Botta unwrapped and dressed the horrible red stump. Rachel only glanced briefly at the bloody gore and then closed her eyes.

The next patient was a wizened little man who lay strapped down to the cot. As Botta approached, he rolled his eyes wildly and jerked at his restraints.

"This man should be released. I have urged it. He suffers from dementia and there is little I can do for him." Botta measured fluid in a syringe, "Miss Mason, please restrain his right arm while I administer this shot."

Rachel grasped the man's arm, but thin and fragile as it was, she could barely hold it still. Botta gave him the shot and almost immediately he calmed and seemed to sleep.

Botta skipped the next two cots.

"These men are soon to be released. They are the unlucky ones. They will fight again."

At the fifth cot, Rachel saw only a bandaged head. There was a small slit at the nose so he could breathe.

"This will take a few minutes. I suggest you not observe this too closely." Botta began to unwrap the gauze from the head. Rachel heard a deep moaning sound and the body twitched as each wrap was unfolded.

Morbid fascination made her look as the final strips of gauze were removed. She choked in disbelief; a recognizable face was gone, only a gruesome jumble of flesh was visible. She glanced away and felt her stomach heave.

"I have to go outside," she mumbled and fled out of the tent. Botta had not looked up.

Despite these experiences, or perhaps because of them, Rachel forced herself to accompany the doctor on his round every day. Each day she challenged herself to go at least one bed farther. It was two weeks before she could make the complete tour. Then, gradually, she began to assist Botta with his ministrations. She was able to close her eyes to the physical damage and think only of the tiny second of peace she might be giving. Daily, she became stronger and of greater help to the doctor.

* * * *

Rachel had been assisting Dr. Botta for about two weeks when he told her that his wife worked at an adjoining camp for women. Would she like to meet her? Rachel's only companion for more than two months had been the irrepressible Scot. Toomey's legs had mended to a point where he was able to move around slowly with crutches he had fashioned out of tree limbs. He was extremely restless and talked constantly of escape. Talk of escape seemed so unrealistic that Rachel tried to avoid him as much as possible and she welcomed the idea of meeting another woman.

The women's camp was a short mile from Rachel's area.

"Why was I not put with the other women, Dr. Botta?"

"The security is greater at our camp and I was able to care for you and Reginald more conveniently. The camp where my wife works is quite different, Miss Mason, these women have all been raped severely by Nepalese soldiers, some many times. These are the women the Chinese choose to treat. The irony is that their soldiers rape other Nepalese women yet they provide no care for them. It is a perplexing distortion of moral ethics that I do not pretend to understand. So, we are here, Rinchen should be over in tent five."

Walking into tent five, Rachel saw a tiny woman, certainly no more than five feet tall, standing at the end of a cot.

"Rinchen!" Botta called.

The woman turned and came toward Botta. The closer she came, the younger Rachel saw her to be. The first thing she noticed were large almond-shaped eyes, with a wide, smiling mouth. As she came to know Rinchen, she found that the expression never varied, nor did her sunny attitude, regardless of the circumstances. She was someone you instantly liked. She radiated a happiness that was infectious.

"Rinchen, I would like you to know, Miss Mason. She has been of tremendous help to me."

Rachel could feel the love the doctor had for this diminutive, smiling doll.

"Miss Mason, I am very pleased to make your acquaintance. Pietre has spoken so often of you!" She extended her tiny hand to Rachel.

"Thank you. Rinchen, I am forever indebted to your husband for saving my life. It is very nice to meet you." Rachel could not believe the tiny thing was more than fifteen, but she had to assume she was at least in her twenties.

"May I show you some of my ladies?"

"Yes, unless it is a bad time."

"No, I have been expecting you. Please." She indicated for Rachel to follow her. "This tent has ladies who have developed AIDS from their violation. It is not uncommon, but these are the worst cases I have. We do not have proper medicines for them so some suffer badly and will soon die."

They walked by cot after cot of bone-thin cadavers who were desperately clinging to life, each with the bewildered expression Rachel interpreted as asking, "Why?" It broke her heart. Tears filled her eyes and she had to stop.

"Rinchen, I can't do this. Please excuse me." She walked back to the entrance where Botta was talking with an older woman. "Doctor, I'm sorry," was all she could say as she left.

Rinchen followed her out and placed a hand on her arm. "I am so sorry, I should not have done this, it was stupid of me. Let us go to my office, Pietre will find us there."

Richen's office was the corner of a supply tent which was stacked high with folded cots. There was very little evidence of medical supplies as far as Rachel could see.

"Now, we will have our tea." She dumped a generous amount of green tea leaves into a tin of water; then lighted the burner of a small stove fed by a compressed gas cylinder. She sat facing Rachel radiating sincere pleasure at meeting the injured lady from America.

They enjoyed their tea together; and Rachel, benefited from the tremendous lift she got from the strongest tea she had ever drunk.

Her new little friend told Rachel her story of escaping from Tibet, passing over the Himalayas in midwinter and being brought half-dead to Botta's camp in Pokhara. How he had saved her frostbitten legs, and how she had, in time, become his assistant.

"You must know, Miss Mason, that I am not truly Pietre's wife. He only calls me that. He will not marry me because he says he is too old. How silly men are. If one loves, age does not matter. We know that, don't we, Miss Mason?"

"I believe you are right, Rinchen, but I am a child compared to you who have lived a life so full of danger. Please, you must call me Rachel. I would like that."

"Ray-choll, that is a pretty name. Pietre tells me you may go back to American soon?"

"Oh, I don't know. It is being discussed, I guess."

"If you do stay, would you come to see me sometime?" Rinchen had put her hand on Rachel's arm."

"I would like to very much. If I am able, I would like to help you. I will not be so silly as I was again."

"That is the reason I like you, Ray-choll. These ladies cannot have the life we have—you feel that as I do. We are so lucky!" The bright shining face looked up at Rachel telling her in unspoken words that life, whatever its temporary problems, was a thing to be cherished.

* * * *

Durgan listened to the voice on the other end of the line, his face a weary mask of irritation.

"Who screwed up?.... So it's one of two or three guys, find out who!" The voice went on, but Durgan wasn't listening, finally he slammed down the receiver and sat staring at the distant peaks. He found no peace in the majestic view, instead he seethed with frustration. After a time, he dialed a number.

"Durgan.... Let me talk to the Ambassador. Bullshit! Put him on!" There was a short pause, "The shit has hit the fan. One of your boys weaseled, trying to be a hero—talked to some reporter from the *Baltimore Sun* and told the whole story."

Durgan listened for a short time.

"Yeah, yeah, well he is working on it. You find somebody who can do it better! So what are you going to tell Madame Secretary? "He waited briefly again. "That won't fly and you know it. I say we hold the line on the terrorist issue—we don't negotiate. If they don't want what we've offered, let the little do-gooder squirm for a while. She shouldn't be over here in the first place!"

Durgan slammed down the phone a second time, then stood looking out the window for a long time. Finally, he returned to the phone and punched in a number.

"Durgan.... Come over here, I need to talk to you!" He hung up and slumped in his chair waiting.

No more than half an hour later, there was a gentle knock on the door. "Come!"

The door opened to Rachel's Karachi companion on the Qatar flight.

"Siddown! What the hell is going on? You've frigged around with this for two months and produced nothing. You claimed you slept with this monkey, what's it got you?"

"It is difficult, Mr. Durgan. I have had several conversations with Mr.

Lawa. He has expressed his appreciation for the offer of two hundred and fifty thousand dollars, but he says that Mr. Prachandra feels it is not enough. So far they are unwilling to alter their demands. I believe the longer it goes the more likely we will be to see an amelioration of their views."

"You know you are so full of bullshit, you don't know your ass from your elbow, Rai. I got a quarter of a mil, and that's it!"

"Mr. Durgan, sir, I believe I can be of service to you, but it will require patience."

"Listen to me, Charlie, don't get your loyalties mixed up! You are being paid by Uncle Sammy, not some two-bit Chink Mao-Mao outfit. You're only as good as you can deliver and you ain't delivering. Now get your ass outta here and spring that damn broad!"

Mr. Rai rose slowly and walked to the door, "I will do my best, Mr. Durgan." He bowed and closed the door.

* * * *

Sam and Caroline were up at four knowing the paper wouldn't be delivered until five, but both had spent a restless night in anticipation of Andrews' story. Sam shaved and showered, made coffee and it was still only ten minutes to five. Largely due to the enormity of the story, the paper was not delivered until five-thirty.

Female Cleric Captive of Chinese Communists, with a sub-head of *Government Silent on Details*

The headline, in one-inch type, was emblazoned across the front page. The story they had approved—centered in a framed black border, was largely unchanged. They had barely opened the paper when the phone rang.

"Sam Adams speaking...."

"Sam! In heaven's name, what does this mean?" It was Dwight.

"Dwight, it is pretty much all we know. I would have told you except that we have been cautioned to tell as few people as possible."

"How long have you known?"

"I guess it's approaching two weeks, Dwight. We have tried to get information from the State Department, but they have denied any knowledge of the affair."

"She's been gone, what—two months?"

"Almost nine weeks, Dwight."

"And no word, nothing?"

"She wrote us a note the evening she arrived, but nothing since."

"Well, I'll be damned! I'm so sorry about this, Sam. Anything I can do? I know some people in Washington."

"No, Dwight, thanks. We believe the fact that the newspapers have it, we'll get some action."

"I would think so, too. Well, please call me if you think I could help. Convey my sympathies to Caroline."

"Thank you, Dwight. We appreciate your kind thoughts."

The phone rang as soon as Sam hung up.

"Sam! *What* is going on? Did you know about this? Whose doing something about it?" It was Marcy.

"I only knew we hadn't heard from Rachel and we got very uneasy, Marcy. Some of the other information we just got."

"Well, it's a bloody disgrace! Why is the Government stone-walling this?"

"The story we get, Marcy, is that, from the top down, we are taking the position that we won't negotiate in any way with terrorists, that is, the Chinese Communists, who have Rachel."

"Ridiculous! If you lie down with the dogs, you get up with the fleas—and we lie down with a bunch of dogs all the time. *Don't negotiate with terrorists!* What a lot of balderdash!"

"Well, Marcy, that's where it stands at the moment. Maybe the newspaper article will help, let's hope so."

"Please call me if you hear anything hopeful, Sam, will you?"

"I will Marcy, thanks."

The phone rang constantly all day, each person expressing either outrage or sympathy. Sam and Caroline alternated taking the calls.

Caroline called Russell early in the morning and read the article to him. He was overjoyed it had finally reached this point and decided to come to Afton in the next few days to be "closer to the action", as he called it.

* * * *

Sam had called the Bishop the night before to forewarn him of the publication, he, in turn had called Digger Hawley, his friend, who took it all philosophically.

"Don't panic, Chaunce. This will bounce around at several levels until they gauge public opinion. If enough people react negatively to the length of time it has been kept secret, we'll have an easier time. However, don't think they won't use whatever intimidation appeals to them to get to the bottom of this. Don't worry about old Dig, I've had thirty years of this and can walk away with a clear conscience if it gets too heavy."

"We are indebted to you, Dig. I only hope it doesn't hurt you."

"You've ruined my chances of being Secretary of State, but then, Madge would have divorced me if I'd taken the job. She'll be pleased."

* * * *

Among the many personal calls were calls from newspaper reporters requesting interviews. Sam demurred seeing anyone, referring them to *The Baltimore Sun.* This did not preclude a half dozen TV news reporters and photographers from taking footage of the Rectory and the Church. Sam tried to maintain some semblance of equanimity when he was confronted by reporters every time he stepped outside the house, each time referring them to the Baltimore paper.

Toward evening, Andrews called and gave Sam an account of the White House press briefing that he had just attended.

"Let me read my notes to you, 'These are serious allegations which warrant a full investigation. The President extends his sympathies to the family of Pastor Mason. He assures the American people that if it is proven that Pastor Mason has indeed been made captive by the Communists, the US Government will do everything within its power to secure the release of this unfortunate person.'

Interpreted, this means everyone is scrambling to take cover and the last guy who doesn't gets burned. I have to think that the man at State's days are numbered. Also, they've sent 'collegial' friends to our publisher to find out our sources, but he, thank goodness, told them it is privileged information that he is not willing to divulge. Are you all right down there, Father?"

"Yes, thanks. Many phone calls, many requests for interviews, many TV trucks up and down our lane and so on. We're just happy it's started."

"Good! So are we. I'll call as soon as I hear anything."

* * * *

By weird coincidence, Lance had scheduled another of his congregational meetings for the day the bombshell about Rachel hit the press. Of the ninety or so who had voted for a new church at a new location, some sixty showed up for the meeting.

Lance was disappointed at the turn out, but rationalized it was because of the shock of the news about Rachel.

"Thanks for coming tonight," he greeted the gathering. "It is a fascinating bit of news *The Sun* has published, were it to be proven true, it would be disheartening. When all the facts are known, however, I'm sure it will be proven to be another liberal attack on our Presidency. So, let us concentrate on the really vital issue of how to proceed with our plan for a new, more representative parish. We have a minimum of sixty to one hundred solid souls who will join in this effort. The figures you heard at the Parish Meeting were inflated to weaken our case, for obvious reasons. I believe we can build a beautiful edifice for our people for less than a million dollars. Sure we'll have to dig deep, but that is a healthy step—invest in a church that will say what we want it to say; strengthen God's purpose in combating the insidious erosion of morals that is so pervasive in our society. Can we not do this? Of course we can and will!

I have consulted my tax attorney and he tells me I can contribute, on a loan basis, of course, two hundred and fifty thousand dollars to the building of this monument. Any of you who feel you can match or exceed that will be among those who will guide our future. I think it is time for us to put up or shut up, to put it crudely. I have asked Carson Brothers, our good friend, to act as our financial secretary so, as we enjoy our coffee and cakes and draw closer together, let us, each of us, give Carson an idea of the kind of monetary support we are willing to give. As you do so, please remember the grave crossroads the traditional churches are at— stumbling along blindly without a coherent creed of social behavior that is acceptable to us who have made up these congregations mindlessly, like sheep!"

There was very little socializing over coffee and cakes; each family in turn quickly speaking to Brothers and recording their pledge. At the end of the meeting only one hundred thousand dollars had been pledged to supplement Lance's offer of two hundred and fifty thousand.

Chapter Fifteen

Toomey's recuperation took longer than Rachel's and like a leashed tiger, he grew more and more frustrated by his physical limitations. Unable to walk or exercise, he grew almost violent in his confinement. He spent time devising ways of escape, each one more complex and risky than the last. Having flown over the area only once, he did not really know the western terrain as he did the more eastern part of Nepal. Botta had told him they were somewhere in the Kalikot District, he thought, which he knew to be the western-most district in Nepal. He also knew that Maoists controlled the western half of Nepal, but challenging the odds of success seemed to make him more determined. Botta tried in everyway possible to discourage Toomey, but he only succeeded in challenging him even more.

He was able to exercise the upper parts of his body in the days before he attempted to walk. As soon as he could, however, he crept, crawled, or staggered for hours at a time. He went without meals to train himself for the days ahead. Gradually, he reached the condition he felt was necessary for an escape attempt.

Rachel anxiously watched his fanatical routine and tried to reason with him about the dangers and the unlikely probability of being successful. She pleaded with him to be patient; that the negotiations for their release might come at any time.

"Lass, I know you mean well; I respect your opinion and I wish you

Godspeed if you do get released, but I cannot stay still here forever. What if I am not repatriated? Am I to stay here until I am an old man? When will the war be over in Nepal? Soon? I don't think so. No, I must at least try to get back to a normal life."

What Toomey did not tell Rachel about her negotiations was that he knew Durgan was CIA and that Rai was an extremely unreliable employee of Durgan's, one who would make the best deal for himself regardless of his current employer. He sensed that if Rachel's release depended on Durgan and Rai, she might be a captive for a long time. Knowing Durgan over the years, he felt the man had been left out in the jungle too long, following jungle rules more naturally than anything recognizable as "civilized."

"But, Toomey, won't you please wait until I get some response to my letter. Isn't it possible that something might come of it?" She gripped his hand, fully realizing that she could not sway him.

"No, lass, I have to go when the opportunity arises and it may well be if Prachandra comes back for another session with you. I will take that opportunity to leave. My heart will be with you. Don't think too badly of old Toomey because he dumped his plane. I sure wish it had never happened."

"Oh, Toomey, may I hug you? You are a part of my life and always will be!" She put her arms around the rigid body of the pilot; embarrassed, he drew back.

"You're a plucky lass, Miss Rachel. I will see you in Kathmandu. 'We'll tak' a cup o' kindness yet for Auld Lang Syne.' What da ye say, lass?"

* * * *

"Reverend Adams, this is Guido Spanosino. I am with the Federal Bureau of Investigation in Washington. Good morning, sir."

"Good morning, Mr. Spanosino."

"I would like, sir, to arrange a convenient time for me to talk to you, preferably this afternoon or tomorrow morning."

"My goodness! May I ask the reason for such a sudden visit, Mr. Spanosino?"

"It is simple a routine follow-up to Miss Mason's trip to Nepal."

"I wonder if I might answer your questions on the phone? Save you a trip, don't you know."

"I would rather talk with you in person, Reverend, if you don't object."

"I don't object, of course, but.... Oh, I see! Would it be because of the *Baltimore Sun* article?"

"No, it has nothing to do with that, it is simply a routine follow-up of anyone who goes to a dangerous country."

"But Miss Mason has been gone, let me see, more than nine weeks. Do you then suspect foul play, sir?"

"Reverend, I simply want to talk to you in person. Is that going to be possible?" Mr. Spanosino's voice had taken a hard edge.

"I will be more than happy to talk with you. I am simply trying to understand the need for you to make such a long trip."

"In order to trace Miss Mason, we will need all the information we can get."

"Then it is not just a routine check-up, as you first said, but more of an in depth investigation because, as the paper suggests, she is missing. Is that correct?"

"Reverend, however you choose to see it. May I expect to talk to you either this afternoon or tomorrow morning?"

"Most certainly, Mr. Spanosino, whichever day you may prefer."

"I will be there at four o'clock this afternoon, then."

"My, that is prompt! I hope this doesn't bode ill for Miss Mason?"

"Thank you, Reverend Adams, I will see you soon."

Sam heard the phone strike its cradle with what he hoped was a frustrated bang.

"I know it was childish, God, but you've known for a long time I'm not perfect."

* * * *

The interview with Spanosino turned out to be anything but routine. He asked about Rachel's experience in Afton and specifically about her relationship with Ben. On several occasions Sam corrected implications

Spanosino made that there was a sexual relationship between the two. The third time the agent referred to Ben as her probable lover, Sam objected.

"Mr. Spanosino, I would suggest that if this interview is to continue, you refrain from implying actions or feelings that are just not appropriate. My wife and I know a great deal more of Miss Mason's life and feeling than the F.B.I. Do I make myself perfectly clear, sir?"

Spanosino smiled condescendingly, "I guess we can come to different conclusions, sir. I have all the information I need. I do thank you for your cooperation. We will hope that we can straighten out this apparent confusion about Miss Mason's captivity. Good day, Mrs. Adams, Reverend Adams."

"Ugh!" was Caroline's comment when Spanosino had left.

* * * *

As fate would have it, Caroline and Sam received Rachel's letter the day after Spanosino's visit. Having read her strange wording several times, they thought they understood the real message: that she was being forced to write the letter and that the obstacle to her release was the government's reluctance to pay the fee the Chinese were asking for her release. She had not said what the amount of money was so they were left in the dark as to how much was being asked.

Overjoyed to receive even this fragile message, Sam knew it was the proof they needed of Rachel's capture by the Chinese. He called Andrews and told him of the letter.

"Holy Smoke! What a wonderful surprise! May I come and get the letter so we can publish it?"

"By all means. Obviously you will need to explain her use of Mommy and Daddy, etc."

"I understand, but that makes it even more ideal, her trying to conceal her message in this way. I will be there in an hour."

* * * *

So, the next morning's edition of the *Sun* printed the letter in toto, in bold print under the headline: *Proof of What Administration Denies,* with a subhead, *Letter Received From Captive Cleric.*

Tad called after attending the hastily called White House briefing.

"Father Sam, you should have been there, except for the grime circumstances, it was hilarious. Scott Meacham told a long, tortured story about 'failed communication in an internet age'. The essence of his story was that somehow there was a horrible failure to communicate at the very source of the incident. Without naming names, it sounds like they are going to make the CIA agent in Kathmandu the goat, claiming that he did not follow procedures so that Miss Mason's capture was unknown in Washington. Obviously, we know that is not the case and they know it isn't. They are simply getting more and more ensnared in their own lies with everything they say. Perhaps, for our purposes, it's a good thing; your source at the State Department may escape the fury of the gods."

"Now, the question is, will they be forced to do something?"

"That's the question, but I can't guess the answer. There always seems to be more squirming room."

"Diplomatically, wouldn't it make sense to try to woo the Communists back to the negotiating table with King Gyanendra by using Rachel as a chip?"

"Sir! 'We don't negotiate with terrorists!' Yes, I agree, but one-way Charlie does not change course, come hell or high water."

"Well, all right then. Let's see how it plays out. Thanks for calling, Tad."

* * * *

Rachel had lived in dread of Prachandra's return, knowing that Toomey would seize it as his opportunity to escape. Lawa had alerted Botta that Prachandra was expected any day.

By this time, Lawa was almost friendly to Rachel. He had been informed of her many services to the wounded men and Botta had praised her work both at his camp and his wife's.

Rachel worked seven days a week and, although she could hardly use the word "enjoy", she had a deep feeling of satisfaction; doing work that had a distinct meaning. It was frequently heart breaking, but as she got to know the men, who were really boys, she felt accepted in a magical, wordless way.

She had developed a great fondness for Botta's young wife. It dawned on her that it had been years since she had had a "girl friend." She had been so competitive in school that it had left little time for socializing, least of all with women her own age, as competitive as she. Rinchen, on the other hand, was several years younger, and vastly more experienced in dealing with the hard edges of life.

Botta, himself, had usurped Sam's role in her life. He did not replace Sam, but in his absence she found Botta to have the same mature common sense philosophy she had found so reassuring at St. James.

As the weeks went by and the monsoon season began, Rachel would, periodically, wonder at the bizarre events that had brought her to this far-distant corner of Nepal—not working to aid poor Tibetan refugees, but ministering to the enemies of Nepal in a land so far from what she had known as civilized that she might as well have been on the moon. Yet, perversely, the satisfaction she gained and the genuine affection she received from the afflicted patients, served to let her rejoice in what she felt was God's mysterious hand in her life.

A month or more (she had trouble keeping track of time) after she had been asked to write her letter home, Prachandra returned. Toomey, who had been waiting for his return to make his escape, was in a final frenzy to leave. Rachel tried one last time to persuade him to stay, at least until they knew what Prachandra might tell them about the negotiations, but Toomey was too ready to test himself to brook any further delay. They parted when Prachandra was announced, Toomey disappearing into the forest as Rachel left for her meeting.

* * * *

Lance had called Sam after the initial headlines appeared in the *Sun*. He expressed concern for Rachel's safety, but it was obvious he was far more concerned about his flock's future. He asked Sam for a convenient time to discuss the future. In the meantime, the Vestry had signed for a contractor in Baltimore to modify the original church building.

Sam agreed to meet with Lance the following day.

The meeting was cordial, but kept at a superficial level. Lance again expressing concern for Rachel's safety, but did not explore the subject, opting to say only that the President will find the right path for her safety, guided by his prayers.

"Father Adams, you are well aware of the different paths your congregation is choosing to follow. The group I represent would like to formally leave St. James and establish a new parish. This is no surprise to you, it has been developing, I understand, for some years."

"Excuse me for a second, Lance. I have been here nine, almost ten years. I am not aware of any dissatisfaction with ecclesiastical matters until, perhaps, two years ago." Sam's point, that could hardly be misunderstood, was that Lance had become a member of St. James two years ago.

"I had understood it was a bit longer than that, but I don't wish to quibble. The issue is more profound than St. James, of course, it involves the Episcopal Church's policy, or lack thereof, on a number of social issues. It is these policies that are forcing us to react. I, personally, feel very strongly that there should be an almost militant defense of ancient beliefs. Our society has reached a point in its development that morals are considered passé. It is a return to the orgiastic Roman culture. Our President is trying manfully to direct us in the proper course and he needs every voice we can raise to support him."

"Lance, please, I am fully aware of your passionate fears; let us both acknowledge them and move on, shall we? Now, you are formally announcing a schism, I gather?"

Disgruntled that Sam had interrupted his impassioned statement of faith, he responded only, "Yes."

"I am deeply sorry it has come to this. I prayerfully hope you know where you are going with this, Lance. I sense a resentment and anger in your decision and I question the wisdom of a schism decided in that mood. However, know that you and any and all of your group that choose to stay, or, in time, choose to return, will be welcomed back with open arms."

"I would disagree with your analysis, Father Adams, but you are entitled to your opinion. I can only hope that you, in time, will come to realize the dire need to muster all God's troops before it is too late."

To divert Lance's mind for the moment, Sam asked where his flock would meet.

"We have leased the old Safeway building downtown until such time as our new church is built. Well, thank you Father Adams. I wish you well and that your curate will be found unharmed."

Lance rose and without further words, left the rectory and St. James.

* * * *

Xavier received his acceptance letter from the University of Maryland while Lisa had been in Connecticut, making a command return to her parent's home. Her parents' marital difficulties had reached a point of no return. Lisa's father had broken off the marital counseling they had initially agreed to undergo. Her mother, then, had formally filed for divorce. Giving up the pretense of living in the same house, her father, a stock broker in Manhattan, had taken an apartment in the upper Sixties just off Park Avenue.

During this final breakdown, Lisa watched her parents tear at each other the few times they were together. She could hardly remember days that had been harmonious, let alone joyful. Individually, she liked her parents, but when they attempted to pretend their marriage had life it always turned into a stressful tug of war for control. Her father worked long hours in New York so that it was usually seven-thirty—eight o'clock before he got home. Her mother refused to prepare meals at that hour, so she had hired a cook/housekeeper. The weekends were the worst; there was always a ritual cocktail party or two that they attended, not infrequently arriving home separately, and always intoxicated. Her mother would sleep until noon or later, either to recuperate from the alcohol or to avoid her husband, Lisa was never sure which.

It was this chaotic lifestyle that made it easy and natural for Lisa to fall into casual sex with several of the smoother, more aggressive boys; Todd Beach was the leader of that group.

Over the years, Lisa had developed a hard protective shell so that her parents searing, hateful words no longer hurt, or she could deny that they hurt. Angry and resentful that she was forced to remain in this ugly atmosphere, she manipulated each of her parents; by expressing a superficial love she extorted her father's agreement to sign over the sole ownership of the Jaguar, and from her mother she gained permission to attend the University of Maryland in the fall.

Her mother had always wanted Lisa to follow her to Miss Porter's School in Farmington, Connecticut. Lisa had heard her mother talk about "Farmington", as the old grads called it, for years and she knew how much the school meant to her. She also knew how much it would hurt her mother to let her go to a college like Maryland, a socially meaningless school.

When her mother brought home the father of one of her classmates after a particularly riotous night of drinking, neither appearing until early afternoon, Lisa called Grandfather Brown and asked if she could come back to Afton.

* * * *

An acquaintance of Durgan's called to tell him of Meacham's press conference during which he had implied that the CIA in Nepal had been the cause of the White House's ignorance of the Mason woman's captivity.

Durgan, who had been with the agency since the mid-sixties, knew every ploy that had ever been used to obfuscate the truth; he had employed most of them himself, but rarely had he been the victim of this deadly game.

Sitting slouched in a chair in his office, looking balefully out at the distant mountains, Durgan let his mind touch briefly on the many crises he had been involved in. His days as a junior agent in Vietnam were a harsh beginning for an eager but naive young man. The distortions of fact that he was forced to author very quickly blurred his understanding of truth and awakened him to a new form of reality, political truth. Dispatches that were specifically designed to create support for an unpopular war were the modus operandi, where old-fashioned truth had negative value. His ready accommodation to this requirement boosted his career very quickly. He later served in Moscow, Thailand, Pakistan, Bosnia and Afghanistan, with several tours at the Pentagon where his ability to write the most positive news releases based on the dire reports from the field won him high praise. The posting to Kathmandu late in his career was, he felt, a demotion. One of the more durable late night partiers along Connecticut Avenue, he found Kathmandu to be a pit. His wife, the third in a succession of women who had initially been thrilled by his profession, had refused to accompany him to Nepal and had since filed for divorce.

The heavy-lidded eyes that looked out toward the high peaks saw nothing of their majesty, he could only see the names of those who might have been responsible for dumping on him.

He had heard nothing from Rai in more than two weeks. In the meantime, the Maoists had taken over several more villages and had bombed a crowded market in the very heart of Kathmandu, leaving a dozen dead.

His determination to find out who had dumped on him mixed with his frustration with Rai, prompted him to go to his desk and open the bottom drawer that held his not-so-secret cache of bourbon. He poured a tumbler full and resumed his seat. As he was taking several large swallows, his secretary, Miss Sessions walked in. Her expression was unperturbed, familiar as she had become with his habits. Durgan continued to consume the burning liquid.

"So?"

"Mr. Durgan, you have a confidential cable from Mr.—"

"Cole, so what?"

"I think you should read it, Mr. Durgan."

"Bull crap! You read it, I'm sure you have already."
She opened the envelope and read:

Dan,

I guess you've heard the news. Someone rather high up has given you the black spot. I know better, that your hands are tied. There's still time to throw it back at them. If I make a little more available do you think you can spring this pain in the ass? I have another hundred to make the offer three fifty.

Unless the guy is a complete idiot, he'll take it. Try it with your buddy Rai and let me know.

Cole

"On the desk, Sessions. Try to get a hold of your Hindu lover on the radio."
Miss Sessions blushed deep scarlet and left the room.

After several hours Rai responded and Durgan gave him permission to raise the ante. Rai said he would try to contact Lawa immediately. Durgan said he would be in his office all night. Signing off, he refilled his glass and settled down to wait.

His answer came more quickly than he expected.

"Mr. Durgan, sir, I reached Mr. Lawa when he was, in fact, in conference with Mr. Prachandra and the captive. I communicated...."

"Cut the crap, Rai. Yes or no?"

"Mr. Prachandra was effusively thankful for your efforts in gaining more recognition, but he continues to believe Miss Mason's safety is worth far more than three hundred and fifty thousand dollars. I am sorry to tell you this."

"Sure, sure! Same old shit! Fine, forget it!" Durgan had switched off the receiver. "Let the son of a bitch have her," he mumbled as he fell back into a stupor.

* * * *

When Hawley read the White House briefing, he had to laugh. He remembered meeting Durgan several years ago and he remembered

199

taking an instant dislike to him—brash, impolite, full of himself were the words that come to mind. Served him right, he thought, or does it? If the poor sap is made the goat, the real blame goes unrecognized. He knew for a fact that there was strong suspicion of Miss Mason's capture within hours of the plane being reported missing. He had read Durgan's original cable to that effect. It was the State Department, and undoubtedly the White House, that had altered the actual facts. Durgan was entirely blameless.

As he mulled over the implication of Durgan being held responsible for the mess, he found, ironically, that it was too blatant a miscarriage to let pass.

Hawley had served in the State Department for twenty-nine years and had set his thirty-year anniversary as his retirement goal. Feeling his anger build at the injustice to the low man on the totem pole, unpleasant as he was, made Hawley reconsider his retirement plans.

At lunch, he phoned his old college buddy, Chauncey Phillips.

"CP, Digger. You probably have read the latest from our White House spokesman: that the CIA man in Kathmandu is the reason the Administration didn't know of Miss Mason's capture. That is a patent lie and I want to issue such a denial, but I wanted you to know, as well as the clergyman.

"What will that do to you at the State Department."

"I've decided to retire, Chaunce. There is too much of this going around and I don't want to be tarred by that kind of brush."

"Well, I can't say I blame you, Dig. I'll call Sam Adams immediately. I'm sure he will only applaud what you are doing."

"Thanks, Chaunce. Let's plan to get together later this month?"

"Great! I'll get the ladies on it. So long, and thanks for all you have done, Dig!"

* * * *

Hawley called a friend at *The Washington Post* and asked if they could meet for a drink after work. Quickly arranged, Harriet Vollmer met him at *The Senator* at five.

He explained his role in the Mason affair, his knowledge of it and when he had first heard of it. He cited both conversations and secret inter-office memos that told of the need for secrecy in this affair. He mentioned the Reverend Sam Adams' attempts to find out officially what had happened and his consequent rebuff. He told her of a letter that could be made available, if necessary, telling Bishop Phillips of Rachel's possible death or capture.

Vollmer listened intently until Hawley had finished.

"Fascinating and damning, but it would be difficult to make a case for obstruction of justice. We do not know what, if anything has been done. Let's assume they have moved heaven and earth to free Miss Mason, but to no avail. You can't contemn them for that, only the secrecy part. If, on the other hand, they are trying to negotiate with the Communists in the face of our President's stated policy against negotiating with terrorists, we have a two-faced embarrassment, but not a crime. If they have done nothing to seek her release, they will have a monumental human relations problem. Of the choices, I would bet they are negotiating, but haven't found the combination, either not enough money or simply distrust of each other. It could be all three. As far as you are concerned, your statements will clear the geek in Kat and blow the cover of the secrecy moguls. It will help some poor sap and embarrass the Administration. That's my take."

"Masterfully explained. I agree. I will proceed in any case. I have written out my story, read it and do whatever you need to do to publish it. If there are significant changes in fact, call me and only say 'Sap" and I'll call you back at the paper

* * * *

Hawley's letter was published with only minor changes under the headline: *High State Dept. Official Resigns in Protest,* with the subhead: *CIA Official Defended*

The story ran in the morning *Post.*

By now the press was clamoring for answers that Scott Meacham could not answer. The President, reluctant to face hostile questions, delegated the job to the Secretary of State. Her short speech did little to still the ground swell of negative public opinion. She stressed "the need to keep a perspective on this delicate situation." The government's only interest, she said, was the safety and well being of this unfortunate young lady. It had been considered only prudent to keep her capture a secret while the government used its every effort to locate and free her, she said.

The first question from the *New York Times;* reporter was, "Would you itemize the efforts that had been made?"

The answer from the Secretary was that much of the effort was still too sensitive to discuss.

The next question from the *St. Louis Post Dispatch* was, "Mr. Hawley, a high ranking member of the State Department with twenty-nine years of service, raised several questions about the need for secrecy in this case. What, in your mind, would have been the danger in keeping the public informed?"

"Mr. Hawley is one of many fine employees of the State Department. I do not personally know him, but he is certainly entitled to his own opinion. I will take one more question." She called on a reporter from *The San Francisco Chronicle.*

"Do you know, Madame Secretary, where Miss Mason is and that, in fact, she is alive and well?"

"Again, I would have to repeat, there is so much that is still sensitive in this case that I cannot answer that question. Thank you ladies and gentlemen." She hurriedly left the rostrum to the irate babble of unhappy reporters.

Rachel's meeting with Prachandra was short, but more cordial than the first. Botta again acted as interpreter.

"Miss Mason, your letter was delivered to your parents. It has caused much consternation among the American people. I thank you for that. It may yet be possible for you to go home to your family. We will see. Mr. Lawa commends you for your work. I add my thanks. Do you wish to say anything?"

"No, sir, other than I have the greatest respect for Dr. Botta and his wife and the work they are doing for you."

Prachandra nodded at Botta and left the meeting.

As she left the session with Prachantra, she was aware of a feeling of peace. Her emotions no longer rebelled at her captivity. It had been a very gradual, almost unconscious, change. Her work with the gentle doctor and Rinchen filled all her waking hours and gave her a reason to live and a deeper understanding of the tenuous line between life and death. She had been able to compartmentalize her mind, concentrating on the dire needs of the wounded and sick, and closing the door on her past life, sacred and achingly dear, but a door that she seldom allowed herself to open.

She was constantly aware of the mountains. The camp was located in a forest glen with a wide break in the trees that allowed an unobstructed view of Dhalaguri, one of the highest of the Himalayan peaks. Called the Snow Mountain, it cast a spell on Rachel. Whether she actually thought about its mysterious power, or whether she had become subtly hypnotized by its overwhelming presence, her surrender to it seemed to give her life a freedom she had never known. In this freedom, she lost control of her old way of life, or, at least, the life in which she had been educated to participate. Here there was no achievement to be gained or lost, there were no measures against which she could judge herself, nor was there ever the subtlest hint of inadequacy.

Rachel had studied the Hindu religion only casually at divinity school, yet there were times when she allowed these mystical beliefs to invade what she thought of as her rational education. Some subtle power was at work in the silence of these mountains that drew her to them and in her surrender, gave her heart a healing peace.

CHAPTER SIXTEEN

Life had been hectic; practically from the time he had invited Tom Farley to join him at St. James that he was thankful when the Bishop asked if he could delay Farley's arrival for two months. Apparently Ambrose Tibbets, the priest in charge at St. Mark's, Shepardstown, had had a heart attack and Farley was needed on an interim basis. Sam readily agreed, in fact, he thought it was fortuitous that Tom would avoid the acrimony of the threatened divisiveness in the parish.

Then, in June, the Bishop called to say that Tibbets had died and that the Shepardstown Vestry wanted Tom to stay on as Rector. Sam, obviously, had no choice but to wish him well.

"I'm terribly sorry, Sam. This is the last thing you need to happen right now." The Bishop was well aware of the on-going tension in the parish.

"It may be a blessing in disguise, Bishop. There were some raised eyebrows when I announced that Tom was coming and, of course, if there were to be a break in our ranks, we will have fewer in the parish to minister to."

"You poor, guy! You don't deserve this, Sam. Please call on me whenever you think I may be of help."

"Thanks, Chauncey, I appreciate that. We'll just muddle through. I will admit to being terribly worried about Rachel. If we could just get some valid information about her!"

"I know. Possibly Stuart Hawley's resignation will open things up? Let's hope so."

Russell had come to Afton a month ago in order to be closer to Sam's efforts of trying to get information about Rachel. He felt like a fifth wheel, however; unable to present himself as anything other than an "interested party." He groused and scowled around the house so much that to give him some useful purpose, Caroline asked him to handle all requests from the press or TV for interviews. He had been masterful at rejecting all but a very few, in most cases without offending them.

* * * *

After Hawley's resignation, everyone following the story felt there would be some concrete news forthcoming, but when a week had elapsed and nothing further had been learned, several of the larger papers dispatched reporters to Nepal.

Among those sent were Tad Andrews of *The Baltimore Sun* and Harriet Vollmer of *The Washington Post;* Tad's friend, Claire Tremont of *The Times* was already in Kathmandu. On landing in Kathmandu, each of them was vetted by Durgan who, now exonerated by Hawley's statements, had become even more difficult to deal with. Durgan did his practiced best to intimidate the correspondents with dire consequences if they interfered with *his* investigation. Harriet Vollmer was far too experienced to give him any credence. Tad, for whom this was a first foreign assignment, saw the man as just another used up man and from his six feet five inch height packed with two hundred and thirty pounds, he looked pityingly at the old agent.

They were, however, all aware of the real danger to themselves and particularly to the captured woman if they attempted any grandstand maneuver to gain access to her. They each began slowly by sifting and eliminating possible legitimate sources of information. At the end of the first week, they put their heads together and shared what they had learned. When they realized that each had come up with nothing of value, they decided to work as a team.

"Obviously, language is a barrier, plus there are enough cross-currents between the monarchists and those that support the insurgents to make you question anything you do hear," Claire, the most experienced, summed up.

Tad, whose interview with Durgan was still festering when he left his offce, had rolled his eyes in disbelief as he passed Durgan's secretary. The woman, he was quite sure, had smiled sympathetically. He related the experience to the two women.

"I could be wrong, but knowing how brutal that turkey is, she probably has scars from her experiences with him. I wonder whether she'd be the logical weak link in Czar Durgan's impregnable fortress?"

"I wonder?" Vollmer said pensively.

"Why not try and find out?" Tremont suggested. "Let's assume she's heterosexual; that being the case, I guess you, oh bronzed gladiator, should be the first into the arena. What say you, Taddo?"

"I might try to buy her a drink," Tad answered, impishly.

"Fine! I suspect she would welcome a sarsaparilla." Vollmer laughed, winking at Claire.

They went to dinner, feeling that perhaps they might make a little progress with Marjorie Sessions, if, hopefully, she were thirsty.

* * * *

As soon as Lisa had returned to Afton, she drove to the church looking for Xavier. He was nowhere to be found, but in going into the Parish House, she bumped into Father Sam.

"Lisa! What a pleasant surprise! Won't you sit a bit and have a talk?"

Reluctantly, but not because of any dislike of the minister, Lisa agreed to go into Sam's office.

"Well, you've been away a long time, how did you find your family?" Sam knew only fragments of Lisa's family's problems, but he decided to bring it out into the open between them.

"Pretty much the same, or worse, Mr. Adams." She had deliberately used "Mr." rather than Reverend thinking it might be a psychological "stopper."

"Oh, your grandfather had felt it was, perhaps, looking brighter. Do you mind my questions, Lisa?"

"No, I guess not. It doesn't seem to be a secret." Her tone verged on being rude.

"Can you talk about it, Lisa, or would you rather not?"

Lisa studied her hands, glanced briefly at the man in front of her, sighed and replied, "Maybe I could talk about it a little."

"Only as much as you want, Lisa."

At first dreading to talk about it, she suddenly felt an urge to tell someone how she felt.

"I hate them, Father!"

"You probably have your reasons."

"They are so stupid!"

"Many of us are, unfortunately."

"I don't mean dumb stupid, I mean they do things they know are wrong just to get at the other guy!"

"Like they are punishing either themselves or the other guy?"

"Why would they be punishing themselves?"

"Sometimes we feel so guilty we do things we know are wrong so that we can feel more guilty."

"That's stupid!"

"I agree, but you and I are sort of sitting on the sidelines, don't you think?"

"I wish I was on the sidelines. I get messed up in their fights whenever I'm in Connecticut."

"Can you talk to either of your parents, Lisa?"

"I used to be able to talk to my Dad, but since I got pregnant he doesn't like me."

"I wonder if he really doesn't? It probably was a shock to him."

"So? What about the shock of his, you know, doing the things he does?"

"I know some things don't seem to have an explanation, Lisa, and that some things hurt us. These are things we are not smart enough to understand and they seem unfair. At times like that we ask God to help us understand. Many times He can speak to us so that it takes away some of the hurt, like having a friend like Xavier we can rely on."

As Sam watched, tears welled up in Lisa's eyes. It was one of the rare moments in her life that her bravado failed her and she was left terribly vulnerable. Sam, never having had children, nonetheless, could feel her desperate loneliness and opened his arms to her. Sobbing bitterly, she let herself be held by a stranger whose loving protection let her release her hurt.

They sat together for some time until her body calmed and her breathing regained a normal rhythm. Sam was uncertain whether she might not have fallen asleep, her emotions having drained her.

"I'm sorry." Her small voice murmured.

"Lisa, Lisa, never apologize for being honest with your feelings."

She lay with her head against Sam's chest, breathing in the total acceptance of this man.

* * * *

Tad created a need to see Durgan, something incoherent, that he knew Durgan would be at his caustic best to answer. When he got to the office, however, Miss Sessions told him Mr. Durgan was out for the day.

"Oh, durn! That's too bad. I guess it's not too important. Miss Sessions, I sort of feel guilty taking Mr. Durgan's time, he seems real busy."

Miss Sessions pushed her glasses down on her nose and looked more closely at Andrews.

"He is, *always* busy, Mr. Andrews." Her voice dripped with sarcasm.

Her tone reinforced the suspicion that she was weary of offering Mr. Durgan any compassion.

"Maybe you could help me, if you have a moment?"

"I will certainly try, Mr. Andrews. Please sit down." She removed her glasses.

"Thank you so much. Please call me Tad."

"Well, thanks, I will if you call me Marge."

"That's nice, Marge. You see the thing is from what Mr. Durgan says, I will probably be here some time and I'd like to see as much of Kathmandu as Mr. Durgan thinks is safe. You know, the pretty places and maybe some of the places only you long-timers may know about that would be...fun." Andrews winked at her to let her know what he meant.

Marge appraised the man sitting next to her before she replied. Nice looking, tall, with an open, innocent expression; he was an appealing sight to eyes that had so long been resigned to the sterile Central Intelligence Agency way of life in Kathmandu. Durgan's cutting remark about Rai being her Hindu lover could not have been further from the truth, as he well knew. As soon as she arrived to be his secretary, he had threatened her, in the crudest language, that any hanky-panky and she would be sent home in disgrace.

"Well, Tad, I don't know a lot about Kathmandu, but I have been here for two years. I hear people talk about some places."

Andrews looked down in his lap, then sort of stammered, "Miss.... Marge, this is rude, I know, but would you ever consider showing me some of these places, say maybe this weekend?" His large brown eyes were those of a lonesome little boy.

"Oh, I don't know, Tad. I probably shouldn't. Mr. Durgan probably wouldn't approve, you being a newspaper reporter and all."

"Don't hold that against me, Marge. My interest would be like a tourist. *The Sun* maybe would be interested in some background on this city."

"You wouldn't mention me in the article, would you?"

"No, I wouldn't. I would really like it if you could show me around, Marge."

"Well," she looked furtively around the office as though there might be open mikes waiting for her reply. "I guess it would be alright. I'd like to go with you."

"Wonderful! I'm so pleased. How about tomorrow, Saturday, at about ten?"

"That would be fine. I will meet you then at the public library at ten."

"I could pick you up at your place?"

"No, I think the public library would be safer...better, Tad."

"Super! Tomorrow then, Marge. I'll look forward to it!"

"Thank you. See you at the library."

* * * *

Sam and the Vestry had met twice with the architect who had designed the church remodeling. He had suggested a graceful extension of the roof on either side of the ridgepole, lending the impression of a giant bird poised for flight. He had retained, but moved outward, the original sidewalls with their simple stained glass scenes of Jesus' life. The Vestry had opted to keep the conventional pew seating which would increase the seating capacity to three hundred, with two side aisles.

Caroline and Sam had had several searching discussions as to how the church might honor Rachel. Still uncertain of her safety, they were even more determined that she be given appropriate recognition. Their ideas ranged from entirely new vestments, a fountain under the old dogwood tree, perhaps even new doors to the church. Each idea met with problems for various reasons. Finally, Caroline tentatively made a suggestion she had secretly harbored for weeks.

"Sam, what would you think if we gave a new belfry, perhaps even a new bell?"

"Goodness gracious, Caroline, do you have any idea what that would cost?"

"No, really I don't, but I have some money and I'd love to see Rachel remembered in that way."

Sam studied his wife's face and knew this was not an impulsive suggestion.

"Well, of course it would be wonderful. I think a new bell could be toned to offset the sound of our present bell. I like the idea. Let me find out what it will cost."

"I'd rather not, Sam. I know that's the practical way to go about it, but if the Vestry approves, I will simply pay whatever it costs."

"Are you sure, my dear?"

"Yes, Sam. I want it to be from both of us."

And so, when the Vestry had finished their final approval of the architect's plans, Sam introduced Caroline's idea. The Vestry enthusiastically accepted the gift and the architect was commissioned to draw up a plan for the Rachel Mason Belfry.

* * * *

Toomey's absence was not officially discovered for twelve hours. When it was found out, Rachel, Botta and his wife were each grilled.

Lawa, however, was not unduly alarmed by Toomey's escape knowing the very slim likelihood of his surviving in the primitive mountain areas around their camp. Not only did bandits roam the remote areas, but all forms of wild animals inhabited the forests, the most dangerous of them being tigers. Almost daily there were reports of Nepalis dying or being seriously injured by tigers. So his departure was reported and some searching attempted, but it was very limited and short-lived. His very existence seemed to have been erased except by Rachel who tenaciously held to her belief that this enigmatic Scot would somehow survive.

Toomey, in the meantime, had headed directly south. He knew that his only chance of survival depended on reaching friendly India. He did not know how far India was, but whatever the distance he was determined to conquer it. He had scavenged enough food for three days if he ate small quantities. Water was not a problem because of streams that criss-crossed his route. He saw rhinos and elephants, but no tigers for the first few days. Sleeping lightly at night for two or three hours, he made torturous progress south. The fourth day the forests began to thin and he would occasionally see the flatter southern lands of the Terai, the most barren and disease-ridden region in Nepal.

At the end of the fifth day since leaving camp, his food was exhausted and he was forced to chew the bark of trees to stay alive. Pausing at the edge of the forest on his sixth day, he searched in vain to see any sign of a village. From flying over this area once, he knew how sparsely settled it was, largely because of the heat and disease during the summer months. He also knew that June was the beginning of the monsoon. Satisfied with his progress so far, yet weak from lack of food, he took off for the distant dust obscured horizon.

* * * *

Tad, arriving promptly at ten at the library steps, saw no sign of Miss Sessions. Uneasy that she might have gotten cold feet, he went into the library to look for her. Strolling casually among the tables, he saw a woman studying a newspaper rather more stylishly dressed than a library visit might warrant. Coming up behind her he saw she was reading a week-old copy of *The New York Times*. The headline happened to read, *Secrecy Surrounds Disappearance of American Cleric*.

"Hi, Marge!"

Startled, she dropped the paper.

Tad scooped it up, "Sorry, I didn't mean to startle you."

She forced a laugh, "No,no. Silly of me."

He replaced the paper.

"I don't see *The Times* very often in our office."

Ted decided he wanted to minimize attention on Miss Mason. "She'll turn up, sound as a dollar, I'm sure. Shall we go?"

As they turned to leave, Tad was flattered and, at the same time, concerned that the woman had dressed so elaborately. The first semblance of guilt crept into his mind. He knew he was expected to exploit her, it had been his idea in the first place—but was it really that necessary to perform his job? To make matters worse, she appeared excited and happy to be out with him. Come on, Tad, loosen up, he chided himself.

He had hired a rickshaw for the day that seemed to please her very much. After they had settled themselves in the cab, she asked if he wanted her to give him some background on the city, or would he prefer her to simply answer any questions he might have as they drove along.

"I'd be pleased if you'd give me a running commentary, Marge, I'm pretty ignorant about Kathmandu."

"Most people are. Nepal is a tiny country squashed in between two giants, China and India. Well, first of all, it's a monarchy, actually the oldest continuous monarchy in the world. The present king, Gyanendra, became king in 2001, after his nephew, the Crown Prince murdered his entire family—an ugly story.

Gyanendra is under heavy assault from an insurgent Communist army that is trying to overthrow him and establish a Communist state a la Mao Tse-tung vintage. It is really a very ticklish situation and it's the reason that your friend, Miss Mason, is in the precarious spot she is. Our present administration has labeled the Maoists, terrorists, which most countries of the world do not agree with, incidentally, and, in doing so, we are in a position where, by policy, we can't negotiate with them as terrorists. I know you want to talk more about that, but I'll just tease you with that lest you might suddenly find me less fascinating."

Andrews had the feeling that she was way ahead of him; that she knew she was being used, but chose to overlook it.

"I am interested in the history, Marge, please go on."

"Well, this building on your right...." She asked the driver to slow down. "The building on your right, Kasthamandap, is supposed to have been built in the sixteenth century from the wood of a single tree. The city was named for this temple." They got out of the rickshaw and walked around the remarkable building.

Five minutes away they examined the erotic carvings of Sjaishi Dewal. Marge pointed out the more explicit examples of the art, delighting in Tad's embarrassment.

"Now really, Mr. Andrews, tell me Baltimore doesn't have temples of love like this? I love Buddhist, or is it Hindu candor, don't you," she teased?

Next she showed him Singha Dunbar, the Secretariat of the Government, once a palace, then the Temple of Kumai, the residence of the Living Goddess, Kumari, and finally, Machehendranath Temple.

"This is my favorite, Tad! So beautiful! I love it!" She was visibly excited and clapped her hands like a little child. "Don't you like it?"

"It is beautiful," he agreed.

It was almost noon, so she directed the driver to take them to a restaurant she knew of nearby. They had a leisurely lunch on the patio over several glasses of rice wine.

She told him of the tragic and gruesome murders of nine members of the royal family in 2001 and the rise of the Maoist movement that had philosophical ties with the *Shining Path*, the Peruvian terrorist movement.

Tad found he enjoyed her company and her refreshing evenhanded comments on Nepal. She had been posted to several foreign countries that she described nostalgically, quickly passing over her marriage that had ended several years ago, largely, Tad concluded, because of her foreign assignments. He guessed her age to be the mid-thirties, at least ten years his senior, but as she relaxed with him, with help from the wine, she became a very charming companion. He had trouble relating this person to the bespectacled, intimidated woman in Durgan's office.

The afternoon touring went much more slowly, but was now mixed with much good humor and laughter. She took him to Thamel, the real tourist center of Kathmandu, where they shopped without buying any of the many unique trinkets that usually tempted tourists. Toward five, she took him to the Rum Doodle Bar where they each had a native beer.

Looking over the edge of his beer glass, Tad deliberated whether to ask her to dinner. He had not really pressed her for the information they were seeking so he realized he hadn't performed his function, yet he was still feeling constrained by the feeling that what he was asking himself to do was dishonest, and he had grown to like the woman. Confronted by her obvious friendliness, if not naiveté, he cringed at his own deviousness, but what had he learned?

"Marge, I would like very much to take you to dinner. You have been so gracious taking so much of your time showing me around. I want you to know that I appreciate it very much. I don't want to intrude in your private life, if you have made plans for the evening." He felt that he had, at least, given her an out to escape.

She looked at him, searchingly, uncertain what his pleasure might be?

"Tad, I'd like to invite you to my place and let me prepare my own version of Nepali food." Her voice had an honest warmth that Tad could not mistake.

"You don't have to do that. Why not go to a quiet restaurant where you can relax? We're both tired and it would be easier for you."

"I like to cook. I know a real easy recipe I'd like to cook for you."

Why, oh why, must she be so nice, he thought.

"Well, sure, I guess. That would be very pleasant."

Delighted, she told the rickshaw driver her address.

Her apartment was in a complex of two-story buildings on the eastern edge of the city.

As soon as he entered, he was conscious of her artistic touches: a carefully placed vase on a small table, a marble egg on a small niche shelf, a photograph of Zion National Park in deep sepia, all creating a distinctly female atmosphere.

"Sorry it looks so feminine—not really a man's space, but it's the private retreat I need after dealing with Danny-boy all day."

There it was, an open invitation for him to exploit. It was so easy it bothered him.

"This is really nice, Marge. I can see your touch everywhere."

She was visibly flattered. "Oh, thanks, I like it."

She tied on a dainty pink apron, "May I fix you something to drink. I have a pretty good variety and, no, I am not a closet drinker."

"Well, I'm a Scotch drinker, Marge, but anything will do."

"Oh, dear! I guess you are too young to appreciate martinis. Well, I do have Scotch for young men."

"Just for that downer, give me one of your martinis, old lady!"

"That really hurts, but I will take pleasure in initiating you into the sacred society of martini-hood."

"Perfect! You are spoiling me."

I think I'd like that, she said to herself and turned to the kitchen.

She returned some minutes later with two frosted martini glasses filled to the brim and a bowl of peanuts. She put the tray on the coffee table and sat at the other end of the sofa.

Tad handed her a glass and touched his own to hers, "This is thanks for a wonderful day, Marge. I really appreciate all you have done for me."

She flushed slightly. "You are fun company. I've enjoyed myself more today than I have in years. Skoal!"

They sipped the icy fire, Marge studying the man across from her, fully aware that he wanted information; that he had ulterior motives. Who doesn't in this crazy world? He was cute and very nice and she was free, white and an aging thirty-five, so why not relax and enjoy it.

Tad, now on the defensive, made small talk about the day until she had replenished their glasses. The second went more quickly than the first and as she was finishing hers, she moved closer to him.

"Tell me why did you ask me to go out with you? Be honest, I'm a big girl," she smiled almost shyly, but yet challengingly.

There it was, right between his conniving eyes.

"I…Marge, you are too much! Why do you have to be so damned devious? You make me feel like a fool."

"I'm thirty-five, not a Hollywood beauty, and I'm smart enough to know that handsome, young men who are about twenty-five don't usually beat down my door. Did you ask me out to get information about the missing girl?"

He refused to lie to her, but he struggled for the right words.

"Tell you what," she continued. "I'll make us a third. That will give you time to think of a reply, then we'll eat. Fair enough?" She rose and, somewhat unsteadily, found her way to the kitchen leaving Tad hopelessly defeated.

When she had placed the brimming glasses next each other, she sat close to him, her eyes teasingly challenging him.

Tad inhaled a large swallow, looking at her, "Marge, all right, I will be honest, though it shames me. Sure, I had hoped to get a lead on the girl's whereabouts or health. I sensed you had been, at least, verbally abused by our friend, Durgan, and that you might be a source of information. We newspaper people are a greedy lot, Marge, do anything for a scoop. I'm sorry and I am embarrassed to have to admit it. I don't want you to tell me anything, *absolutely nothing!* Promise?"

She laughed, "How silly of you, but thanks for telling me the truth. I didn't flatter myself that you were breathing hard to date me just to take me out." As she laughed, she put her hand on his arm.

"Don't, Marge, please! I have been the fool, but I have genuinely, honestly enjoyed being with you today. Please believe at least that of me."

She leaned forward and kissed him. "I do, but sometimes old ladies like I am get a kick out of thinking they can be attractive to virile, young bucks like you. Pretend I'm twenty, just for tonight," she whispered.

Instead of kissing her, Tad put his arms around her and held her. "It won't work, Marge. I can't *pretend* anything. You are a sexy, attractive woman. It's you who would have to pretend...that I wasn't a horse's you-know-what."

"You talk too much, newspaper man. Kiss me and I will tell you everything I know about your missing missionary," she whispered.

Tad, never a candidate for monastic orders, could no longer condemn himself, nor deny her very obvious charms.

* * * *

The reporter returned to his hotel around eleven Sunday morning. After showering and shaving, he felt obliged to meet with the two women who had been silent partners in his ill-conceived quest. They met for lunch in the hotel dining room and immediately pressed him for details.

"Before we start, gals, let me say two things: one, I am ashamed of the crude idea I came up with, believe me, I am. Second, all of us need to be extremely careful about protecting the source of our information—Marge Sessions works for a vindictive individual. Please believe what I have just said."

The women exchanged glances, but didn't comment, only nodded agreement.

"So, the story is that Durgan is using a Pakastani named Rai to negotiate with the Commies. There is no question that we are negotiating with the terrorists. Rai is on the CIA payroll, but they know he is working both sides of the street. The CIA, through Rai, has offered a man named Prachandra three hundred and fifty thousand bucks for the girl's release, but Prachandra wants a million, so has turned them down. Washington is still presenting a 'no negotiation with terrorists face'. The CIA doesn't know where to go from here. Rai believes something short of a million will do it, but there is *big* resistance to those kind of dollars from Washington, to say nothing of Gyanendra."

"Where is the girl, Tad, and is she safe?"

"Rai has been cagey about her location, but he implies she is as far from Kathmandu as you can get and that she is well."

"What about the pilot?"

"Rai seems to know nothing except he believes he may have survived and is with her."

"How can we use this information without tipping your friend's cover?"

"Marge says Rai has a girl friend, a Chinese, who lives here—I have her address. She lives a rather free life, according to Durgan, when Rai is away. Durgan has warned Rai a number of times about her. Now, in case you are getting any ideas, I am not your boy on this one, ladies," Andrews said ruefully.

The two women laughed.

"Sounds to me like you got in over your head with Miss Sessions, Tad," Harriet needled.

"I found I didn't like myself for using her. She's a very nice lady."

"Sorry, Tad. I think we can work around Sessions and build our fire with the Chinese woman," Claire concluded.

CHAPTER SEVENTEEN

One of Rachel's rules at the camp had been not to keep track of the days. She could not avoid the fact that when the monsoon began it had to be early June. It had been more than three months since she had been brought to Botta's camp. It seemed impossible! Every day was so busy and fraught with potential tragedy that calendar time had no meaning. It was only the speed and efficiency with which Botta applied his skills to the broken bodies that time had any significance.

Each day Rachel felt a little more confident dealing with the horror of the men's wounds. Botta instructed her as he would a nurse in training when he performed whatever was possible within the limits of his equipment and supplies. For those men who survived their wounds, Rachel established an elemental, non-verbal relationship. They were amazed to see a white woman ministering to them, and it lightened the darkness of their lives. In time, they were able to express a self-conscious, but sincere affection toward her. Botta repeatedly told her that her form of medicine was far superior to his more mechanical methods.

As one bloody day followed another, Rachel, Rinchen and Botta lived only for one success at a time, and then moved on to one more challenge. The type of wound was the name of the patient to Botta; the nose shape, cracked teeth, or wondrous dark eyes were the name Rachel used to remember the men. The work for Rinchen was more harrowing, for at her camp there were few cures, only further decay of already wasted bodies.

* * * *

After Toomey's escape, the three virtually lived together. Botta had been granted a generous sized tent in which he had devised a walled-off room with a canvas drape where Rachel slept. Viewed from any other than their primitive captivity, it would have seemed a questionable arrangement, certainly compromising.

Her idle time was so infrequent that she seldom had time to feel sorry for herself and bemoan her captivity. Russell's face would appear in her mind's eye at unexpected intervals. Her life, however, had become so bizarre and unrelated to her previous life that as the days sped by she would confuse Russell's face with Scott's or sometimes Ben's. This concerned her and she wondered if she could be suffering some form of mental aberration? She told Botta about these experiences, but he reassured her that both he and Rinchon them had gone through the same experience and that it would pass.

At the end of each day, Rachel lay down exhausted, fulfilled by her work, but with a prayer for those she struggled to remember from a million lifetimes ago.

* * * *

The three reporters decided they needed to be seen going into Rai's mistress' apartment so that if it was under surveillance, Durgan would assume it had been she who had leaked information. How they would have discovered her existence, they could not answer, so they had to leave it unresolved.

The woman's apartment was in a rickety two-story building in the heart of the Thamel district. The three climbed the narrow staircase to the second floor and knocked on the door. Moments later the door was opened by a fragilely pretty oriental woman, prematurely aged, but with the brightest eyes they had ever seen. She showed no surprise at confronting the three Americans.

"Miss Sakya, I am Claire Tremont, from an American magazine. We are doing a special edition on Chinese women living in Kathmandu and wondered whether we might talk to you"

The woman nodded agreeably and bowed them into her apartment. Andrews had brought his Nikon camera so as to appear to be a photographer.

Claire continued the interview, stressing their interest in China, women in Nepal, her work, how she entertained herself, et cetera. On the subject of her work, Miss Sakya was prompted to say, evasively, that she did not presently work because she was contemplating marriage.

"Oh, how nice! May I assume you will marry a native Chinese?" Harriet asked.

"Oh, no. My suitor is a high caste Hindu from Karachi. He is employed by the United States Government."

"Really! How very interesting! Does he live here in Kathmandu?"

"Yes, but he travels frequently in Nepal. He is on a very secret mission right now to western Nepal."

"Really! We are planning a trip to western Nepal ourselves. It would be interesting if we went to the same places. You don't remember where he was going?"

"He would be angry with me, but I will tell you it is near the mountain, Dhaulagiri. It has something to do with a western woman who is with the Chinese forces."

"That sounds exciting. What is your fiancé's name?"

"Sher Rai. He is an upper caste Hindu," she repeated proudly.

"This will make an exciting story, Miss Sakya. Have you gotten enough pictures, Tad, if so, I think we have taken enough of Miss Sakya's time. May we offer you fifty American dollars for a nice dinner with your fiancé?"

"I would be pleased, but I will not tell him how I got it. Thank you kindly!"

The reporters left the apartment and went back to the hotel.

Combining what Marge Sessions had told Tad and the information that Rai's friend had provided, they each filed a story, but they agreed to let Tad's story run first because of his greater contribution. Each identified his source as a person close to a Pakistani employee of the CIA.

To avoid Durgan's news blackout, they were forced to phone their stories, an onerous task made uncertain by constant static. The following morning, nonetheless, each of the papers broke the story in large headlines, citing the amount of money the government had offered the Communists and Rachel's approximate location. The stories stressed that her capture had been known from the earliest moment of her disappearance and listed the number of denials the Administration had authorized.

The furor from these articles forced the President to claim personal ignorance, but in an attempt to distance himself, he criticized several State Department officers, again claiming the mix-up had originated at the Kathmandu level. The Ambassador was recalled for consultation and the White House issued internal instructions to all Departments that there would be no information released on any foreign activities except that which Scott Meacham provided.

Official Washington was buttoned up tight, which only heightened the zeal of reporters to find those still willing to talk "off the record."

* * * *

Rai had again reported failure to gain any concessions from Prachandra. Nothing had been gained in the four months of the secret negotiations except that it had finally become known that the President's vow never to negotiate with terrorists had been proved duplicitous. An angry public demanded that the woman be ransomed whatever the cost.

When the Ambassador returned to Nepal, Durgan was recalled. Outraged at this second official insult, he took his frustration out on Rai and Sessions; he cancelled Rai's contract and told Sessions she had been released by the Agency. The Ambassador reiterated the President's resolve to never negotiate with terrorists and reaffirmed US support for the beleaguered Gyanendra monarchy.

Andrews, hearing from Marge of Durgan's recall, her firing, and Rai's termination, corralled his colleagues and returned to Miss Sakya's apartment in the hope that they might find out how they could get to see Rai. When they arrived, they were met by a tall, distinguished looking Asian about to leave the apartment.

"Mr. Rai, Tad Andrews of *The Baltimore Sun*. We have just heard the unfortunate news of your severance from the CIA." Tad, gambling that this man must be Rai, saw no reason to be obscure. "I wonder if we might be able to tell your story, perhaps in a more reasonable way?"

Rai had been involved in so many devious schemes both with the CIA and many other groups that functioned just below the margin of legitimacy that this recent turn of events apparently left him unruffled. He took some time to respond, studying the group.

"I do not know *The Baltimore Sun.* Who are these other people?"

"Miss Tremont represents *The New York Times* and Miss Vollmer is with *The Washington Post.*"

"Ladies," Rai bowed. "What is it you want to know?"

Claire answered, "Most people in the United States want to gain Miss Mason's release and they feel our government has destroyed any possibility, because of their stated policy of not dealing with terrorists which has been demonstrated to be a lie. We believe that if her safety is assured and the amount of ransom is known, we could gain her release."

Rai studied the young woman. He rarely dealt with women in any significant way other than for his own pleasure. Turning to Andrews, he said, "If it were to be that I could supply the information you seek, how might you recognize my service?"

Tad had never been involved in any news story larger than neighborhood murders, yet instinctively certain that they were on the verge of breaking open the logjam, replied, "You would be suitably rewarded. First of all, we would need to know the final amount the Communists would be willing to accept; we would need to be assured of Miss Mason's health and safety, and we would need some proof her captors would honor her release if the ransom is paid."

Rai turned and walked to the windows of the apartment.

"Sit down, ladies, if you will. I met Miss Mason on the flight to Nepal months ago and again the following the day when she agreed to accompany the pilot, Mr. Reginald Toomey, to Pokhara."

The reporters exchanged raised eyebrows.

"I respect Miss Mason for her desire to aid Tibetan refugees. It is most unfortunate that she became a captive of the insurgents; they are a most determined group. I have had dealings with several of their officials, including the man, Prachandra, who is their leader. I have advised Mr. Durgan several times that the offers made for Miss Mason's release would be considered inadequate, but he did not agree, so nothing has been accomplished. The amount of money is ridiculously unimportant to your country. It is only their so-called policy regarding terrorists that makes her release overly complicated. The United States is entitled to define groups hostile to their policies by any term they choose. It is certainly true that the Communists have performed savage acts. It is also well documented that the government of King Gyanendra has performed equally appalling acts against the insurgents, but more basically, they have done nothing to alleviate the degrading poverty of the low-class Nepali. Is one policy more inhuman than the other? I will not waste our time debating the issue.

The Communists seek one million dollars for Miss Mason's release. I know where she is being held and I believe, given assurance that the money will be paid, I can get them to guarantee this agreement." He turned and looked at each of the reporters; his look was boldly challenging and yet each of them saw the faint flickering in the eyes of the compromised power broker.

"Before we could get approval for the payment, someone would have to see Miss Mason to verify her health. The money would be placed in a Swiss bank and released when Miss Mason was freed." Andrews, again, spoke as though international intrigue was his normal beat.

"I believe that could be arranged."

"You have some means of communicating with her captors?"

"I do."

"I suggest we meet again in twenty-four hours to finalize the arrangements. Is that agreeable?" Andrews again.

"Excuse me, sir, but I did not hear the stipend I might expect for this delicate negotiation?"

The three Americans looked at each other already well beyond any legitimate authority.

"I believe we might provide one hundred and fifty thousand dollars for your services, if safely concluded," Claire said, haltingly.

"That is not what I would have hoped to receive, but under the circumstances, I will agree to it."

"All right, then you will get permission for our people to go to this camp to verify Miss Mason's condition and we will attempt to raise the one million dollars. Needless to say, our agreements will require ultimate secrecy."

"It is not I who will violate such a stricture; it will more probably be your citizens who will divulge it. I must warn you, however, that Prachandra wearies of the many false starts in this process."

The three rose, nodded to Rai, and let themselves out of the apartment.

* * * *

After they had left Miss Sakya's apartment, they went to Claire's hotel room to discuss what they had learned and what their next steps would be. The news blackout that the Durgan had imposed on all reporters in Nepal made it impossible to communicate confidentially with their papers, so it became obvious that one of them would have to fly back to the US. Harriet volunteered, in part because she had a husband and two children where the other two had no immediate families.

It was agreed that Harriet would first talk to her editors and get their reaction to what had been proposed to Rai. If there were agreement, then *The Times* and *Sun* people would be brought in. They did not dwell on the possibility that they might find no support at all. Assuming everyone was on board, the three papers would have to decide how the ransom was to be raised in view of the State Department's order forbidding Americans from contributing funds, goods, or services for the benefit of the Maoists, an officially labeled terrorist group. Would an out-pouring of citizen support be enough to allow the ransom to be paid? The amount of money was not the problem; it was more circumventing the letter of the law.

"Wait a minute," Tad shouted, "We're making this far too difficult. We know the CIA has been negotiating with the Commies and offering ransom money, but just not enough, therefore the *precedent* has been established! If there is an argument, we subpoena whoever from the CIA and State who knew about this whole thing, including Hawley, and prove that the Administration was secretly violating its own orders; ipso facto, we are only following White House precedent," Tad smiled, smugly.

"Hmm, I guess that makes sense? We should be on solid ground. Good! What do you think, Claire," Harriet asked?

"I guess so. I'm just thinking about that poor girl's future being horsed around this cavalierly. OK, let's go with it. Hat, would you cable us saying something about a happy birthday if this will fly with the papers, or, if it won't, cable something about a serious illness, OK?"

"I'll do that."

"We will have to wait for Rai to get back to us, but why don't you make a reservation on tomorrow night's eleven o'clock flight. We should hear by then."

It was five o'clock when they had concluded all their discussions and plans so Claire suggested they go out to dinner.

Tad excused himself. "I apologize, Claire, but I'm having dinner with Marge—sort of a thank you affair. She's flying out at noon tomorrow."

"She's probably pretty upset about losing her job, even though it was to that turkey, Durgan, I guess," Claire sympathized.

"No, actually, she's happy as a lark. She gets a decent severance and she's rid of old foul-mouth."

"Thank her for us, Tad." Tad did not see Harriet's wink at Claire.

* * * *

Marge had chosen a quiet, expensive little restaurant not far from her apartment. Sitting across the table from her, Tad still struggled with his conscience over how he had attempted to use her. It was obvious that she bore him no hard feelings. She was determined to make this dinner a happy occasion; she wore an elegantly simple satin dress, with an Oriental flare, including the long slit up the side of the skirt; not normally the clothes of American secretaries in Nepal. Her long blonde hair had been dressed professionally that afternoon, Tad guessed. Her face was illuminated with the same happy, open expression that had he had noticed on their first "date."

"You seem preoccupied, Tad, why?"

"Oh, nothing. I will be sad to see you leave, Marge."

"Thanks. You're the only thing that would make me regret leaving. I've gotten sort of fond of you, Scoop." She attempted to laugh, but failed.

"You could stay."

"I wonder if that would be good for either of us, Tad? You don't need a mother and I need someone to be with always, not just some nights."

"You make our age difference seem like fifty years, not ten."

"It's thirteen, Tad. That's a long time when the woman gets to be sixty-five and the man is only fifty-two."

"Think of the years in between, Marge."

"I have, believe me, but I've had most of my romantic ideas drained out of me. You were a marvelous surprise and I am very grateful."

"You won't reconsider staying?"

"Don't, Tad, please! I want to retain some dignity. I don't sleep around, as the saying goes."

"Could I call you when I get back to the States?"

When she looked into Tad's guileless face, her eyes filled with tears and she reached for his hand and gripped it tightly to help her control her emotions.

"Perhaps, but *only* perhaps, my dear Tad. Perhaps after the beguiling magic of this chaotic mountain world has faded—when we are back in our normal, humdrum lives and we want to reminisce, yes, then call, but, and I say this in the gentlest way possible, I will not sit by the phone waiting for your call, Tad."

Afterwards, at her apartment, she asked him to come in for a brandy.

Sitting quietly, sipping pensively, she asked, "Would you come to the plane with me tomorrow, Tad?"

He put down his glass and drew her to him. They lay quietly, talking until he left at midnight.

* * * *

Andrews had just returned to the hotel from seeing Marge off when his phone rang.

"Mr. Andrews, Rai here. I hope you are well?"

"Very, Mr. Rai. What news do you have?"

"I prefer to visit you, possibly at the Public Library, if that would be convenient?"

"Of course. What time, sir?"

"It is now moments after three o'clock, would four o'clock be too precipitous?"

"No, I believe we can do that. I will see you there, Mr. Rai. Thank you."

Tad called Claire and Harriet and they decided to get a quick bite at the hotel restaurant before heading for the library.

"Interesting," he said, as much to himself as to the women. "This is where Marge wanted to meet. This must be where Kathmandu-ers meet, apparently."

"Everybody's bugged these days, Tad," Claire told him.

He thought back to the nights he had spent with Marge—how she wanted the radio playing and would only whisper to him when she talked. He had thought that an intimate touch, if a bit unusual. She must have assumed she was bugged, poor thing. She was well off to be out of this crazy place, he realized.

They spotted Rai immediately upon entering the library. He had reserved a cubicle to the rear of the main reading room. Gesturing to Tad, he retreated into the room.

He formally greeted the women, and then proceeded to speak only to Tad.

"I have spoken with the responsible party in regard to Miss Mason. He assures me that under the circumstances you described, he will guarantee Miss Mason's safety and release. He is agreeable to having two Americans visit Miss Mason to verify her condition. He stipulates, however, that no one associated with the American government be a member of this team. Because the Communists must transport these men to Miss Mason's camp, a suitable airport far enough from Kathmandu, to assure the safety of their aircraft, be selected. The money, one million US dollars must be deposited in a Swiss bank to an account he will specify. I trust these advices will be satisfactory?" Rai waited expectantly for Tad to respond.

"What do you say, is that good enough?" Tad asked the two girls.

"Sounds good to me. I would have to warn your people that if the Commies try any tricks, they can expect to be annihilated," Claire added.

"I do not believe such a thing is conceivable. Mr. Pranchadra needs the money, he is not a fool, I assure you."

"Well, then, let's go. Harriet, you are free to get ready to go. Mr. Rai, Miss Vollmer will fly to the United States to discuss our arrangements with our employers."

"They do not yet know of these arrangements?" Rai, for all his sophistication, sounded shocked.

"No, but we don't anticipate a problem."

"Well, I trust not. My contact will take it very badly if this were to be another disappointment, I caution you."

"I hear you," Tad replied, feeling very vulnerable.

"When will I hear from you, sir?" Rai asked Tad.

"Hopefully within the week, Mr. Rai."

"And my commission for arranging this transaction?"

"It will be paid when the Commies are paid. It will also be in a Swiss bank in your name, released when everything is completed satisfactorily."

Mr. Rai nodded at the women and left.

Alone, the three stared at each other questioningly.

"Boy, he scares me to death when he talks darkly about what happens if we screw up." Claire whistled softy.

"We've gone too far to screw up!" Tad tried to sound reassuring.

They said goodbye to Harriet, each literally holding his breath that the precarious ledge they had climbed out on would hold just a little longer.

* * * *

Harriet used the phone on the plane to call her editor. Not sure of the hour in the US, she dialed his home.

"Hello," a hoarse female voice answered.

Harriet knew instantly that she must have wakened Joan, Frank's wife.

"Joan, I'm terribly sorry, I didn't know the time. This is Harriet Vollmer. I'm flying into Dulles today, or is it tomorrow? What time is it?"

"Oh, hello, Harriet. It's one-thirty in the morning. Everything all right, I hope?"

"Yes, great, thanks. I hate to do this to Frank, but I need to talk to him."

"Sure, of course. He is pretending to be asleep, but I'll get him."

There was a muffled conversation, then her boss came on the line.

"Vollmer, you can pick up your final check as soon as you land. Don't *ever* call me at this ungodly hour again!"

"Fine! I'll just file my story with *The Tribune*."

"So, bribe me. Hopefully you've learned *something* about the Mason fiasco?"

"Much more than something, Frank. We've arranged for her release."

There was a dead silence on the line.

"Vollmer, if this your idea of humor, you *are* in trouble!"

"No joke, Frank. That's the reason I'm calling. You will need to get the biggies together today, tomorrow or whenever this thing lands so that I can spill all this stuff to them. It will probably loosen a few bowels, but I believe they'll think it's worth it."

"Tell me more, you sexy, exciting, slice of fantastic pulchritude!"

"If you're going to talk dirty, I'm hanging up."

She told him the story from beginning to end, but even on the plane at forty thousand feet over somewhere in Asia, she was paranoid about unknown ears hearing any part of her story.

* * * *

Twenty-one hours later, Harriet had told the management group of *The Post* the same story, then had answered a short hour of questions. They were all satisfied that the Government had established the precedent for negotiating with the terrorists, so they were not concerned about any backlash. They were, however, nervous about the girl's safety during the tenuous period until the deal had been consummated. They anticipated that government officials would generate a lot of flack in defense of their own efforts.

Harriet stressed Rai's warning if these negotiations fell through which, of course, gave them further concern.

Although not having finalized exactly how they should proceed, the Chairman asked Frank and Harriet to go to both *The Sun* and *The Times* to bring them up to date. He would alert his counter-parts that they were coming, and that it was imperative that the meetings be held today, regardless of the time. He provided his private plane in order to expedite their appointments.

* * * *

Unnoticed by most readers, was a small notice in the Kathmandu paper stating that a native of Scotland, had been found unconscious outside the city limits of Rupaidia, India, a town on Nepal's border. The man had been hospitalized with a virulent case of malaria. Where he had come from was unknown. With no identity, the news was quickly forgotten.

The British Consul in New Delhi had, as a matter of routine, been contacted by Indian officials in Rupaidia concerning the Scot. A final comment on the report stated that the subject claimed Nepal as his home. In due course, when his disease had been medicated, the patient took a flight back to Kathmandu.

* * * *

Vollmer and Frank Saunders, her editor, completed their mission to the other two papers. The reactions were identical to that of The Post; each confident that they could legally usurp the government's secret and hesitant ransom initiative and effect Miss Mason's freedom.

The papers formed a select group of executives from each paper who would direct the ransom planning. Rather then threaten dire consequences for anyone who leaked their plans, they simply asked that everyone privy to the news Harriet Vollmer had brought back from Nepal give the papers three days to publish their stories.

Only an hour before the first edition that would carry the story were the final decisions agreed to: The papers would finance the one million dollar ransom money equally; a fund would be set up soliciting citizen support for Miss Mason, the money to be used for Tibetan relief; the two Americans who would determine Miss Mason's state of health would be named later. Unless otherwise delayed, the two would leave within three days.

The reason for the delay at the last minute concerned the men originally designated to go to Nepal.

* * * *

Sam had answered the phone on a Wednesday evening. Caroline had already gone to bed and he was dozing over a copy of *The New Yorker*.

"Yes, Sam Adams here. May I help you?"

"The Reverend Mr. Adams, this is Charles Biddle. I am Chairman of the Board of *The Baltimore Sun*. I apologize for calling you at this hour. I would not do so if it were not an urgent matter."

Sam's heart sank! Now fully awake, he thought, bad news about Rachel.

"That's fine, Mr. Biddle, I wasn't sleeping. You have my attention, sir?"

"This is good news, Father. To the best of our knowledge, Miss Mason is well. I am calling for another reason, however."

"Oh? What would that be?"

"I would like to talk to you at your earliest convenience, sir, preferably early tomorrow morning. Would that be possible?"

"Well, yes, I would be happy to see you in the morning, but you have me extremely curious at the moment."

"To be completely honest with you, I am at the Canvasback right now as I am calling you. If you would prefer, I could come up to the Rectory yet this evening?"

Sam's head was spinning; he looked at the clock; it was ten thirty.

"Well, I guess. Certainly, give us fifteen minutes. Do you know how to get here?"

"Yes, thanks, they have already told me here at the motel."

"Well, then, we'll look forward to seeing you shortly."

When he hung up, he reached for Caroline's shoulder.

"Caroline."

She had heard the mumble of his conversation, but had been able to go back to sleep.

"Caroline!" He increased his pressure on her shoulder.

"Yes, what is it?" Not irritated, but certainly unwilling to be wakened.

"Caroline, wake up, I have to tell you something important."

Now fully awake, she turned toward him, "What, Sam? Has someone died?"

"No, no. A Mr. Biddle who is Chairman of *The Baltimore Sun* is coming here in fifteen minutes."

"*What!*" Caroline sat bolt upright in bed and stared at her husband as though he were demented.

"It's true. I can't explain why, but it has to be urgent. Rachel is well so it can't be bad news. Let's get dressed!"

Caroline moaned, "Oh, goodness, my hair!"

"I don't think he is coming to grade us on our late-night appearance, my dear. Just put on a robe."

"Never! I'll be ready before you are."

They each pulled on casual clothes, then Sam went down and turned on the living room lights and those on the porch. He had no more than done so, when automobile lights illuminated the driveway.

"Caroline, he's here," he called.

She came downstairs still fussing with her hair.

Sam anticipated his guest by opening the door and greeting him.

Quickly settled, the polite small talk disposed of, Biddle began.

"I apologize once again, but I believe what I am about to tell you will explain the urgency." He, then, told them the complete story as related to him by Harriet Vollmer.

"The three papers will publish this story in the next two days. We would like to publish the names of those who will go to Nepal. They should be ones who have known Miss Mason, preferably one of them should be a doctor. We are suggesting that you, Father Adams, and a doctor here in Afton by the name of James Crawford be the two representatives. If this meets with your approval?"

Sam and Caroline sat in stunned silence.

"I realize this whole thing is moving so fast that few of us can keep track of it, but speed is essential, we believe."

Caroline was studying her husband's reaction to this astounding story. More personally, she thought of his suggested role in this bizarre affair. She saw a man whose face, though deeply lined, had good color, even at this hour; eyes with heavy sacs of age under them and his hair artfully combed so that the thin places were disguised. What was not readily visible was a man who had, not too long ago, recovered from a heart attack, whose heart was already stressed because of the divisive efforts of Lance Bosley, a man who still had no curate after more than five months, and, finally, a husband with whom she hoped to spend many more years. It was too much of a challenge, she knew.

"Well, what can I say? Astounding! You people have done a wonderful job, Mr. Biddle! As far as my part, of course I will go. Dr. Crawford is the ideal person to assess Rachel's condition, but he will have to answer for himself."

"Excuse me, Sam. I feel I need to participate. I don't think you, personally, are essential to this adventure. Of course, you would love to see Rachel as soon as possible, but I do not think, all things considered, that you should go. I won't enumerate the reasons for my opinion. I believe you are honest enough with yourself to come to the same conclusion, Sam. I will, of course, leave it up to you, but think carefully about all that is involved."

Sam quietly listened to his wife's position. He could not defend the idea that *he* was essential to the trip. It would be arduous, yet, childish as he knew it to be, he would welcome the challenge; it would be one of the most unique opportunities that anyone could be offered. Old enough, however, to recognize that he was romanticizing what was a deadly serious and highly hazardous venture, he had to concede that he might not be the man for the job. If not he, however, who?

"Alright, my more balanced half, I concede I may not be quite up to it. Who would you suggest?"

"How about my son? He is far more fit and he had gained some rapport with Rachel as well as gaining a little insight as to why she felt the need to go to Nepal in the first place. I suspect that if anyone has an incentive to go, it would be Russell."

Biddle listened to their exchange.

"Does your son live locally, Mrs. Adams?"

"No, he lives in Naples, Florida. Ironically, he has been here for the last month only leaving for Florida yesterday."

"It will be essential for us to determine his availability as soon as possible, if you feel he is the appropriate person to make the trip."

"Sam, what do you think?"

"I think it is a good idea. I think he should be the one to go."

"Fine! Do you think we might call him right now?"

"Oh, sure, he usually watches Dave Letterman, so he would be awake. Shall I call?"

"If you would, Mrs. Adams, please."

Caroline dialed the number, but soon got his answering machine.

"Hmm, well he's either out late or on the road. I have his cell phone number, I'll try that."

Caroline was thwarted the second time when his cell phone did not ring at all, so then she called his home phone again and left a message.

"I'm sorry. That's a bit unusual. I should hear from him in the morning, however."

"That's fine. I will need to talk to Dr. Crawford in the morning. Would you think it would be kinder for you to alert the doctor, Father? We could even meet here, if it were convenient?"

"Yes, that would be a good idea. What time is it?"

"Almost midnight," Caroline replied.

"I hate to call him at this hour, Mr. Biddle, he gets so many late-night calls as it is. I would rather call him first thing in the morning."

"Certainly. Well, we've done some ground-breaking, but we've also got some loose ends." He rose and shook their hands. "I'm sorry this is so sort of cloak and dagger-ish. I hope you are able to sleep for whatever is left of the night. Thank you so much! You will call me when we can see Dr. Crawford?"

"Yes, of course. Thank you for all you are doing for Rachel, Mr. Biddle. We needed something like this to happen; everything seemed to be going around in circles getting nowhere."

"We're not home free yet, but I think we've got the key. Good night, sleep well."

Sam and Caroline sat together for another hour sipping glasses of milk, rehashing what Biddle had told them.

* * * *

The meeting with Jim Crawford was short and enthusiastically affirmative.

"I will welcome the opportunity to see Rachel, as soon as possible," he told Biddle.

Biddle confirmed that Jim had a valid passport and, thanking them all profusely, got in his car and returned to Baltimore.

All that remained was to hear from Russell.

As the hours dragged by without having heard, his mother became more and more concerned. Finally, in desperation, she redialed his home phone and he answered.

"Hi, Mom. How are you?"

"Russell, what is happening with your phone? I called you last night on this phone and when I got no response, I called your cell phone and it didn't work at all."

"I've had trouble with both of them, Mom, I'm sorry. We had a terrific electrical storm yesterday and it's caused all sorts of trouble. Why'd you call?"

"Russ, things are about to open up in Rachel's situation. Three of the big papers, *The Times, The Washington Post,* and *The Baltimore Sun* are going to publish a special edition late tonight that will force the government to allow the papers to provide the ransom money and get Rachel released."

"Holy Toledo! Wonderful!"

"As part of an agreement the papers made with the Communists, two Americans, not associated with the government, would be allowed to meet Rachel to determine whether she is in good health. I have suggested you as one of the two Americans—you and Dr. Crawford whom you met when you were here."

"Oh, bless you, bless you, Mom! Wonderful! When do we leave?"

"I don't know yet, but it will be soon. Your passport is up to date, I hope?"

"Sure is! I used it when I went to Finland."

"Good! Well, I need to call the gentleman from *The Sun* and tell him that you are willing to go."

"Willing! Must you say it that way? How about *raring*?"

"Calm down, Russell. It is a long, difficult and very serious mission. It will not be a walk in the park."

"I know, Mom, it's just that it will be such a relief to finally do *something*!"

"Bye for now, Russ. I love you."

"I love you, too, Mom, and thanks!"

CHAPTER EIGHTEEN

Rachel could not sleep. It had been a normal day, even a better day than most because no one had died and the black helicopter had not brought any new wounded. Yet, something was causing her to lie awake, staring at the gray canvas sagging over her head. Sleep had never been a problem since she'd arrived at Botta's camp. Her days were normally so full that she fell asleep as soon as she lay down. Tonight was different for some reason. In her struggle to sleep, and against her better judgment, she allowed herself to think about Afton. What were Sam and Caroline doing? How was the discussion of the new church building progressing? Had Xavier been able to buy Sam's car yet? Would he go to college in the fall? What about Lisa? Had her parents reconciled so that she could go home? If she had gone home, what about Xavier? Had Sam's new curate, Farley (was that his name?) started?

And Russell, what about Russell? What were her feelings about him after all this time? If he were suddenly to appear, how would she feel toward him, or he about her? Would she have changed? How could she not have been changed? Would he still like her? How would she be able to have the same feelings after all she'd been through? Could she turn these experiences into something positive when she returned to a "normal" life? What if she never were freed? When she confronted this ultimate question, her mind retreated and reran the same questions over and over again, unable to deal with that too real a possibility.

Exhausted, she threw off the damp sheet and walked outside. The moon was full, tingeing the trees with a silvery luminescence, the air heavy from a rain that had fallen in the early evening. She shivered at the feel of the damp soil on her feet. Preoccupied by the endlessly circling questions, she raised her head, as though by an ultimate command, to see the moonlit brilliance of Dhaulagiri looming over her. The sense of its untainted purity seemed to shame her pitiful, self-indulgent questions. In the thrall of its magnetism, she could only walk toward it.

Why did the mountain seem so powerful a force? Why did she let it draw her closer, almost against her will? Was there some hidden truth in its power? Scott had known its terrible attraction; how else to see it than a powerful and dangerous drug, deadly for Scott. Or was it, rather, a meaningless form of hypnotism, over with the slap of a hand, a thrill, but nothing learned? Or could, on the other hand, its purity wash away the stagnant, weary self-doubts of a lifetime; allow a vision beyond the ability of eyes to see; a baptism that purged the soul and gave rebirth? Was its awe-full silence she felt so strongly, be beckoning her to embrace a new vision of her life? Or was she only a lonely and confused soul creating storybook illusions?

Overcome with the never-ending questions with no certain answers, she knelt, unable to find her way. In the brilliance and purity of the snow-covered mountain, with tears in her eyes, she prayed to a God who had created this mystical, unknowable force.

* * * *

Dr. Botta had heard Rachel leave the tent and, concerned, he had gotten up when she had not returned. The light from the moon showed him a wide area of the campsite; Rachel was not to be seen. Striking off randomly toward the mountain, he had not gone more than two hundred yards when he thought he saw her, bent over on her knees. He approached her quietly, but when she did not respond to his presence, he put his hand on her shoulder.

"Rachel?"

Her response was as if from a long way off. "Yes, Sam, here I am."

"Rachel, dear, let me take you back to your tent, it is too cool and damp here. You'll catch a cold. Come with me, won't you?" He lifted her to her feet.

Looking at the man she had gotten to know like a father, her eyes reflected fear.

"Where are you taking me?"

"Rachel, I am Dr. Botta. You are tired; let me take you back to your tent.

Slowly, she seemed to regain an awareness of where she was.

"I'm so sorry, Dr. Botta, I guess I must have walked in my sleep. I don't seem to remember why I came out here. I am sorry to have disturbed you."

Botta listened to her words, but he heard the deeper sound of distress. He knew she had been working too hard, almost fanatically, filling in every waking moment to escape the reality of her imprisonment. He had cautioned her several times to take time away from the daily ugliness to refresh herself; to walk in the forests, spend time simply looking at the beauty around her, but she seemed afraid to give herself time to think. He blamed himself for selfishly using her single-mindedness to his own advantage.

When they reached the tent, Rinchen met them. She could immediately see that the girl had cried and seemed confused.

"Rachel, come with me for just a minute. You are tired. My monstrous husband is destroying you. Come, lie down and let me sing to you." She took Rachel's hand and led her to bed and helped her lie down. She shooed her husband away and softly sang ancient Tibetan songs her mother had sung to her long ago.

Rachel slept late into the morning, the first time she had not risen with the Botta's since she had recovered her vision. Botta thought little of it, knowing she had not had much sleep the night before, but he did ask Rinchen to check on Rachel as she was able.

When Rinchen looked in on her, Rachel's forehead was feverish and the sheet was damp. She found her husband and told him, but he was unable to go to her until noon. As soon as he entered the tent, he sensed a problem. Rachel was awake, her face flushed and her body shaking with chills and fever. It might not be malaria, he thought, but she had the classical symptoms.

* * * *

Joseph Callahan, one of the largest stockholders on *The Baltimore Sun's* Board of Directors, had been a very substantial contributor to the President's 2004 campaign. It had only been in the last six months that he had become disenchanted with the President. He had watched his ratings drop in all the public opinion polls, especially on Iraq. His greatest concern, however, was the ballooning deficit. It became clear to him that the President was bent on hewing, slavishly, to his own single-minded course, regardless of the consequences. Callahan had made his opinions abundantly known to the few Administration officials willing to listen, but to no avail. The Nepal Conspiracy, as Rachel's captivity became known at *The Sun*, was the final straw for Callahan.

Fully aware, however, that the mission *The Sun* and the two other papers were embarked on, was fraught with hazardous political implications, he had convinced the owners of the papers that one last effort should be made to gain some measure of support from the government rather then have to fight them all the way. They all knew that the official reaction to their plan could be vicious.

Two days before the scheduled special edition was to run, Callahan called the White House and requested a meeting with the President on matters he considered "of the greatest urgency."

The White House Counsel replied that he and the Vice President would see his group at three o'clock that afternoon. Callahan replied that it was urgent that he see the President himself. There was an hour's delay that Callahan assumed was spent debating the value of his contributions, then he received word that the President could see his group, briefly, at five o'clock.

The three Chairmen and Callahan arrived promptly at the White House at four-thirty. At quarter of five, they were ushered into the Oval Office.

With the President were the Secretary of State, the Vice President, the White House Counsel, and the Director of the CIA.

"Joe! How nice to see you again! Gentlemen sit down, please. I'm afraid time is terribly important, as I'm sure it is with you, too."

"Mr. President," Callahan began, "I want these gentlemen to tell you what we believe is *terribly important* for you to know." Callahan had deliberately used the words "terribly important" with the same emphasis the President had used.

"Certainly, certainly! And I'm very eager to hear what you have to say, gentlemen."

"Mr. President." The Chairman of the Board of *The New York Times* had been selected to speak for the group. "We have been concerned about the seeming confusion that exists in the government's attempt to gain Miss Mason's release in Nepal."

"Nepal, yes, I, too, am concerned. Go ahead."

"It seems that elements of the government, shall we call them, have acted independently to gain her release, but that, seemingly, the negotiations are being conducted secretly in order to avoid conflict with your stated policy that there can be no negotiation with terrorists."

"Exactly, I am resolved that we will not negotiate with terrorists."

"But, Mr. President, evidence shows that government negotiations have existed from the very first and that the inability to gain Miss Mason's release has been the amount of money the Communists are seeking, not the fact that they are terrorists."

The President looked at the Director of the CIA for help, "Is that true, George?"

"I believe the gentleman has used the word "elements of the government." That would be my understanding, sir," he replied.

"So, some of our people are trying to be heroes, gentlemen," the President smiled dismissively.

"I may not have phrased my statement clearly; it is our understanding from first hand accounts, that the negotiations have your approval, Mr. President, and it is at the highest level that the maximum ransom figure has been known."

There was an embarrassed silence.

The Vice President broke the silence, "We certainly will look into this, Mr. President. I believe some of this information has been distorted."

Callahan was getting impatient with the polite puffball that was being played.

"Mr. President, within these walls, let's just level with each other. You knew what was going on. You're to be commended for trying to help Miss Mason, but I'm afraid you just got all tangled up in your own underwear. What's the difference between $350,000 and $1,000,000 once you start playing footie with the Commies? Tell the President what we are going to do, Ted." He handed the ball back to the *Times'* Chairman.

Color rose in the President's face and his lieutenants found the pattern of the carpet to be extremely interesting.

"Mr. President, our papers are going to pay the one million dollar ransom to the Communists. We believe that our freedom to act in this way is determined by your precedent; that you, secretly, have contradicted your policy of not negotiating with terrorists in this case. We are, therefore, going to publish a special edition of our papers tomorrow stating our intentions. We will assume that, with the reasoning we have given you, we might count on your assistance if there were a need as far as the Nepalese government is concerned. We hope to make this as non-contentious as possible."

George Templeton, CIA, spoke up, "There is nothing we can do from here, gentlemen. King Gyanendra would not permit such a large amount of money to fall into the enemy's hands."

"Well, that's true as far as it goes, George, but how many millions have we already poured into Gyanendra's coffers? Is it twenty million or more? We don't need to advertise the amount of ransom we will pay."

The President had been getting visibly restless, "Gentlemen, I am embarrassed to say that I have another important meeting. I believe we can find common ground, George. Let's all put our shoulders to the wheel and get this poor girl back home to the good old US of A. You will excuse me, Joe? The Vice President will work with you to find a common path. Dick, you know our position, do what you can to make this work." He shook Callahan's hand, nodded at the other three and he was gone.

After he had left, the Vice President asked to read a copy of the story to be printed. When he had finished, he put down his glasses and studied each of the newspapermen.

"Obviously, this is a venomous story and we take grave exception to its statements and implications. You must not use the word "precedent" as your grounds for entering into this ransom robbery. There can be no allusion to the President's involvement in the negotiations; there is too much involved worldwide for this kind of slander to be implied. And, you must not mention the amount of money involved."

Aware that the President had given them wide latitude to proceed with the girl's release, they were taken aback by the censoring the Vice President was attempting to impose.

"Mr. Vice President, we understood the President to give us permission to proceed with few constraints. We cannot, in good conscience, agree to your restrictions. First of all, it is clearly understood that the negotiations were authorized at the highest level of this Administration. If the President were not involved, it would have to be you yourself, sir. As we volunteered, we will not mention the amount of money involved, but it will find the light of day from any number of sources, I'm afraid."

Staring malevolently at the newspapermen, from under his brows, the Vice President growled. "Choose your own poison, gentlemen. I would caution you, however, that what goes around comes around. Charges that cannot be verified lead to very serious trouble. We will have our own investigation of the negotiations and publish the truthful version of this miscarriage of justice."

"Sir? With all due respect…."

"Gentlemen, I believe you understand my position. The meeting is over as far as I am concerned. Good afternoon." The Vice President left the room followed obediently by the Secretary of State, George Templeton of the CIA, and the President's legal counsel.

An usher came into the office and led them to the exit area.

Everyone in the group was fuming at the crude ending of the meeting. They went back to the Executive Offices of *The Post* and made the final decisions about the story. They agreed not to mention the amount of the ransom. They would, however, make it plain that someone in the Administration with the "highest authority" had approved the negotiations.

Satisfied that they had shone a bright light on the tangled, secret negotiations by opening it to the light of day, they parted with a feeling of satisfaction, but not without the nervous feeling that the Vice President might yet derail their efforts.

* * * *

Back in Kathmandu, when Claire and Tad received Harriet's "birthday" cable, they immediately contacted Rai. He treated the news without apparent enthusiasm, but promised to contact Prachandra as soon as possible. In the meantime, they learned that a new CIA man had been assigned to Nepal, Edward Tugwell. His first act was to call Claire and Tad to his office.

Tugwell kept them waiting for forty-five minutes before he had them ushered in by a new "Miss Sessions."

"Well, this is a real thrill for me to meet you two super sleuths. I understand you are the heroes who will rescue our forlorn prisoner?" Tugwell's tone of voice dripped with venom.

"Mr. Tugwell, if you have something to say to us, please say it. We do not have to be subjected to your form of ridicule." In retrospect, Claire realized this was not the best attitude to take with such a man.

"My, my! Touchy aren't we? O.K., here it is. I will have you watched twenty-four seven. If you so much as look cross-eyed, I'll have you sent home. Your people want to play hardball; I'll show them how it's played. Fair enough?"

Tad stood up and approached Tugwell, "Who in the hell do you think you are, talking to us like that? You have no right whatsoever. If you harass us in anyway, you'll be extremely sorry." Tad's size and tone of voice left little doubt as to his intentions.

"Just test me, little boy, just test me! Alright, I'm busy, you are dismissed."

Neither of them moved to leave until, at their leisure, they walked calmly out leaving his door open.

On the street, Tad looked at his companion, "Well, I guess I didn't think they could top Durgan."

"I don't like this, Tad. We are really isolated now. I know he will censor our cables so how can we communicate. Why must everything be so difficult?"

"I would guess that our people have ruffled official feathers by their intention to go public and this is harass-the-little-guy time. It will be annoying, but it can't last for long."

They found a message from Rai waiting for them when they got back to the hotel. He asked them to meet him at the library at two o'clock.

Following the same routine as their previous session, he closed the door of the cubicle. Everything they had proposed was agreeable with Prachandra, he told them, but Prachandra wanted to know who the two Americans would be and insisted on bringing them to his camp in his own helicopter.

"He also warns against landing the Americans in Kathmandu, sure that Gyanendra would try to prevent them from leaving," Rai reported. "Therefore, your people will have to find a suitable airport farther west in Nepal or in India where he can ferry them to his camp. It is important that this detail be worked out, as you can understand."

"We will get back to you as soon as we know something, Mr. Rai," Tad said, with a conviction that he really did not feel.

After Rai had left, Tad turned to Claire, "How the devil are we going to communicate these details without Tugwell finding out everything we plan to do?"

"I don't know for sure, but I'm thinking that one of us needs to get out of Kathmandu so that we have some freedom to tie up these details with the people in the States."

"Sure, but then *we* can't communicate. I wonder if our cell phones would work over a couple of hundred miles?"

"I don't know, but I left mine home anyway. I think I'm going to go to Pokhara, then sort of disappear to the border town of Nepalganj. I can send cables from there."

"How do you know Nepalganj?"

"I went there a couple of months ago. Nepal and India had a meeting to discuss immigration control. It's kind of a dump, but it has some geographic virtues."

"I'd rather go, Claire; it sounds kind of iffy."

246

"You would do better here, Tad. Tugwell can't physically intimidate you as he might try to do with me."

"Hmm, possibly."

"The other thing is Harriet will be coming back, as far as we know, and will know all that has gone on in the meantime. She'll need a strong right arm."

* * * *

Sam and Caroline read and re-read the special edition of *The Sun*. It wasn't until the second time through that they realized that neither Jim nor Russell's names had been mentioned as the two Americans who would go to Nepal.

"What do you think that means, Sam?"

"I have no idea. They were the logical choices and the gentleman from *The Sun* seemed agreeable. Maybe we should call them and find out?"

"I think I will. Russell is due here any minute and he will really be upset if they've decided to use someone else."

She dialed the number Biddle had left them. A secretary answered and said that Mr. Biddle would return her call in a few minutes; he was on another call.

"Mrs. Adams, Charles Biddle. I'm sorry I could not take your call. I was, as a matter fact, about to call you. I can guess why you are calling— the omission of your son's name and Dr. Crawford's?"

"Yes, that is the reason I called."

"Mrs. Adams, I have asked one of our people to come to Afton and discuss with you more of the details of our mission than were available when we first talked. Nothing has changed as far as your son and Dr. Crawford are concerned. Frank Saunders will be calling you in just a few minutes to arrange a convenient time to talk."

"Well, thank you Mr. Biddle. My son will be arriving this afternoon and I know he will be eager to get any information you may have."

"Things are working out, Mrs. Adams, but there are twists and turns."

"I'm sure there are. Well, thanks for your call. We will look forward to Mr. Saunders' call."

She hung up with a puzzled expression on her face.

"They are sending a man here to explain some more of the details about the trip, Sam."

The ring of the phone cut her off. It was Frank Saunders who asked if he could see them early tomorrow morning; they agreed on nine-thirty.

Russell arrived at five-thirty and immediately raised the same question; he had read *The Times* account.

Reassured, he said, "Well, as long as nothing has changed, I'm OK. I suspect this whole deal is rather complicated, especially with the government looking over their shoulder. For example, how and who is coordinating this with the Communists, for goodness sake? You can't just make a phone call and talk to them."

"I'm sure I don't know. This gets more and more like a John Grisham yarn by the minute and it makes me nervous," Sam grumbled.

They alerted Jim Crawford to the nine-thirty meeting the next day. He had been so busy he had failed to note the omission of their names in the article.

* * * *

Promptly at nine-thirty a car drove up to the Rectory. Jim Crawford had arrived minutes earlier.

"Mr. Saunders, welcome to suburban Baltimore. Thanks for coming," Sam greeted him.

"Probably not too far from the truth in another fifty years, if that. Good morning, sir." They shook hands.

Caroline had made coffee and had bought small, unglazed doughnuts. They settled in the sunroom and after casual small talk, Saunders began.

"You all know the broad outlines of what we propose to do. Some of the details have become a little more difficult than we at first thought— not surprising. We are shooting for your departure, gentlemen," he nodded at Russell and Jim, "on Saturday afternoon. Will that work for you?"

Both nodded that it would.

"Great! Now, to the nitty-gritty: you will fly in Mr. Biddle's private jet.

Because it only has a range of thirty-eight hundred miles, you'll have to do it in several hops. You will travel in luxury, however, I assure you. A commercial flight is scheduled to leave Dulles carrying two men to Nepal who will present themselves as the two Americans who will pretend to be charged with verifying Miss Mason's well being.

Why this bit of subterfuge, you ask? We anticipate difficulty in Kathmandu. We have been led to believe that the King, Gyanendra, will endeavor to prohibit these two men from leaving the city on the pretext that he will not permit such a large ransom be paid to the Communists. There is some indication that someone from the Administration prompted this action.

In order to free Miss Mason, per our agreement with the Communists, we will have to fly you two gentlemen from Qatar to a smaller airport in Lucknow, India, toward the western part of Nepal. There, the Communists will send a helicopter to take you to Miss Mason. In this way, we believe we can avoid any unpleasantness.

We don't know the exact time it will take to reach Lucknow, but we think it will take the better part of two days. Before leaving Qatar, you will contact our man, a Mr. Choate, in Lucknow, and tell him of your estimated time of arrival. He will be in contact with the Communists as far as the helicopter is concerned. Are you thoroughly confused? I assure you that this will all be given to you in written form before you take off."

"Where will we leave from, what airport here in the states?' Russell asked.

"Probably Baltimore, but that could change; we intend that flight to be completely secret."

"I'm not clear about Rachel," Jim asked, "Will she return with us?"

"In all probability, yes, unless there are problems."

"Like?"

"The release of the ransom money from the Swiss bank."

"Then what? How does she get out?"

"We'll have to go back in and get her."

"What other problems do you see around the corner?"

"Only what our friendly government chooses to throw up as road blocks. They've just named a new CIA agent-in-charge in Kathmandu who has a rough-as-a-cob reputation."

"Well, we'll soon see, the sooner the better!" Russell said.

"If there are no further questions, I'll get back on my horse and go back to Baltimore. You two gentlemen should stay close to your cell phones; I will notify you instantly when I am told the departure day, hour, and place. Incidentally, the Commies will insist on seeing your passports before they take you to their camp, just be sure you have them handy!"

Sam, reflecting on the complicated plan after Saunders had left, admitted he would have been too old for all that was involved. How, he wondered, did simple, innocent Rachel get ensnared in such an ugly, unbelievable affair? Her naïve hope to find a personal peace in Nepal had turned out to be anything but.

* * * *

Saunders called Russell and Jim at nine that night.

"Well, it gets trickier and trickier," Russell reported as he hung up the phone. "They want us to fly out of the Frederick, Maryland airport at ten tomorrow night, and to rent a car, not drive there in our own car, thus leaving no trail, or at least a trial harder to follow."

"They certainly are being cautious, but that's all to the good," Sam responded. "Well, Russell, you are about to embark on adventure that, God willing, will return our Rachel to us safe and sound. You know you have our prayers."

CHAPTER NINETEEN

Thankful they had the remodeling of the church to divert them, Sam and Caroline watched it grow to completion. Having acceded to Caroline's plea that he not go to Nepal, he tried doubly hard to concentrate on parish matters.

The roof of the new building had been shingled over, the walls moved outward and the original stained glass scenes reset. What remained was the completion of the bell tower and a new floor in the nave. Each day he watched as the tower rose above the entry; where the old steeple had appeared truncated because of its lack of height and round dome, the new belfry rose higher, lending a gracefully high counterpoint to the wide, gull-like roofline.

Caroline took particular pleasure as her gift to Rachel rose.

The contractor estimated that he would be finished in another thirty days, but, as always with an "if." Apparently the new bell had cracked in the casting process requiring a new one to be made, but he still hoped to be finished in thirty days.

This prompted Sam to consider how the new building should be celebrated.

* * * *

The day after Tad and Claire had concluded that she should leave Kathmandu, Tad received an unexpected call.

"Tad, this is Ben Choate, with *The Washington Post* calling. I'm staying at the hotel. Could I come to your room for a chat?"

Taken aback at a call from an unknown person from *The Post*, and becoming more cautious every day, Tad replied, "*The Washington Post?* Harriet Vollmer is your correspondent here."

"Yes, she is, but I'm replacing her on an interim basis, that's what I'd like to talk to you about."

"Do you know *The New York Times* correspondent?"

"Claire Tremont? Only by name."

"I'd like her to be involved in our conversation."

"That would be a good idea, save me doing two sessions."

"All right. I'm free now, if you want to come over."

Still puzzled by the call, Tad alerted Claire who quickly came to his room.

When Choate arrived, they saw a middle-aged man, bearded and carrying far too much weight to be an active correspondent.

"Hi, guys. Let me immediately dispel any idea you may have that I am an ace correspondent. I am a lawyer and have worked for *The Post* for ten years. The reason I'm here rather then Harriet is that I'm just a messenger boy. It is the safest way to bring you up to date and cross some other t's that needed crossing."

Ben rehearsed for them the sequence of events that had been planned. He told them of the difficulty they anticipated when the two men arrived in Kathmandu and how they deliberately planned this to obscure their real efforts. He told them about the alternate plan to send Dr. Crawford and Mr. Pickering by private plane to Lucknow, India, and their eventual pick-up by the Communists to take them to Miss Mason's camp.

"It all sounds doable, *but* we desperately need the method of contacting the Communists. They are the only way to Miss Mason's camp, yet we have no way of contacting them directly except through the contact you two have established. It is too risky for us to rely solely on this man at this stage. We *have* to know the method of communicating with them? Can we get it?"

"We can try. Mr. Rai is deliberately vague on many things. I'm sure it's to protect his own interests, but I can understand why we need the information. We've wondered about this gap in the chain ourselves," Claire replied.

"Get a hold of him, please! We need to get that information as soon as possible, the success of this whole deal depends on it."

Tad told him that their contact point was through Miss Sakya, a "friend" of Mr. Rai's.

Assuming that Tugwell would have Andrews and Claire watched, they agreed to meet in an hour at The Kathmandu Guest House, one of Nepal's favorite hotels. Tad requested one of their curtained, private alcoves. These "private dining rooms" were artfully designed in such a way that each had a rear entry, presumably to make a rendezvous with certain ladies less noticeable. Tad and Ben reversed the intended purpose, sneaking out the rear door, leaving a lady waiting. Claire, reluctantly, watched them go, keeping her fingers crossed that they would find Rai.

Miss Sakya greeted Tad's knock and apologetically told them that her fiancé, Mr. Rai, was not there at the moment. Displaying a thick billfold, Ben suggested that she might know where he might be found. Hesitating only briefly, she told them that an address on Four Temple Street might be a place to look. Handing her a fifty-dollar bill, the two left and hailed a rickshaw.

Four Temple Street had an up-town appearance compared to Miss Sakya's modest quarters. Knocking at the door, Rai, himself, answered. Visibly disturbed that his home had been compromised, he reluctantly let them in.

Choate made short work of his demand for the necessary method of contact. He told Rai that there would be no pay-off for him without it.

"Why may I not communicate with them myself when the two gentlemen arrive in Kathmandu?"

"Because it could become too problematical." Choate did not choose to tell Rai of their alternate plans. "We will not proceed until we have this information!" Ben's flat, unemotional demand gambled much, but there was no alternative.

"I would reluctantly give this information, but you can see how this jeopardizes the fee I hoped to receive for performing this service?"

"Mr. Rai, you are dealing with honorable men, not thugs and

scoundrels. We will pay you exactly the amount we agreed to, but only if you give us this information."

Rai decided he had no alternative so he took a piece of paper and wrote down the radio frequency and call letters to Lawa's camp.

Thanking Rai profusely, Choate and Tad retraced their steps to the restaurant and entered by the rear door. They rejoined Claire who had shredded three napkins in anxious anticipation of their return.

"You have no shame, madam! Entertaining *two* men in your little love nest," Tad chided her.

Ben told her they had been successful and that that called for a bottle of champagne to celebrate a vital victory. Then he proceeded to tell them that he would have to leave Kathmandu so that he could get to Lucknow with the radio contact information to give it to Crawford and Pickering when they arrived. Claire told him the route she had thought of using: Pokhara to Nepalanj to Lucknow.

Choate booked a six A.M. flight to Pokhara the next day and so was gone before Tugwell was aware he had arrived.

* * * *

Botta had monitored Rachel very closely as the fever raged through her body. He did not have the most modern medicines, but he had years of familiarity with malaria. He was quite certain she suffered from the disease, but there were peculiarities with her sickness that made him question whether his diagnosis had been right. The speed with which she recovered made him more uncertain. After four days, Rachel's fever lessened and her eyes cleared. When she took more interest in her food, Botta was sure the worst was over. Lawa made regular visits to check on her progress and seemed relieved to hear she was recovering.

On the seventh day, Rachel walked tentatively and began the slow process of gaining her strength back.

During one of Botta's visits to her bedside, she asked, hesitantly, about the night he had found her far from her tent.

"Dr. Botta, the night I first got the fever, you found me outside. I don't remember what I was doing out there. Did I say anything to you?"

"No. You did mistake me for a man you called Sam Adams, but you were in the early stages of your fever by then, I believe."

"I did, really? Dr. Botta, I never have told you, or anyone else for that matter, that I am an Episcopal priest. I didn't think it was important, but I want you to know. Sam Adams was the Rector of the parish I left to come out here."

Botta was not, visibly, surprised by her revelation.

"I could tell you were a person of deep convictions, but I did not know you were ordained to the priesthood. I have admitted to you, I believe, that I am not a religious man, Miss Mason, but I am in awe of the unprejudiced sacrifice you have made to these poor men and women. Some would have refused to help as you have, defending some hollow, rote principle. You have given everything you have to help these poor people regardless of the stigma of being "the enemy", seeing only their humanity, not their label."

"It is because of your example, Dr. Botta. You are the reason I have survived at all. I am content to stay here and work with you until this horrible war is over."

"You are too generous, Miss Mason. No, if it were to be that you are allowed to return to the outside world, you must go. You have much to give to the world and are far too young to be buried here. I am different; I am seventy-one years old and cannot live forever. I will stay, but you must go, if your God allows it to happen."

Rachel shut her eyes to stop the tears. She could not bear the thought of leaving this gentle, dedicated man.

Then, quietly, he said, "If, when this is all over and Rinchen is free, you could be of assistance to her, I would be deeply indebted to you."

Gripping the old doctor's hand, she whispered hoarsely, "You know that I will."

* * * *

Sam had asked Charles Biddle to keep them abreast of any news, good or bad, whatever the time of day or night. Biddle had cautioned them that it would take at least seventy-two hours for them to expect to hear anything. It was as stressful a time as either of them had ever experienced. To get some relief during the hours of waiting, they listened to all their favorite symphonies, then took turns reading to each other. They allowed themselves to go to the church to watch the final installation of the new bell, but even with that "outing" they were within earshot of the cell phone.

Finally, seventy-five hours later, by their clock, they received a call from Charles Biddle's secretary. It was brief, "Mr. Biddle asked me to call to tell you his plane has landed in India. That is all the information he has at the moment."

"Thank you so much!" Sam exclaimed.

They went to the church and knelt to pray; the first hurdle had been cleared.

* * * *

The commercial flight from Qatar arrived in Kathmandu on schedule at eight in the evening. Tugwell and several of his staff had waited impatiently until the passengers had entered the building and were lined up to have their visas checked. His counterparts in Washington had cabled that the two men's names that were assumed to be the party to contact Miss Mason, were Stanley Good and Harry Warner—employees of *The Washington Post* newspaper. When the two men had reached the Inspector's desk, Tugwell asked them to step around the kiosk and follow him. Seemingly unconcerned, Good and Warner followed him to a private room at the rear of the check-in area.

"Please sit down, gentlemen. My name is Tugwell. I am the Station Chief of the CIA in Kathmandu. I have information that you are here to contact a Miss Rachel Mason and to seek her release. Is that the case?"

Stanley Good looked bewildered. Harry Warner, his eyebrows highly arched, appeared equally confused.

"Mr. Tugwell, I have no idea what you are talking about. My friend, Stanley and I are here to do some trekking and maybe a little night activity." Good winked at Tugwell. "We don't know a Miss Mason. Are our passports and visas not in order?"

"I do not have time for games, gentlemen. If you refuse to cooperate, I will have to place you in temporary custody. What you are party to is a crime in this country. The King is aware of your plans and he will not permit you to stay in Nepal. I have to refuse your admittance and send you back on the next plane. Is this clear to you?"

"It is absolutely not clear at all and I resent the implications you are making. What crime? What King and what plans are you talking about?"

"You both work for *The Washington Post* newspaper, do you not?"

"Why, yes, of course, how would you know that?"

"And what are two *Washington Post* reporters here to do, pray tell?"

"I have told you we are here to do some trekking. We are not, incidentally, reporters. Stan is the Assistant Manager of Advertising, and I handle the Obituary section."

The two "decoys" continued to harass Tugwell until he was convinced that they were too ignorant or stupid to be a part of the ransom plan. He was sufficiently aggravated with them that he ordered the local police to confine them until they could be loaded on the next plane back to the US.

Enraged that these men had not been properly identified as the agents of the newspapers at Dulles, he could not do anything but cable back to the Pentagon that some asinine error had been made.

* * * *

When the graceful, silver Gulfstream had rolled to a stop, Curtis, the co-pilot, called to Russell, "I think you might try to reach Mr. Choate now. It's ten o'clock and dark as pitch so the Commies will have to wait until tomorrow, but no harm in having Mr. Choate alert them."

Russell called the number he had for Ben Choate and he came on the line immediately.

"Mr. Choate, Russell Pickering. How are you?"

"Boy! Am I glad to hear your voice! You are in Lucknow, I gather?"

"Yes, just landed. Do you think you should call the people at Rachel's camp?"

"I will, Russell. Let me do that and I'll call you right back. Give me your number."

Russell handed the phone to Curtis, "Wants the plane's phone number, Curtis."

That done, they waited for Choate's reply.

Minutes later he called to say the Communist helicopter would be in Lucknow by 9:00 AM tomorrow."

"Thanks, Ben. Hope to see you soon."

"Well, that's done. I guess we sleep on the plane, Curtis," Russell asked?

"Without a visa you have no choice. We have to check in and park this baby."

"You guys did a marvelous job," Jim Crawford told the pilot and Curtis. This is one beautiful airplane!"

"We stretched its limits, I believe, sir," Steve Bassett, the pilot said, with a weary smile.

* * * *

Up at dawn the next day, Jim and Russell showered and shaved not knowing how long they'd be away nor what the sanitary conditions of the camp would be like.

Russell forced himself to think about the strange scenery, the red ball of a sun streaming through the oval window of the plane, the odor of the coffee the crew was brewing, the crackle of the plane's radio, anything to keep from anticipating his meeting with Rachel. How could he prepare himself to see this woman he had known only briefly in Maryland almost six months ago—one who had been forced to live what kind of life he shuddered to imagine. What would they have to say to each other?

Then his common sense surfaced briefly; it was his job to go to her, see that she was safe, and arrange for her return. He was not there to turn into some sort of mooning adolescent; he had a job to do. But his common sense could not prevail very long before his imagination took over again. Time would not move! When would the bloody helicopter arrive? He looked outside for the umpteenth time.

"Russell, sit down, boy. You are making *me* nervous," Jim Crawford laughed.

"Jim, do you have any sedatives?"

"Yes, I do, but I'm not giving you any. We're almost there, Russ, take a deep breath or two."

Very shortly, they heard the roar of a helicopter's rotors. The pilot was given permission to land in the area of the Gulfstream, so Crawford and Russell shook hands with their crew and walked toward the ugly black aircraft.

They were met by the two oriental pilots who immediately made sign language gestures indicating "passports?"

They produced their documents and then tried hard to restrain themselves as the pilots chattered excitedly, studying the pictures, looked at their faces, then back to the pictures. Finally they seemed satisfied that they were who the document proclaimed them to be.

Pointing for them to get into the Vietnam vintage Huey, they revved the rotors and took off at a wild angle with very little altitude.

"Holy Smoke! This could be the end of us, lad," Jim Crawford joked, though his color was ashen.

The battered old Huey was open on both sides, the doors long-since torn off to more easily load the wounded. The result was that a wild rush of air pounded in on them as the pilot raced along the treetops. Both men clung to a stanchion and held on for dear life, convinced that the pilot, by his wild flying, was expressing his personal distaste for foreigners, especially Americans. At times the plane flew so close to the trees that the branches lashed the undercarriage. The flight took an hour and a half, so by the time they felt a slowing of the rotors, indicating an approach, Jim Crawford was livid with rage.

The pilot deposited the plane as he had flown it, with a hard landing.

Several men were on hand to tie down the plane, one of whom gestured to Jim and Russell to follow him. He led them along a narrow forest path to a clearing where there were a number of tents. Separated from the others was a larger tent reinforced with wooden walls and flooring. They were led to this tent and urged inside.

Seated at a long table, was a man they assumed to be the person they were to meet, with a colleague at his side. There was no sign of Rachel.

Prachandra had decided he would speak in English to obviate the need for an interpreter.

"Gentlemen, please to sit down. Please to tell me who you are."

Jim Crawford introduced himself as a physician and Russell as a family friend of the prisoner.

"Good! I am Prachandra and this is Comrade Lawa. It is his camp to which the prisoner Mason was assigned. You are prepared to arrange her release?"

"That is the reason we are here," Jim replied.

"Good! I will bring prisoner Mason here shortly, but first, the ransom money, one million dollars US is available to be released?"

"Yes, it is."

"How is this to be done?"

"You will radio to this person whose name is Choate and identify yourself." He showed him a radio signal address, "I will then authorize this person to release the money to an account in the name of Pushpan Kamal Dahal, which we understand to be your real name? When they radio back that this has been done, you will release Miss Mason to us and you will transport us back to Lucknow.

"How do I know you will not withhold the ransom at the last minute by some trick or another?"

"You don't, nor do we know you will actually free Miss Mason when the money is released." The Americans had built a fail-safe device for just such a possibility by requiring a second approval to the bank after Rachel had been safely freed.

Prachandra laughed loudly and slapped the table, "A good game we play. I assure you I want Miss Mason gone, so you have no fear of my changing my mind."

"Then, sir, could we see Miss Mason and get on with our mission?"

Prachandra barked a command in Nepali to a guard outside the tent.

Waiting for Rachel to arrive, Jim spoke to Prachandra, "Mr. Prachandra, I would respectfully ask that your pilot fly less aggressively when Miss Mason is on board. We found him to fly far too low and with unnecessary speed. It was a very difficult flight and Miss Mason should not have to be subjected to that experience. I need not remind you that had we crashed because of the carelessness of this pilot there could have been no ransom." The longer he spoke, the more irate he became.

Prachandra understood Crawford clearly and guessed they had been subjected to unnecessary hazards because of the pilot's own agenda. He barked another command and minutes later the pilot appeared. When the pilot approached, Prachandra hit him across the face so hard that the man's cheek turned scarlet. He, then, delivered a tirade to the sullen man. Prachandra had waited six months for this much-needed money and the pilot was being made to understand the stupidity of his behavior.

Finished with the pilot, Prachandra dismissed him and turned to Crawford, "I am sorry that the imbecile acted badly. You will have a good flight returning."

Rachel walked through the tent opening.

Absolutely unprepared for what she saw, she stood rigid in disbelief.

"Rachel, dear," Jim Crawford began.

His voice and the use of her name were like an electric shock. She trembled and tried to speak, but her voice was so hoarse it couldn't be heard.

"Rachel?" Russell spoke her name again and walked toward her.

Still in shock from the thoughtless way in which she had been brought to them, totally unaware of her imminent release, she simply stood, unable to respond.

Russell reached her and slowly, very gently, put his hands on her shoulders. "Rachel, I'm sorry it is such a surprise; they must not have forewarned you. I'm terribly sorry. Jim and I are here to take you home. Are you all right?"

She stared at him with unbelieving eyes. Russell? It couldn't be Russell. Why was he here? How did they get here? Is this a cruel joke? This can't be happening. It must be just a terrible dream.

"Rachel, look at me. I am Russell, you remember me."

"Russell?" She managed to say.

"Yes, Rachel. We are here to take you home."

Slowly, mechanically, she began to understand that something had happened. Russell and Doctor Crawford had somehow miraculously appeared and were talking about taking her away. Only later, when she rehearsed the scene, could she understand how totally immersed she had become in her work at the camp, and how she had so totally repressed the thought of her release. It was as though she resented their sudden appearance to take her home. This place was her home.

"But I can't leave Dr. Botta." Her voice was low and her words indistinct.

"But you must, Rachel. You need to come home."

Rachel looked at Dr. Crawford, bewildered.

He was concerned by her behavior. "Slowly, Russell, slowly."

Prachandra watched the scene dispassionately.

"Miss Mason has performed well for us. She has helped Dr. Botta and his wife with many difficult operations. We hope she will remember that Communists are not the terrorists that your government labels us, but human beings. We fight for the oppressed, and to end the corruption of this monarchy." Prachandra stood and nodded at the two Americans, "Take Miss Mason, but remember that we are honorable men, not terrorists."

Crawford walked up to Rachel. "Rachel, you have done wonderful work here according to Mr. Prachandra. He has praised your assistance, but he feels you need to go home and rest. We want to take you home to Afton."

The shock was wearing off. What Dr. Crawford said began to make sense to her. She was tired. Maybe she should go home to Afton for a while?

"Yes, I guess I am tired, Doctor," she nodded.

Dr. Botta was brought in as an interpreter if he were needed.

When Rachel saw him, she rushed over to him and threw her arms around him. Embarrassed, but quickly seizing up the reason for the presence of the two Americans, he knew why she was holding him.

"Miss Mason, we knew it might happen. You must go and live a good life. I shall miss you sorely as will my wife—she will be devastated. Think of us, but not with sorrow, only with the warm memory in your heart of how you contributed so much to our work." He gently freed himself from her arms and backed away.

"Is there any reason we can't make the call and release the money now?" Crawford asked Prachandra.

He nodded and led Crawford to an adjoining area of the tent where contact was quickly made with Choate in Lucknow, who had been impatiently awaiting the call.

As they waited for the ransom to clear, Russell stood close to Rachel holding her hand. She still seemed bewildered by what was going on and Russell made no further attempt to explain it to her.

Receiving Choate's OK, Crawford turned to Prachandra, "It is done. May we leave?"

"Yes, you may go,' Prachandra answered. "Thank you, Doctor Crawford, you are an honorable man." They shook hands.

"Thank you, Mr. Prachandra, may you find peace soon."

Seeing that some sort of deal had been made, Rachel appealed to Prachandra for Dr. Botta and his wife's release. Prachandra disregarded her and urged Crawford to leave.

Rachel had nothing to take with her so she was helped to board the helicopter and was quickly lifted out of Botta's camp, but not without a feeling of deep anguish for those she was leaving and the many who had died in her care.

* * * *

As soon as Ben Choate had released the money from the Swiss bank, he cabled the three papers to inform them. Charles Biddle, in turn, called Sam and Caroline. It was 12:53 AM, on a Sunday morning. By arrangement, the papers had agreed not to publish Rachel's release until they knew that the Gulfstream had left the ground in Lucknow. The headlines, however, had been written days ago.

Sam had been so ebullient with the news of Rachel's ransom that after he and Caroline had knelt in church for some time, he felt a compulsion to ring the new bells in the Rachel Mason belfry. The contractor, presciently, had installed them just the day before. So, at 1:45, early on a September morning, residents of the encroaching neighborhoods were wakened by a peeling of bells from the new, invitingly designed Episcopal Church. It was a pleasing sound; so with a passing smile, they fell quickly back to sleep.

* * * *

Despite Prachandra's warning to the pilot, the flight to Lucknow was not a pleasant experience for either Russell or Jim. Rachel, on the other hand, was immersed in the landscape as it flew by, never having seen but a very small part of it. The roar of the air through the door-less cabin prohibited any conversation allowing her precious time to force her mind back to what she remembered of a normal world. Hard as she tried, however, she could not yet reconcile leaving the camp that had been her salvation for so many months.

At the Lucknow airport, the pilot, Steve Bassett, had made all the necessary preparations for an immediate departure. When he sighted the returning helicopter, he started the jets so it was a short half hour after Crawford and Russell landed with Rachel that they were airborne.

Jim Crawford had been able to communicate briefly with the two pilots to tell them of Rachel's fragile emotional state so that little time was spent on introductions. Once on the plane, Rachel seemed to withdraw completely, staring out of the window for hours at a time. Russell, who had been so ebullient about seeing her again, hoped that enough of their feeling for each other remained that they might simply start up where they had left off. But, guided by the doctor's caution not to press Rachel too hard at first, he restricted himself to periodically approaching her to offer snacks or light meals. Only sparingly did she eat anything.

Crawford had been able to talk to Botta before they had left the camp and learned of Rachel's recent fever. Botta told Crawford that Rachel had been delirious on several occasions and had lost considerable weight during the siege.

During the second day's flight, Jim suggested that Russell attempt to draw Rachel out as gently as possible. But the woman Russell talked to and the voice he heard was not that of the Rachel he had known in Afton. Why should it be, he ruefully asked himself? Where he had provided an understanding shoulder for her to lean on, here he sensed she did not need that any longer. Although she seemed pleased to see him, she talked in a remote, almost mechanical, way about her experiences, never approaching anything personal. But yet at times he thought he heard a depth of feeling he not heard before. Though she did not describe the details of her life at the camp, he sensed a determined blurring of culturally accepted beliefs and a dismissal of stereotypes. What he did not hear was the voice of a woman who was now ready to throw herself into the arms of a love affair. Though love softened the words she used, it was not of the more intimate love between a man and a woman that he had hoped to hear.

Rachel, too, listened as they talked. She heard the man she had grown to respect so deeply before going to Nepal talk a different language than she understood. She could feel his desire for her, but it was for the woman he had known in Afton, not the woman she herself was only gradually coming to understand. She became suddenly aware that she could not wrap herself in his arms and go back, and it was a lonely feeling. Where, then, was her life to be lived; was it so altered that she could not adapt to a normal life?

* * * *

It was on the final approach to the Baltimore/Washington Airport that Russell put into words what each of them had been saying, silently, to each other.

"Rachel, you are soon going to be inundated by well-wishers, newspaper and TV people and all sorts of other types. It is a necessary evil of our culture. I don't envy you your task. Tell your amazing story honestly so that you, yourself, can listen and let it guide you. While you are telling it, I sense that I would be something of a distraction and I don't want that to be the case. If, in time, you ever want to talk, I would like to listen. I think you have a lot of sorting out to do which I fully appreciate. Let's part at the plane as best friends and let our future be what fate may want it to be."

Rachel listened quietly, "Russell, you have an amazing ability to see inside me. I have changed, but my feeling for you has not. I do need time to find out who I have become. It wouldn't be fair to you to suffer through that. I'm sure I will want to talk, so I hope you will listen when I do call. My life has been so weird and yet so satisfying, I really don't know how to make it fit inside me, let alone make it meaningful to someone else.

Two experiences that are the contradiction of each other may give some idea of my confusion. Working with Dr. Botta with the ghastly wounded boys, I came to see them as society's wounds inflicted on itself. Man's insatiable cruelty is wounding the life God has given us. The horror I saw made me lose hope for the feeble efforts we make to change ourselves.

The other was a near-mystical experience I had one night near the mountain, Dhaulagiri. The moon had lighted its slopes so brilliantly that it was almost impossible to look at. I was transfixed by the power of it. It seemed, silently, to beckon me closer. The closer I came, the more I felt the strength to persevere despite constant failure. I lost myself to that mountain and I knew, for at least an instant, what inner peace was.

I know how this must sound to you, Russ, but until I am able to understand these experiences and use them in my life, I will be like a wandering blind man. I want so much for you to help me understand, my dearest Russell."